ANOTHER'S CHILD

PATRICIA PLOSS

Joshua Tree Publishing

• Chicago •

ANOTHER'S CHILD
PATRICIA PLOSS

Published by
Joshua Tree Publishing
• Chicago •
JoshuaTreePublishing.com

All rights reserved. No part of this book may be reproduced or transmitted in any form or by any means, electronic or mechanical, including information storage and retrieval system without written permission from the publisher, except by a reviewer who may quote brief passages in a review.

13-Digit ISBN Print: 978-1-956823-24-0
13-Digit ISBN eBook: 978-1-956823-25-7

Copyright © 2022 Patricia Ploss. All Rights Reserved.

Front Cover Image Credit: Patricia Ploss

Disclaimer:
This is a work of fiction. Names, characters, places, and incidents are the product of the author's imagination or have been used fictitiously. Any resemblance to actual persons, living or dead, events, locales or organizations is entirely coincidental.

Printed in the United States of America

Dedication

This book is dedicated first and foremost to my wonderful parents, Tom and Dorothy Cornell.

Though they have both been gone for many years now, they were the best parents any child could ever have hoped for.

This book is also for all the birth parents in the world, who gave up their most precious gift to others. Your bravery and true love for your children will always be a shining beacon of hope.

Finally, this book is for all the adoptees in the world. Our lives may have taken many paths, but we were all loved enough to be given hope and a chance at a better life.

All lives are a precious gift. May we be humble, thankful, hopeful, and helpful in them.

Preface

This story is for all the people out there who've arrived as parents through adoption. Adoption has many facets that all connect and interconnect with many more people than simply the birth parents, adoptive parents, and the adoptee(s).

Adoption changes the course of families forever, and its impact creates new legacies—some good, some bad.

The journey requires bravery, selflessness, trust and most of all, love—love for another's child that you raise as your own.

This story is fictional only because I don't know all the details of my parents' journey to adopting me. Bits and pieces were all they ever shared. I used some of the facts and changed some dates and names to suit my imagination.

Birth parents should be lauded for what they do to give their children a life they are not able to. Giving up something that is literally a part of you—to strangers in many cases—would take all the bravery in the world, in my opinion.

So I wish to thank birth parents who have let their children go for having the heart, the love, and the faith to do this wonderful thing for those people who can't become parents in other ways.

To all the adoptive parents in the world, I thank you for your bravery in taking on the unknown of a child not born to you and for loving that child. You are very much "real parents." As an adoptee, I'm often asked, "Don't you want to know who your REAL parents are?" I say, "I had REAL parents! They raised me, took care of me, supported me and loved me. They were the parents I knew. They were very much my REAL parents."

I had birth parents, but I will never know who they were. I thank them for giving me the opportunity to grow up with people who could give me what they could not. It took me a long time to get to that conclusion. For many years, I felt that I was just thrown away as if I was unwanted trash.

As a parent myself, I realized just how much my birth parents loved me to do what they did by giving me up for adoption.

Please enjoy this story of an adoption that took place way back in 1963, when it was an easy process and took hardly any time at all! Plus, the fee was a whole $2 to file the papers!

God bless all the families, no matter how they came to be.

Chapter One

Dorothy Cornell stood at her kitchen window, watching the birds of early spring as they darted from frozen branches to the still brown grass in the front yard.

She rubbed her belly, so pregnant she had trouble doing just about anything. Sighing, she looked at the calendar on the wall. A whole week overdue, yet the baby still hadn't come.

Just a few days ago, Dorothy and her husband, Tom, had been to the doctor for a checkup. All seemed in order; she was just overdue a few days. The doctor said he'd let her go another two weeks and then do a cesarean section if the baby still didn't come on its own.

It was March of 1961. Dorothy and Tom had been married ten years without having a family to call their own. When she finally became pregnant, Dorothy couldn't wait to tell Tom when he arrived home from work that hot summer June day, so many months ago! She still recalled the look of joy on his face as he took her in his arms and held her close.

Dorothy had been a schoolteacher since just before their marriage in August of 1951. She loved her third-grade students. Sometimes she would teach either second, fourth, or fifth grade, but third was her favorite. The kids still enjoyed school, they were old enough to catch on to the curriculum, and they still liked their teachers. Each one was precious to her, and she did her best to instill confidence and guide them through the school year.

Having a child of her very own was a dream she'd chased all these years. Tom, too, wanted to have a family. He wanted to spend time with Dorothy and whatever kids they might have, going on vacations, teaching them gardening, and bringing them up with love, respect, and goals for their futures.

Dorothy poured herself a glass of water and took two pork chops out of the refrigerator to prepare for dinner. Tom worked at the Dow Chemical Company downtown. He was the manager of the patent department. He enjoyed his work and sometimes brought home interesting stamps from across the world. Dorothy saved them in parchment sleeves, hoping one day to start a stamp-collecting book with her children.

Unwrapping the fresh chops from the butcher's paper, Dorothy considered what side dishes to make to go with them. Carefully she rubbed oil, seasonings and breadcrumbs onto the large chops and placed them in a glass pan.

She washed her hands and turned to the cupboard to see what was available to make. Stretching, she reached to the second shelf and retrieved a can of peas and carrots. As she lifted the can, she felt a sharp pain in her side. Quickly her arm dropped as she gasped and clutched her belly. Her other hand on the edge of the counter helped steady her balance as she took long, slow breaths. The pain ebbed away, and she stood for a moment, waiting to see what would happen next. Could that have been labor? She wasn't sure. Nothing else happened for a few minutes, so she took down the can of vegetables, leaving them on the counter and reached down for a saucepan from the lower cupboard. Bending down had been nearly impossible for several weeks, and Dorothy strained as she felt, more than saw, her favorite saucepan on the bottom shelf of her cabinet.

Finally grasping the handle, she brought the pan up and set it on the gas stove. Thinking of what else to have, she decided that making mashed potatoes would be too much work, so she pulled a bag of bread from the bread box and decided that would just have to suffice. She knew Tom wouldn't mind. He'd eat about anything she put in front of him, and she was thankful for that! Tom could grill a mean steak and chicken, too, but that was mostly reserved for the summer months and weekends.

Carefully, Dorothy stepped to the other side of the sink and took plates and table settings out of the cupboards on that side of the kitchen. She was worn out by the time she had everything ready to go for dinner and had put the chops back in the fridge until it was time to cook.

Thinking of napping but feeling like she should be doing something productive instead, Dorothy walked down the hall to the baby's nursery. Just walking into the room made her smile. Opening the window a bit to let fresh air in, she watched as the light-green curtains fluttered in the breeze. There was a big maple tree outside the baby's window, and the leaves were just starting to bud.

Springtime was a lovely time to have a baby, Dorothy always thought. Everything is new, clean and fresh. It'd still be chilly in Mid Michigan in the spring, but she wasn't planning to take her baby out too much at first anyway. It was a perfect time to become a mom.

Lovingly, Dorothy went to the crib her parents had bought for them. Stroking the smooth white wood, she reached over to smooth the yellow-and-green fitted sheet. Her mother had knit a blanket of pure white for the baby, and it was tucked into the corner of the crib. She touched the softness of the blanket, treasuring it because her own mother had made it. Alongside the blanket was a tiny teddy bear in a soft shade of tan. Tom's sister Joan had sent it for the baby. It'd be the very first toy their baby would receive! Lastly, there was a little white sleeper and tiny cap lying on the blanket in the crib. This would be the outfit their baby would come home from the hospital in! Soft, snowy white, wrapped in the cozy blanket, surrounded by love! They had packed a diaper bag as well, and it was at the ready for when the time came!

Dorothy had two older sisters. Betty Jean was married and had three kids, and her other sister, Phyllis, had four! She'd married a redhead named Stan, who played football for Michigan State. Everyone called him Red due to his vibrant red curls! Each of their four children had inherited his gorgeous hair and their mom's sunny disposition! Dorothy loved her nieces and nephews dearly but always felt as if she was on the outside looking in, not quite part of the family scene. The longer she and Tom didn't have kids, the more isolated she felt. So finally, when she found out she was pregnant, she was over the moon, and her mother set to knitting this beautiful blanket, as she had for all the grandkids before hers.

Turning to the two dressers, one tall and the other set up for a changing table, as well as clothing storage, Dorothy smiled at the drawers. Tom had painted them in alternating colors of pink and blue. They were excited to meet their baby, and since there was no way to know whether it was a boy or a girl, he decided to paint the drawers in both colors. Dorothy didn't think a girl would mind some blue drawers, but she wasn't sure if a boy would appreciate the pink ones later on! It was still a sweet and thoughtful thing for Tom to do, and she loved it.

Opening a drawer, she took out a tiny onesie in a buttery-yellow shade. She laid it across her stomach and laughed! Her stomach was so big, this tiny slip of cotton would never fit on a baby, she thought. Carefully she folded the onesie, placing it on top of the others in a rainbow of pastel hues. Next to that were tiny white socks and several pairs of booties. Sleepers were in the next drawer, and several receiving blankets filled drawers in the other dressers.

Dorothy's sisters and mother had thrown her a wonderful baby shower, and all her friends were there. Dorothy was nearly the only one who was a first-time mom at thirty. Most of her friends had had their kids in their early twenties, either right out of high school or shortly after college.

Dorothy had gone to Michigan State, as had her sisters, and gotten a teaching degree. She still recalled how scared she was, walking into orientation at the huge school! She quickly made her way around, though, and enjoyed her college years.

Tom had started at MSU as well but then transferred to a business school up in Chicago. There he learned to be a stenographer and worked for an attorney for a while. Soon, though, he joined the Navy. He traveled the world during World War II, typing up meeting notes for all kinds of events and officers. He continued on into the Korean Conflict, eventually discharging and finding his way to Midland. There he'd gotten a job in the patent department at Dow Chemical.

Dorothy had met Tom on a blind date on New Year's Eve, heralding 1951. Theirs was a whirlwind romance, and they married in August that same year. Everyone thought they'd start a family right away. But when that didn't happen year after year, Dorothy felt left behind by some of her friends who'd had kids young. Some of the kids were already in junior high, for heaven's sake!

Finally, it was her turn, and she couldn't be more excited.

Dorothy hadn't felt any more pains, but she was feeling warm and very tired, so she decided to take a short nap on the sofa.

Making her way to the living room, she once again rubbed her belly and felt like a trundling bear! First, she opened a couple of the windows to let in the fresh, cool spring breeze. Birds sang, and the clear sunlight of March pushed its way through the sheer white curtains they'd hung long ago when they had moved into their home.

Memories filtered through her mind and heart as she slowly eased down onto the dark-brown sofa they'd purchased just a few years ago. Carefully lying on her side, Dorothy promised herself she'd only close her eyes for a little bit. She still felt warm and uncomfortable.

Since she'd been to the doctor last week, she'd felt the baby move less and less. All of her friends who'd already had babies assured her that this was normal. The baby was just moving into place, getting ready to be born. Even the doctor said this was normal and not to worry. As Dr. Brooks had delivered several babies over the years, Dorothy tried not to worry. She passed her concerns off as a first-time mother. Certainly, they were all right. The baby was just getting ready to be born, especially since it was so late! There couldn't be much room left inside to move! She still wondered, though, as she had felt so much movement for several months now.

Quietly she rubbed her belly once again and whispered soft words to her baby, asking it to come soon, as she was so anxious to meet him or her and become a family of three. She pressed on her belly in the usual spots that received a kick, or movement, but, again, felt nothing. Tendrils of alarm began to snake through her mind. Surely nothing was wrong. Her pregnancy had been text book. Nothing horrible. Hardly a day of morning sickness, no crazy cravings, nothing to indicate anything was wrong. In her fourth month, the doctor had told her to expect to start feeling the baby move. And he was right! The movements and kicks had grown stronger with each passing week. At every doctor visit, all reports were fine, and Dr. Brooks said she was right on schedule.

It was only a few weeks ago, when she neared her due date, that the baby's movements became less and her belly grew even bigger. Dr. Brooks said he'd let her go almost two weeks past the window of her due date, and then they'd discuss a cesarean section. Dorothy hoped she wouldn't have to go through that and so didn't pay much attention when the doctor told her about the relatively new procedure that'd only been around for about ten years. After all, her sisters never had any problems giving birth, and there were seven kids between the two of them.

Dorothy just felt like her baby wanted to take its time and be as healthy as possible, and she was OK with that. Until last week, when most all movement stopped.

Gazing toward the windows, Dorothy tried to recall the last time she'd felt any movement from her baby at all. As far as she could remember, it had been at least four days. Saying a silent prayer for everything to be all right, she drifted off into a restless sleep, nightmares of darkness, crying and looking for her baby, sending her down darkened paths, calling out a name she didn't know.

Chapter Two

Dorothy tossed and turned on the couch, never quite waking up until she felt a hand on her shoulder, gently shaking her.

Slowly she opened her eyes. As she began to focus, she saw Tom there on the edge of the couch, his dark eyes filled with concern.

"Dottie, are you OK? I just got home, and you were crying out in your sleep!"

Dorothy took a few moments and looked toward the window. The slant of the sun told her that it was way past dinner time, and she immediately tried to sit up. She had to make dinner!

Tom eased her back down and shushed her. "Hey, it's all right, don't try to move much. I know you must be really tired. Don't worry about dinner."

"I'm so sorry, Tom! I just meant to lie down for a few moments. I . . . I had a pain earlier, and I'm just so tired! I just needed to close my eyes for a minute!"

"Honey, it's OK! Listen, you feel really warm, and I'm going to go find the thermometer and get you some water. You just lie back and relax," Tom said, standing up and heading toward the bathroom. She watched as he loosened his tie and made his way down the short hall to the bathroom.

Slowly Dorothy sat up. She did feel really hot and something else she couldn't quite identify. She felt sore all over, and her stomach was upset too. Certainly, she wasn't getting the flu at this point!

Tom returned, shaking the thermometer to get the mercury down. She opened her mouth, and he placed it under her tongue.

"There now, just hold that in there, and I'm going to go get you some water. Sit tight, and I'll be right back," he said, squeezing her shoulder gently.

Dorothy again watched as her husband left the room and felt something akin to fear. She didn't want to be alone, yet she knew he was just in the next room.

She heard the water run and ice cubes clink into a glass. Then in a moment, Tom was right there with her again, placing the glass on a coaster atop the coffee table.

"OK, let's see now," he said, settling next to her on the couch.

Dutifully, he took the thermometer from her mouth and held it to the fading light. Silently, Dorothy watched as he held the glass thermometer to the fading sunlight. His brow furrowed as he squinted. Turning the stick this way and that, he faced her and once again felt her forehead.

"Dorothy, this says you have a temperature of 103. I think we should call the doctor. How do you feel?"

Clearing her throat and reaching for the glass of water, Dorothy took a mental status of what she was feeling. Nausea rang through her gut as she sipped the cold water. She also felt a headache, and sweat was trickling down her back.

Looking up at Tom, she told him how she felt and placed a hand on her belly. "Tom, I haven't felt the baby move in a few days. I'm really scared."

"Oh, honey, I think the baby's fine. I think your body is just ready to give birth and get back to normal. I'm going to call Dr. Brooks's answering service and see what they want us to do. How does that sound?"

"OK, that sounds good. I'm going to go to the bathroom while you do that," replied Dorothy.

Tom helped her get to her feet and held her arms until she felt steady. He watched closely as his wife slowly walked down the hall to the bathroom. Quickly he dialed the doctor's number and left a message with his service, detailing his wife's symptoms.

Hanging up, he heard Dorothy scream and ran toward the bathroom, his heart pounding!

"Tom, there's blood! So much blood!" Dorothy exclaimed, holding her belly and a washcloth soaked in blood!

"OK, OK! We're going to the hospital. Here, I'm going to help you to the kitchen and go get the car! Just hold on, honey. It will be OK!" He fervently hoped what he was saying would be true, but in his heart, he was terrified and felt helpless.

As quickly as he could, Tom helped Dorothy navigate to the kitchen and then down the porch steps to an empty lawn chair. Jumping into their baby-blue 1955 DeSoto car, he quickly but carefully backed up to the porch where Dorothy was holding her belly, bent over and crying.

He exited the car as fast as he could, ran to the other side, yanked open the passenger door and ran to his wife's side. Carefully he helped her to stand and half carried her the short steps to the car. As gently as he could, he eased her down into the seat. Shutting the door, he practically flew to the driver's side and jumped in.

There was no time to latch his seat belt, and he wasn't even going to attempt to latch Dorothy's as he threw the car into reverse and backed out of the driveway.

Thankfully, Midland General Hospital was only a few miles away, but it felt like fifty as he careened around curves and slowed just barely for stop signs in the waning sunlight.

Screeching into the hospital emergency entrance, Tom threw the car into Park and bolted inside the doors, calling out to Dorothy that he'd be right back!

Flying to the nurses' desk, he was out of breath as he explained to an older nurse what was happening with his wife.

From years of experience, the nurse was able to keep calm and understand what the harried man was yelling about. Quickly she called orderlies with a wheelchair to go retrieve the woman in the car and calmly told the husband to go move his car into the parking lot, and the staff would take things with Dorothy from there.

Tom rushed with the orderlies to his car outside. They quickly got Dorothy out of the car and into the wheelchair.

"Tom, don't leave me!" Dorothy called out.

"Honey, it's going to be OK. I have to move the car, and I'll be right there. I promise!"

Dorothy stared at him, terror in her eyes. She was holding the blood-soaked washcloth down low and had her other hand pressed against her swollen belly.

"Hurry, Tom! Hurry!" she called out.

Tom kissed her quick and promised to be there as soon as he parked. He slammed the passenger side door, but not before noticing a dark-red stain on the cloth seat. His heart lurched with pain and worry as he ran to the other side and jumped back in the car.

The hospital parking lot was nearly empty, so Tom was able to get a spot close by. He slammed the door without bothering to even lock the car, shoved his keys in his pocket and ran back to the entrance of the hospital.

Once inside, he again jogged to the nurses' station. This time, the same nurse took his name, Dorothy's and the name of their doctor. The nurse called Dr. Brooks's answering service and stated there was an emergency. After listening for a few moments, she hung up the phone and turned to Tom.

"Sir, Dr. Brooks will be on his way. We are examining your wife. You can see her in a few minutes. Please have a seat over there in the waiting area, and we'll be with you as soon as we can." She gestured to several rows of white leatherette chairs, all connected together by metal rails.

Tom didn't know if he could sit and paced the floor. The intake nurse didn't look all that concerned and went about her business.

There weren't any other emergencies going on at the time, so Tom figured there was plenty of staff to help Dorothy. He tried to think of what could be wrong. Maybe her water broke, and she was finally having the baby. But why would there be so much blood? Why did she have such a high fever? Just the other day, Dr. Brooks had given her a clean bill of health; she was just a little past her due date. What could possibly go wrong now?

Tom looked out at the parking lot to see if Dr. Brooks was anywhere in sight, but all he saw were a few cars and heard birds singing as the sun set.

Pacing, he went to look for something to drink. He didn't want to call any family, as he didn't have anything to report, really. Maybe it'd all be fine. He didn't want to make a second set of calls, so he searched, instead, for some water or maybe coffee.

Around a corner and down a short hall, he came to a coffee station. There, a candy striper volunteer was just making a fresh pot.

"Hello, sir, would you like a coffee?" she asked, smiling at him.

"Yes, please."

"It will just be a minute. How do you take it?"

"Just black is fine."

"Sir, are you all right?" the candy striper asked.

"Oh yes, sorry. My wife, she's in the emergency." He didn't want to say too much.

"Oh, I see. Well, there are many fine doctors and nurses here. She'll be OK. Oh, here you are, sir. Coffee's all ready."

She handed him a steaming cup. The scent was fresh and strong, but Tom didn't have the stomach to drink it just now. Instead, he carried it back down the hall to the main waiting room to see if there was any news.

He placed the cup down on an end table and walked to the nurses' station to inquire about Dorothy. His Dottie was so strong and loving. He hated that this was happening to her and that he could not help. They wouldn't even let him see her, and he'd promised her he'd be right back.

The nurse smiled up at him from her desk chair and let him know that Dr. Brooks had arrived and was in the room now with her. As soon as possible, she'd let him know the situation. She again told him to have a seat.

Tom walked the perimeter of the waiting room once again and watched as the late afternoon sunk into twilight. He sat in one of the white chairs and took a sip of coffee. It was almost cold. Looking at the clock, he calculated they'd been there nearly two hours. It was just after 7:00 p.m.

Chapter Three

After a few more minutes, Tom went in search of a restroom. Once there, he splashed his face with cold water and said a prayer to God that everything was going to be OK. He sighed as he dried his hands and once again headed for the lonely waiting room.

This time, a family had come in, and an ambulance crew raced in with a young man on a stretcher! Tom flattened himself against a wall as the men hurried through with a gurney and beyond the doors to the examination rooms!

Tom looked on as a couple clung to one another, the woman crying, the man comforting her, along with a teenage couple who stood by silently. Tom couldn't begin to know what the situation was, but he said a prayer for them as well.

Just then, Dr. Brooks came out of the ER doors, white lab coat smeared with blood, holding his glasses in one hand and rubbing his forehead with the other.

Tom's heart sank. He knew then that something horrible had happened. He just didn't know if it was his wife, his baby, or both!

"Tom, please, come with me." Dr. Brooks turned back to the set of doors he'd just come through, and Tom followed him, head hanging down, preparing for the worst news.

Dr. Brooks stepped into an alcove in the hall and turned to face Tom.

"Listen, Tom, I'm so sorry. I believe the baby has died. I can't find a heartbeat. There's a lot of blood, as you know, and Dorothy might be septic with infection."

"Dr. Brooks! Is she OK? Is my Dottie OK?" That's all Tom cared about at the moment. His baby dying was shattering his heart, but he couldn't also stand to lose his wife!

"I think she'll be OK, Tom. We've stopped the bleeding and gotten her on medications. She's conscious, but we have to get the baby out, Tom. I wanted you to come see her before we do that."

The doctor didn't need to explain that he was afraid Dorothy wouldn't make it either, but it was obvious. She'd lost so much blood, and she was so sick! Tom nodded and followed the doctor as he turned toward the examination room.

"Wait, Dr. Brooks. Does Dorothy know the baby might be gone?" Tom asked, trepidation in his eyes.

"Yes, she knows. She knew when she discovered all the blood, I think. She keeps telling us how she has felt no movement for almost a week. Everything was fine when you two were here the other day. Strong heartbeat, everything was as it should be. But now, I'm unable to locate a heartbeat. Now it just may be that the baby is turned in such a way that I can't get it. And because she's overdue, the placenta may be breaking up, and that would explain the blood. We're going to do a cesarean section as quickly as possible. So you've got just a few minutes, and we need to get her into surgery." Dr. Brooks squeezed Tom's arm and nodded to him.

Tom instinctively knew that time was of the essence, or Dorothy wouldn't make it.

Taking a deep breath, Tom followed Dr. Brooks into the exam room. The lights were bright, which made the blood-soaked towels even brighter. Swallowing a lump in his throat, Tom quickly made his way to his wife's side.

Clasping her hand, he noted she felt cold and clammy now, as opposed to the heat from the fever earlier. He didn't know if this was good or bad, and this wasn't the moment to analyze that. Kissing her forehead, he tasted the salt of her sweat. She was too weak to hug him and just had tears streaming down her face.

"Oh, Tom, the baby, it's . . . it's dead! Our baby is dead!" she sobbed into his chest.

Tom held her close, rocking her, and said softly, "Dorothy, we don't know that yet. They are going to take you into surgery and see what is going on. I'll be right here when you wake up. Shhh, it's all right. I love you so much."

After a moment, Tom stood and patted her hand, enveloped in his. "OK, honey, the doctor is going to take you now. I'll be right here."

Dorothy, still quietly crying, nodded and squeezed his hand back. He could tell by the look in her eyes that she knew their baby didn't make it. She gasped to catch her breath as another contraction ripped through her body.

"OK, nurses, let's go, please," said Dr. Brooks. He was all business as he followed the gurney with Dorothy on it out the doors and quickly to the surgical ward of the small hospital.

Tom had no other option but to wait once again in the front lobby with the white chairs. He thought he'd never forget the sight of that sterile, cold waiting room. It seemed cruel and uncaring, as if the building itself had seen so much pain and suffering, it shielded itself from comfort.

Time seemed to stand still as Tom waited for news. The other family was huddled on a corner couch. The apparent mother was still crying softly, and the teen couple, arms around one another, just stared out the window. The man, who must have been the father of the young man, was asking the nurse for any updates.

Tom wondered idly what had happened and assumed the patient was the couple's son. Perhaps the young girl was their daughter. He didn't know, and he didn't want to intrude on their pain, so he kept to the other side of the room.

Chapter Four

After what seemed like hours, the doors at the end of the surgical hallway opened, and Dr. Brooks slowly walked toward Tom. He had on a surgical cap, white scrubs with blood stains, and white shoe covers that were also splattered with blood.

Tom knew his baby was dead for sure now. But what about Dorothy? He stood and slowly walked toward their trusted doctor. Tom knew it wasn't Dr. Brooks's fault, but he could tell the man was distressed by looking at him. Shoulders slumped, Dr. Brooks pulled off his cap as he raised his gaze to Tom.

"Tom," he said, then cleared his throat. "Tom, Dorothy is OK. She's lost a lot of blood, and she's sick, but I believe she will come out of this OK. It will take a while."

Tom felt instant relief that his wife would be OK. He knew what the doctor was going to say next, but knowing that Dorothy was going to be all right was his top priority. He'd deal with whatever was next later.

"Tom, the baby, I'm sorry. The baby was stillborn," Dr. Brooks said, with his hand on Tom's arm. It wasn't often that a baby didn't make it, but Dr. Brooks had had to have this conversation with parents before. It never got easier, and it always tore at his heart. He had three healthy children of his own, so when a patient of his lost a baby, his heart broke for them, as he thanked God for his own family.

"What . . . what happened? Why was the baby stillborn?" asked Tom.

"Your baby had hydrocephalus," said Dr. Brooks.

Tom's brow furrowed, as he didn't know the term.

"To explain, that means water on the brain, Tom. The spinal fluid in the baby's body went to the brain. It was too much for the underdeveloped brain to handle, and the baby essentially drowned. We don't know what causes it. Most babies with this are stillborn or die shortly after birth. If they do live, it's a short life span filled with endless disabilities and years of doctor visits, surgeries, and treatments. Believe me, Tom, it's no life that anyone would wish for or want to have. I know that isn't what you want to hear right now, that your baby's better off not having lived, but in the long run, you'll see it's true. This child would have been nonverbal and in an infant state for as long as it was alive."

"Dr. Brooks, was my child a boy or a girl?" Tom said, numb with all the information and a pain in his heart he couldn't even identify. Even as the doctor was explaining what happened, Tom thought of Dorothy and couldn't begin to imagine what she was feeling. Thoughts of phone calls and planning a funeral skittered through his mind. He felt fractured, angry, and sad all at once.

"It was a boy, Tom. Now, I'm going to let you see Dorothy as soon as she's awake. Then, if you two wish to see your baby, we'll bring him to you."

Tom nodded, still reeling and not quite believing all that was happening. He stood there, Dr. Brooks still had a hand on Tom's arm, and he knew the doctor was genuinely hurting as well.

"What, uh, what does he look like? Will she be able to stand to see him?" Tom asked, tears slipping down his face.

"Oh. Well, he looks quite normal. He does have darker skin. But that's because I believe he passed away a few days ago, sometime after your last visit here, when Dorothy was no longer feeling him move. Other than that, he looks normal. Now sometimes, a baby born hydrocephalic has a large misshapen head, and the entire body is out of proportion. But your son does not look like that. The back of his head is soft and fluid-filled, but he just appears as if asleep. I'm so sorry, Tom. There's no way to know about these things, and there is no way to prevent it."

Nodding, Tom tried to take deep breaths and continued to try to comprehend the situation.

"Is there any family you'd like to call right now? Anyone you'd like here with you?"

Tom shook his head. Both of their parents lived two hours away in two different directions. There wasn't anything they could do about it anyway. He just wanted to see Dorothy and hold her.

"OK, well, she should be awake soon, and we'll take you in to see her. Then you can decide if you wish to see the baby. I'm so sorry, Tom. I'll come get you when she's awake."

Tom again nodded and watched as Dr. Brooks turned back to the surgery doors.

Watching as the doors swung shut, Tom simply stood there. He felt the weight of the world on his shoulders as they slumped, and his head dropped down, and he stared at the floor. He noticed a smudge of dark-red blood, probably from Dr. Brooks's shoes. Idly he wondered if it was his wife's or his son's.

Slowly he turned to wander back to the waiting room until he was able to see his Dottie. She would be so devastated. They'd tried for so long. How could this have happened?

The family of the young man were standing up, speaking to another doctor Tom didn't know. He watched as they nodded and clung to one another. He heard the words *coma*, *brain injury*, and *surgery* come from the doctor's mouth. The father held the mother, and the young couple were arm-in-arm as they heard the words come. At least their boy was alive, Tom thought. There was hope for that family, but none for his little one.

Sitting down, he leaned forward and pressed his hands to his forehead, a searing headache coming on. All he wanted was to see his Dottie.

After a bit, he looked up and saw the nurse at the desk watching him. He nodded at her, and she stood up.

She came around the side of the desk with a glass of water in hand.

"Mr. Cornell, I've been made aware of your situation, and I'd like to extend my condolences. Dr. Brooks is the best doctor around, and your wife is in very good hands. These things just happen sometimes. It's no one's fault. Truly it isn't." She handed him the glass of water and patted his arm.

"Thank you," Tom replied. He took a sip from the offered glass and watched as the nurse made her way back to her desk. She sat down just as her phone rang and turned away to speak to whoever was on the other end.

Time seemed to stand still in Tom's mind. When would Dr. Brooks come and get him? He could only wonder as he sipped his water and watched as the other family was given instructions to follow an ambulance to a hospital in another town with a bigger surgical crew to help their boy. He managed to nod at them as they made their way out the door. The father nodded back and assisted his wife outside.

Chapter Five

As Tom tried to make sense of the nightmare he was currently awake in, Dorothy slowly awoke from the anesthesia. Groggy and unsure of where she was, her hand automatically went to her belly to protect her baby.

Alarmed when her stomach was no longer hard and round, Dorothy gasped and threw off the light blanket that was stretched over her! She felt her stomach, soft, sore and misshapen, frantic to know what had happened.

Slowly, she took in her surroundings. She was on a white stretcher with metal bars keeping her inside the confines of the single-sized bed. Above were fluorescent lights, dimmed but casting a cold blue light on the room around her.

A door stood partially ajar, and Dorothy struggled to find her voice to call for help.

"Please! Help! Where am I? Where is my baby?" Dorothy croaked out. Idly she wondered why her throat was sore, and she couldn't seem to speak above a whisper.

Fragments of memories raced through her mind, and pieces were sliding together! She remembered pain and blood! So much blood! As she tried to recall more details, a nurse came through the door, a stethoscope in one hand and a chart in the other.

"Dorothy, are you awake? I thought I heard you call."

"Who . . . who are you? Where am I? Where's my baby and my husband?" Dorothy's words tumbled out as fast as she could speak.

"Shh, shh, you just rest now. I'm Nurse Fern Hutchins. Let me take a listen to your heart and get the rest of your vitals, then I'll explain." With that, she put her stethoscope in her ears and placed the head against Dorothy's chest.

Quickly Dorothy pushed it away and tried to sit up. Demanding answers to her questions and refusing to let Nurse Fern touch her until she answered her.

"Dorothy, your baby was in distress. We had to get it out, and so you were put under anesthesia. You've had surgery, and you need to be calm and try to relax. Please let me do what I need to, and then I'll go get Dr. Brooks."

"Answer me! *Where* is my baby? *Where* is my husband!" Dorothy's voice became louder and stronger as the effects of the drugs wore off. She was panicking and not getting the answers she sought from this nurse! Frustration didn't begin to cover the emotions she was feeling.

Since Nurse Fern wasn't going to answer, she'd just have to get up and find those she was looking for! Pushing the nurse away from her once again, Dorothy struggled to sit up in the bed. Crushing pain ripped across her lower abdomen, and she sucked in breath as tears stung her eyes! What had happened to her? What did they do to her? The pain was blinding, and she couldn't move!

Nurse Fern clasped Dorothy's wrists in her hands and looked directly into her eyes. "Mrs. Cornell, Dorothy, you need to stay put. Just lie back and breathe. I'll go get Dr. Brooks, but you have to promise me you won't try to get out of this bed!" She was stern but direct and never broke eye contact with Dorothy. She needed to be clear to this patient because she realized that the news this poor woman was going to receive would devastate her. So Fern needed to calm Dorothy's nerves and help her to relax as much as possible.

Dorothy looked into Fern's eyes and saw compassion and something else she couldn't immediately identify. It scared her, but she also knew the nurse was right, and she wasn't stable enough to get out of bed.

Feeling terrified and wanting to cry, Dorothy looked around the quiet room and thought about all the nurse was telling her. The baby had been in distress, and they had to do surgery to get the baby out. She supposed that meant a cesarean section, and with the shooting pain across her belly, it made sense. She asked Nurse Fern and listened intently to her explanation.

"Yes, Dorothy, Dr. Brooks performed an emergency cesarean on you to get the baby out. As you know, you lost a lot of blood, and both you and the baby were in danger. I'm going to go get Dr. Brooks now, and he can explain more." She quickly stood up, not wanting to deliver the news she was sure Mrs. Cornell knew was coming anyway. It wasn't her place to tell this patient what had happened, and she wasn't about to break that rule.

"I'll be right back, Mrs. Cornell. You just stay put right there!" Nurse Fern stated clearly.

"OK, OK, I'm not going anywhere. Please, just hurry! I want my husband too! Where is he?"

"He'll be along shortly. Don't you worry now," replied Fern as she backed out the door.

Dorothy hugged herself carefully. She knew what was coming. The baby was dead. She knew it just as well as she knew her heart was broken. No one seemed to understand last week when she said how the baby had completely stopped moving. She knew then that something was very wrong. Suddenly angry with everyone, she flung the blanket off and looked at her belly under the hospital gown spread across her body.

Huge bandages crisscrossed her stomach. She could see stains of blood at the edges and a slight one in the middle, probably from when she tried to get up just a few moments ago. Gingerly she ran her fingers across the bandages, assuming it was stitches she felt. It was bumpy and very sore and stretched from one side of the hip to the other. Again, she felt the softness of her belly, her baby no longer in it.

She wondered then, son or daughter? Which would they bury? She knew without a doubt her child was dead. Images from the scattered nightmares she'd suffered from of late now made sense. How did she just know this baby wasn't going to make it? She looked up at the door and wished for the doctor to come and not come! The longer she didn't know the truth, the longer she could believe her sweet baby was in the nursery, just waiting to see her.

Taking a deep breath, she wondered where Tom was and if he was OK. This had to be her fault. She must have done something wrong and caused her baby to die! Would Tom hate her? Leave her?

She started to shake, afraid of what he would say and do when he came through the door!

Pressing her fists against her eyes, Dorothy quietly sobbed, spasms of pain wracking her body as the cold air of the surgical recovery room nipped at her empty, broken body.

Chapter Six

Nurse Fern tracked down Dr. Brooks at the nurses' station, doing some charting. She informed him that Mrs. Cornell was awake and demanding answers.

Dr. Brooks sighed, rubbing his temple. These conversations never went well. He checked his notes once again, anticipating questions Dorothy might ask, making sure he had all the details. He asked Fern to retrieve Mr. Cornell from the waiting room and bring him to his wife's bedside.

As she went off to collect Tom, Dr. Brooks took a moment to sip some water and say a prayer to God to give him the words to comfort this couple and not hurt them any more than they already would be.

Tom jumped up as soon as the waiting room door opened to see a nurse he'd not seen before. She looked young, with reddish-brown hair, kind eyes, and a sad smile.

"Mr. Cornell, I'm Nurse Fern Hutchins. Please come with me. Dr. Brooks is headed to your wife's room, and he will speak to you both now."

Nodding, swallowing a huge lump in his throat, Tom brushed his hands across his pant legs, suddenly feeling clammy and sweating at the same time. Trying to breathe normally, he followed the nurse through the door and down a short hallway, bright with white paint and unforgiving lights above.

Dr. Brooks stood at the end of the hall, in front of the door where Tom assumed Dorothy was.

"Tom, I'm so sorry. Dorothy hasn't been told anything yet, but I wanted you to be here. Please, follow me."

Silently, Tom nodded and watched as Dr. Brooks opened the door. Stepping in ahead of him, Tom saw his wife, shoulders curled forward, cradling her empty belly. His heart felt like it was shattering. He moved to her bedside and sat down with her. Pulling her toward him, he surrounded her body with his arms, rocking her slowly, not saying a word. He could feel her body shaking with silent tears, and he couldn't fix her. He couldn't fix himself. He simply waited for Dr. Brooks to make it all go away.

Clearing his throat and glancing upward to clear his own eyes of tears, Dr. Brooks looked at this couple and started reciting the words he'd had in his mind for the past few hours.

"Your baby had hydrocephalus. That means all the spinal fluid seeped into the brain and, essentially, the baby drowned. There is no way to know a baby has this until it's born. It's a medical mystery. We don't know what causes it. We don't have a way to cure it. Babies born with this are either stillborn or die shortly after birth most of the time. Some of them live, but they have severe, debilitating deficiencies that require round-the-clock care for as long as they are alive. I'm sorry this has happened, Dorothy. We had to do an emergency cesarean section, as I know Nurse Fern informed you of. There was a lot of blood. Your life was in danger. You need to rest as much as possible, and we need to keep you here in the hospital for a week."

Dorothy struggled to understand what the doctor was saying as she clung to her husband, and the tears rolled down her cheeks.

Tom leaned back and looked at his wife. He brushed her tears away and again swallowed the lump in his throat.

"We had a son, Dottie. A little boy." He knew she wanted to know but hadn't found her voice to ask.

This seemed to make her cry harder. She knew how much Tom wanted a little boy, and she knew he must be devastated.

"Dr. Brooks," Dorothy interrupted quietly. "Dr. Brooks, can I see my baby, please? I have to see him."

"Yes, of course, you may see him. I explained to Tom the baby doesn't look like others born with this defect. His head is of normal size. It's just very soft in the back. His skin is dark due to him passing several days ago. But other than that, he looks fine."

"Fine. I'm sure he looks just fine for a dead infant, Dr. Brooks," Dorothy said vehemently. Her anger was spiking again, as no one had listened to her when she said the baby no longer moved within her.

Dr. Brooks had heard these statements before on the rare occasions he'd had patients deliver a hydrocephalus baby. He didn't take it personally. He understood, as much as he could, the loss of a child. He also knew there was nothing that could have been done to prevent it. It was already done, and it was a blessing that this child hadn't lived. It would have suffered greatly and known much pain. He saved these words for later and nodded to Nurse Fern to go fetch the stillborn child.

"Nurse Fern will be back soon with your baby. You can take as much time as you need with him. We'll be right outside if you need us to answer any more questions. I know that this is a lot. It's overwhelming, and I'm very, very sorry."

Tom looked at the doctor while still holding his wife and nodded. He understood that this was no one's fault and couldn't have been prevented or cured. Dorothy was shaking. He wasn't sure if it was shock, anger, frustration, or sadness. Probably all those things, he decided.

Dr. Brooks left them alone for a few minutes to gather themselves and be ready to see the baby that never took a breath. His heart ached for his patients that suffered these losses, and he wanted to give them as much privacy as possible. There'd be time for more explanations later. Dorothy would have to be monitored and examined as the days passed to be sure she was clear of any infection. Dr. Brooks shook his head, recalling how close he was to losing her on the OR table as well. She'd lost a lot of blood, and the deteriorating body of her son inside of her had made her very sick. He knew she was a strong person, though, and felt she would heal in time—physically anyway.

He would have to tell them not to try to have any more children for at least a year, if ever. That was another conversation he hated having with his patients.

Tom reached for a tissue to wipe Dorothy's tears again. They need to gather themselves to meet and then say goodbye to their baby son.

"Dorothy, I love you so much. I'm so sorry."

"What are you sorry for? This wasn't your fault, Tom. I wonder if I did something, though," she whispered back.

"No, honey, no. You heard Dr. Brooks. There's no way to know about these things and no way to stop it. You didn't do anything wrong. Shhhh." He shushed her as fresh, hot tears streamed down her face.

"How can our baby be dead, Tom? How?" Dorothy let him rock her in his arms, so many questions racing through both their minds. Feelings of anger, hurt, and fear coursed through their veins, as well as unfathomable heartbreak.

"I don't know, honey. I don't know. OK, here, let's just breathe and take a minute to get ourselves together. We get to see him and hold him. Let's make the most of that time." He didn't have the right words to say, but he didn't want Dorothy, or himself for that matter, to forget even one hair on their baby's head. This would be a brief moment to savor what could have been, and he wanted to never forget, even though it was never meant to be.

"You're right, Tom. We must always remember him." Through her tears, she sat up a little straighter until the pain in her belly made her gasp sharply.

"Here, let me adjust the pillows," said Tom, aching to do something, anything, to ease his wife's pain.

As they waited for Nurse Fern to bring in their baby, they were each lost in their own silent thoughts.

Tom thought about how all they'd planned and created in their home was all for nothing now. He couldn't see ever going through this again. He'd have to call his parents and his boss. He didn't think he could get through the explanations without completely losing composure.

He also knew he'd have to plan a funeral . . . for his baby. Dorothy wouldn't be there; she'd still be here. He would have to bury his son alone. That thought terrified and angered him. They needed each other to draw strength from, and he wasn't even being given that.

Dorothy's thoughts ran from her empty belly to frustration that no one heard her words about the baby not moving. Then she thought about Dr. Brooks telling her that there was no way to know this would happen. No preventing it. She still felt guilty, though, as if she should have died and her son should have lived if only for Tom's sake. She felt so confused and lost. What was she to do? She'd have to call her parents and her sisters. They'd come; she knew they would come and care for her as long as she needed them. She only wanted her own mother, though. She knew Betty Jean and Phyllis were busy with their own broods, and she also didn't know if she could stand the sight of healthy children playing and laughing. Her own baby would never utter a sound. Never run, play, or go to school. Her baby would be cold in the ground, all alone. These thoughts made her angry and jealous. She tried to force them from her mind as she waited for the nurse to bring her her dead son.

Chapter Seven

Tom turned to face the door and held tightly to Dorothy's hand. He felt they were as ready as they could be to see their son.

Just moments later, they both watched as the door to the room whispered open. Nurse Fern held a white blanket wrapped tightly around a silent infant. From their vantage point of the bed, all they could see was the blanket and a snowy-white cap peeking over the edge.

Nurse Fern felt her own heart break as she looked at this couple whose lifeless baby she held in her arms. Usually, the maternity ward was the happiest place in the hospital, but once in a while, there were days like this when there were no cries from a newborn demanding milk and a warm blanket.

She slowly walked to the bed and leaned down. She placed the bundle into the limp arms of his mother. She watched as Dorothy's gaze fell on the somber face of the child. Tom, too, was looking down at his son, whose eyes were forever closed.

Nurse Fern said not a word as she carefully and silently backed out of the room, allowing the couple to grieve and spend time with their baby.

Walking back to the nurses' station, she found Dr. Brooks waiting there for her. He instructed her to call the funeral home in town, as he had told her a few times before when a baby or a mother didn't survive their journey here. She nodded and jotted down notes as he gave her instructions. He told her to let the Cornells have as much time as they needed to say goodbye and to not disturb them. He said he'd be back in a few hours to check Dorothy.

Nurse Fern went to an empty desk and began charting the details before picking up the phone to make the call she didn't want to make.

Dorothy held her lifeless child, tears pouring silently down her face. She could feel Tom's arms around her and vaguely noticed he was rubbing her arm.

She couldn't take her eyes off her son. His skin was dark, as Dr. Brooks said it was. It wasn't as scary as she thought it would be. His eyes were closed as if he were asleep. His cheeks were soft, and his lips were full.

Carefully Dorothy stroked her baby's cheek with a fingertip. She turned and looked up at Tom. "He's beautiful, isn't he?" It was more of a statement than a question.

"Yes, he is," Tom choked out the words. His own tears left tracks down his face as he tried to bring himself to touch his baby.

"I want to see his hair," said Dorothy. With one hand underneath him, she took her other hand and carefully pulled back the white cap the nurse had placed on the baby's head.

Dark hair curled over his tiny forehead and across his head. "He looks so much like you, Tom! See, he has your cheekbones and your hair. See, he's so handsome!"

Tom could only nod and carefully reached over to stroke the baby's fine, dark hair. Dorothy turned to her side and handed the baby to her husband.

Gingerly Tom took his son in his arms and felt fresh tears sliding down his face. He wanted to be strong for Dorothy, but this was just too much. His precious baby was dead, and he had to figure out how to deal with it and be strong for his wife. Inside he was silently screaming for help. For justice, for answers. He was completely overwhelmed with emotion and simply didn't know what to do except stare at his son and memorize every line of his sweet face.

As Tom held his tiny son in his arms, he thought of all the things that would never be. Letting tears course unchecked down his face, he let the emotions happen. The baby, with eyes closed, didn't move at all, of course, and it only fueled Tom's anger and frustration. He now felt Dorothy's hand on his back, quietly rubbing. He supposed she didn't know what to do either.

Neither of them expected this to happen, so they weren't prepared and didn't really know how to act.

After a bit, Tom slid his hand to the back of the baby's head, wanting to feel the softness the doctor said was there, all the spinal fluid that had made its way to his son's brain and killed him.

Carefully he supported the baby's head and let his fingers explore. Sure enough, it was soft and malleable, not unlike a soft pillow. He looked over at Dorothy. She reached her hand out, and he placed it on the back of the baby's head so she, too, could feel the soft pocket of fluid.

He watched as tears fell from her eyes and landed on their son's face. Carefully, he brushed them with the tip of the blanket that held their baby tight.

After a few moments, Tom handed the baby back to Dorothy. She carefully took him and laid him down on the bed. "I just want to see his body."

Tom nodded in agreement.

Dorothy unwrapped the tiny body to see that he was the same tan-brown color all over. There was a little diaper on him, but that was all. Dorothy thought longingly of the sleeper she'd chosen at home to dress her baby in when they left the hospital. She supposed she'd have Tom bring it in, and they would bury their son in it. This made her cry once again as she thought of all the tiny clothes, booties, and blankets waiting for the baby who would never come home.

She ran her hands over the tiny arms and legs. They were so soft and yet so cold. Tom looked down and touched his son's chest as if feeling for a heartbeat. All he felt was cold, smooth skin. He helped Dorothy as she rewrapped their infant.

Dorothy picked the baby up carefully and held him to her chest. She began to sob. She felt the stitches of her operation pulling and causing pain. It was nothing compared to the pain ripping her heart apart. How could she let this little one go into the ground? He'd be alone, cold, and lost. How could this be happening?

Tom held her close, tucking her head under his chin, and rubbed the back of the receiving blanket. He, too, wondered how this had come to be and how he was going to let go and move on with life. It seemed so unfair to be alive while this innocent baby was not.

Time passed, and they murmured words to each other that sometimes made sense and sometimes didn't. They had no frame of reference for what was happening to them, so they just said whatever came to mind.

Soon an hour had gone by, and it felt like it was time to figure out what came next.

Tom said he would make the phone calls to their parents as Dorothy needed to rest. He'd also take care of the arrangements for their son. He couldn't bring himself to say the word *funeral*, and neither could Dorothy. She asked him to bring the little white sleeper to dress him in. She was going to clothe her son, no one else. She wasn't going to allow it. It would be the only time she would ever have to dress her baby, and she would insist on this happening.

Tom understood and promised her this. He wasn't sure how that would happen, as he figured the hospital would want to have the baby sent to the funeral home as soon as possible, especially since he'd already been gone nearly a week.

Dorothy kissed her baby over and over, trying to warm his little face with her lips. Inevitably, his skin cooled again almost immediately. She told herself to ignore that and continued to kiss his sweet face. She wished she could see his eyes, but she was afraid to open them. She knew she shouldn't, so they didn't try. Tom held his son again, kissed him, and whispered to him that he would always love him and never forget him.

"Tom, should we give him a name?" Dorothy asked, tears brimming over her lashes.

"We talked about Mark for a boy. Do you still like that?"

Dorothy looked at her son. He had, indeed, made a mark on their world. Mark suited him, and she didn't want him to go without a name.

"Yes, Mark. Mark Thomas Cornell. Please, let's name him that."

Tom could only nod and touched the cold cheek of his son, Mark, once again.

"I'll go get Nurse Fern now. Then I'll go home and get the outfit and come right back."

"OK. OK, Tom." Dorothy's voice cracked. The time to say goodbye to her son was coming fast, and she didn't want it to end. She knew it had to, though.

Tom stood and kissed his wife on top of her head. Making his way to the door, he turned to look at her once again. Her head was bent over tiny Mark. She was studying his face. He knew it was so that she would always remember him. He didn't think it would be right to take a photograph, so he turned and pushed open the door.

Nurse Fern was at the nurses' station, waiting for him as he walked toward her.

"Mr. Cornell, what can I do for you?" she asked softly.

"I'm going to go home and get the outfit we planned for the baby to wear home. We want him to wear it for . . . for . . ." His words trailed off. He couldn't speak of burial just yet. It was too permanent.

"Yes, sir, I understand. I'll go check on Mrs. Cornell, and you just be careful going home and coming back."

"Yes, I'll be quick," Tom replied, stepping away from the nurse and heading down the hallway.

He didn't even recall leaving the hospital, but suddenly he was in his car. He sighed and grasped the steering wheel. It was fully dark out, and he had no idea really of what time it was.

He slotted the key into the ignition and started his car. Carefully he backed out of the parking space and turned toward the driveway and out into the street. The drive home provided a bit of normalcy in a day that had wrung him out completely.

Soon he arrived home to a dark house. No lights were on; they'd left too quickly earlier to even think about leaving a light on. He pulled into the driveway and shifted the car into Park.

Sighing again, he slowly got out of the car, never imagining he'd be taking clothes to the hospital that wouldn't be coming back with a baby in them!

Chapter Eight

Tom's heart was heavy yet beating fast as he stepped into the darkened kitchen of his home. He wondered if it was really a home or just a house as he thought about a newborn's cry and laughter he would not hear later on. As he crossed through the doorway into the living room, his fingers ran along the doorjamb where he'd planned to measure the height of his child as he grew. Now he wondered if it would ever come to pass.

He didn't know if he could go through this, should it happen again. And what about Dorothy? He could not imagine the pain she was in. It had to be a million times worse than the emptiness, anger, and frustration he was feeling. After all these years of wanting a child, finally, it was going to happen. Then it was snatched away before it could even begin.

With the dark thoughts rolling through his mind, Tom quickly hurried to the nursery and snapped on the light. He needed to get the baby's outfit and get back to the hospital as quickly as possible. Dorothy shouldn't be alone, and he wanted just a little more time with Mark before the undertaker would pick up the tiny body.

The little white sleeper with the matching cap was lying on the bassinet, all ready, next to a bag filled with cloth diapers, bottles, and baby formula. Tom looked at it forlornly and wondered if there was anything in it he needed. He decided to just put the bag away and deal with it later as he gathered up the sleeper and cap. Looking about the room one last time, he spied a small teddy bear in the crib; it had been a gift from his sister Joan. Next to it was the blanket Dorothy's mother had made. He scooped that up as well and practically ran out of the room. He was in such a hurry, blinded by stinging tears; he left the light on and wound his way through the house, out the door, and slid back into his car.

The drive back to the hospital was a blur. He felt he'd driven it a thousand times, even though it'd only been just the one time a few hours ago. The spot he'd parked in before remained empty, so he pulled right in and jumped out of the car as fast as he could.

He practically ran to the doors of the hospital, wanting to be by Dorothy's side as quickly as possible. The lobby was darkened for the night, with just a few small lamps lit. The nurse from earlier remained at the front desk.

As Tom rushed to the desk to be let into the maternity ward, the nurse nodded and rose to walk him to the maternity wing. She knew what had happened, as Nurse Fern had advised her and let her know Mr. Cornell would be returning and to expect the local undertaker to arrive later as well.

The charge nurse patted Tom on the shoulder and told him she was so sorry for his loss as she opened the door to maternity and saw him through. He seemed oblivious to her, as he just wanted to see his wife and son.

As Tom passed the nurses' station, Fern nodded at him and gave a weak smile. Again, he barely noticed as he made his way to Dorothy's room.

Walking in, he watched as Dorothy held their infant up to her chest and was quietly rocking him in her arms. She hummed a lullaby, tears sliding down her face. Tom was sure that his heart was splitting in half as he watched the heartbreaking scene before him.

Dorothy looked up and met his gaze. Fresh tears rolled from her eyes, and he felt his own hot, angry tears follow suit.

Quickly he walked to the bed and sat down next to her. The clothing, blanket, and teddy bear fell out of his hand onto the foot of the bed. He wanted to get rid of the items as if dropping them would make the reality just a bad dream.

Enveloping Dorothy and Mark in his arms, Tom felt the warmth of Dorothy's body and the cool stillness of Mark's. He simply didn't know what to do as the trio rocked gently back and forth, quiet tears and sobs filling the sterile hospital room where so many before them had celebrated the births of their children. It seemed so unfair, and a rage built inside Tom. He did his best to tamp it down. He knew there would be plenty of time later to be as angry as he felt, but now he had to be there for Dorothy and his baby, even though his baby wasn't really here.

Slowly, Tom released his tight hold on Dorothy and took the corner of the bedsheet to dry her tears. She smiled gently at him.

Silently she handed the baby to Tom. He carefully held his son, memorizing each contour of his face as he had done earlier. This time, he took special care to tuck the image of his baby into his heart, into his mind. Each detail—the tiny upturned nose, the soft hair. Even the dusky tone of the baby's skin. He knew that was due to being not alive for several days. But he also told himself that Mark was part Cherokee, as Tom was, and that would contribute to a darker complexion. It was too painful to think that his son was only dark due to dying before he was born.

He slowly felt the softness of the back of Mark's head and hoped that he hadn't known what was happening when the spinal fluid moved into his brain and snuffed out the life he never got to live. He hoped his baby had felt no pain and simply drifted away and was at peace.

Carefully he laid the baby down on the bed and looked at Dorothy.

"I brought the sleeper for him. I thought he should have the bear from my sister and the blanket from your mom. I . . . I didn't want him to be alone," Tom said, choking on the words, trying not to sob.

Dorothy nodded and leaned down to retrieve the tiny white sleeper and cap.

"Here, help me get this on him. We can do this together," she said, slowly unwrapping the tiny body from the hospital receiving blanket.

The limp arms and legs made Dorothy shudder. He should be waving his arms and legs around, breathing and looking about at his new world, not silent and still. How would she get through this and hand her baby over to strangers? The thought of him in the ground soon almost made her scream. Instead, she sent more prayers to heaven for strength and guidance. Never had she dreamed that she would have a stillborn baby! As time marched on through her marriage, she had finally taken it that she'd never have a baby. So when she finally became pregnant, it never occurred to her that her baby wouldn't live!

She picked up the sleeper. It was soft and warm. Tom carefully helped slide the baby's legs and arms into it. Dorothy snapped the tiny snaps that cozied up under the baby's chin. As Tom lifted Mark's body up, Dorothy carefully tucked the cap around Mark's head so that the soft part in the back was cushioned. She knew it didn't really make any difference, but she felt better somehow, knowing that his little head was protected now since her body hadn't been able to protect him.

Together, they spread out the soft blanket Dorothy's mother had made and laid Mark's tiny body down on it. Tom placed the teddy bear on Mark's chest, and as they folded him within the blanket made with love, they wrapped his tiny arms around the bear for eternity.

The tears were endless as they completed this one task they could do for their child. Soon the undertaker from Ware Smith Funeral Home would come and take their baby away.

Dorothy carefully picked up her son one last time and handed him to her husband. She watched his face as he tucked the baby next to his heart and kissed the top of his head. Her heart wrenched, and she again felt as if it was her fault and that she'd failed her husband miserably.

As Tom held his baby for the last time, he spoke softly to him. "Mark, I love you so much. I had so many plans for us, but God has better plans for you. I know you're safe and loved more than we could ever love you here. But I sure am going to miss you. Please know that I love you so much and that I'm so sorry."

With that, he gazed down at his baby's face and kissed his tiny nose. Then he looked at Dorothy, who again had tears streaming down her face. He held the infant out toward her, and she gingerly took the swaddled body into her arms one last time.

Looking at his face, eyes forever closed, she began to rock him gently one more time. Quietly she sang a lullaby, making up the words as she went along. She wasn't even sure what she was saying but continued on with comforting words, more for herself than anything else. She held him to her shoulder, feeling his weight, measuring the finality of these last few moments with her child.

Finally, she pulled back and looked down at her son. She kissed his darkened face all over. His skin was cold as if he'd just come in from a winter's day.

Looking up at Tom and nodding, he slowly stood and made his way to the door. Looking back at Dorothy and Mark one last time, Tom went to let Nurse Fern know that they were ready for the undertaker to come now.

Nurse Fern dialed the funeral home and let Tom know they'd be there within just a few minutes. Nodding at her, he swiftly walked back to the room.

Stepping in, he saw that Dr. Brooks had arrived and was speaking to Dorothy. She still held Mark in her arms.

"Oh, Tom, I was just telling Dorothy that we're going to keep her here for a few days yet. Make sure she's strong and has no infections."

"Yes, that's a good idea," Tom replied, just staring at his baby, willing him to suddenly take a breath, knowing it would never happen.

Dorothy looked back at him. She was thinking about the funeral and how Tom would have to do that alone. It made her sick and angry, but she couldn't leave the hospital, and the baby had to be buried.

"Tom, Dorothy, please again, know that neither of you caused this. It just happened. There's no preventing it and no stopping it. It is not your fault in any way. Once you're healed in a few months, Dorothy, I want you both to come see me." He didn't say it was to discuss future babies, but they both knew what he meant. Dorothy vaguely wondered if she would ever get pregnant again or if she even wanted to. If this happened again, she didn't know if she could go on.

Chapter Nine

Nurse Fern heard the door of the maternity wing open and knew before she looked up that it was the undertaker from Ware Smith Funeral Home that was walking into the unit. It was near midnight, and no one else was expected at that time of night. Looking up, her eyes met those of the somber man before her. She nodded and said hello. It wasn't often that Mr. Rans was in the maternity ward, but she'd seen him enough to know who he was.

"Mr. Rans, I'll go let the Cornells know you've arrived." She couldn't bring herself to say, "Good evening." There was nothing good about it.

Kyle Rans nodded at the nurse. He had arrived without a gurney. As a baby was so small, he would just carry the infant out to his hearse. Transporting infants and young children was the hardest thing he ever had to do. When an older person passed away, it was oftentimes a blessing for the family. Those who'd been sick or very old were often ready to go. But infants, children, and young adults—those were heartbreaking situations, and he had never really gotten used to those. He would be sure to take the utmost gentle care of this stillborn infant for this couple. Silently he waited near the desk for the nurse to return with the baby.

Gently knocking on the door, Fern waited before going into the room where the Cornells were with their baby. She heard a faint voice beckoning her to enter. She took a deep breath and quietly opened the door.

Gazing at the sad couple holding their infant all wrapped in white, Nurse Fern let them know the undertaker was here whenever they were ready. They nodded at her almost in tandem, and Mr. Cornell asked for just a few more minutes.

Fern nodded back and carefully shut the door behind her as she went back to her station. She told Mr. Rans it would just be a few minutes. He took a seat nearby and patiently waited, knowing letting a loved one actually be taken away was often the most difficult part of the entire funeral process. Once a family allowed the undertaker to remove the body of their loved one, it became all too real.

Back in the room, Tom and Dorothy each took one last turn, holding their son. Dorothy's eyes roamed over her son's face one last time as she was determined to never forget each detail. Finally, she leaned down and kissed her son on his forehead, nose, and lips. Then she placed him gently in Tom's arms.

"Tom, can you take him out? I want to remember you holding him, not the nurse. I don't want to see the undertaker with him. Can you do it?" she pleaded, tears streaming down her face once again.

Tom swallowed a giant lump in his throat and could only nod. The weight of the lifeless body felt solid and cold in his arms despite the blanket his son was wrapped in. He'd do anything to ease his wife's pain.

Standing, he looked down at Mark's face, still and quiet forever more. He, too, pressed a gentle kiss on the baby's forehead and turned to the door. "I'll be right back, Dot."

She could only nod, hugging herself and silently crying as she looked at her husband, holding their son, turn and walk out the door. Knowing she'd never see her baby again as long as she lived, a sorrow drove itself into her heart and mind, crushing her spirit, breaking her heart, and settling in her empty belly. She didn't ever want to go through this again.

Tom slowly walked toward the nurses' station, holding his son in his arms. There was a man seated off to the left who stood, buttoning his suit jacket. Of course, this was Mr. Rans, Tom knew. He'd seen the kindly undertaker at several funerals over the years. He was always very pleasant. Tom never dreamed he'd be meeting with this man to plan a funeral for his child!

"Mr. Cornell, I'm Kyle Rans. I'm sorry to meet you under these circumstances. Please know that I will take special care of your son," said Mr. Rans quietly.

Tom nodded and said, "Yes, I've seen you at many funerals over the years. I just never thought that . . ." Tom couldn't continue his thought as the lump in his throat threatened to choke him. Tears shone in his eyes.

"I understand, sir. Would you be able to come to the funeral home tomorrow morning, say 9 a.m.? We can go over details, and you can take your time."

Tom nodded, still trying to wrap his head around what was happening. It was impossible. His son just couldn't be dead. Yet there he lay, lifeless in Tom's arms. He looked down at the sweet baby and hugged him just a little tighter. Looking first at the nurse, who gazed at him with sympathy, he took a deep breath and looked at Mr. Rans.

"Yes, I can be there. Um, OK, here you go. His name is Mark." Tom looked at the baby once again and kissed his forehead. He looked at Mr. Rans, who'd lifted his hands out to take the infant, and quickly placed the baby in his arms.

"I will see you tomorrow, Mr. Cornell. I'm so very sorry for your loss. Please extend my condolences to your wife."

Tom nodded and quickly turned to go back to Dorothy. He didn't want to see this virtual stranger walk away with his baby. It was becoming all too real, and time was moving on. It never stopped. What was the adage, "Time heals all wounds"? He scoffed and thought he'd never not feel this wound. It was too deep and too hard.

Tom went straight to the bed, sat down, and took Dorothy into his arms. They didn't speak, just held each other, rocking slightly back and forth. Unbelievable pain wracked their souls and bodies. Silent tears mingled together as they each felt their feelings, but neither spoke their thoughts. They were lost in their own versions of the hell they were going through.

After a time, they sat apart and dried their tears. Tom looked at his wife. He noticed how pale and tired she looked. He was sure he didn't look good either.

"So, what did Mr. Rans say?" Dorothy asked in a timid voice.

Clearing his throat, Tom replied, "He said he'd take special care of Mark and asked me to come see him tomorrow at 9 a.m." Staring at his wife, he watched as she nodded.

"OK, I guess that's what you'll do then. I'll be here. I can't leave," she said, tense anger in her voice.

"I know. It's OK, Dorothy. I don't want you to have to do this anyway. I'll do it and take care of it. You just concentrate on healing and getting better." He reached over and intertwined his fingers with hers.

She nodded. Thoughts raced through her mind of what a baby's funeral would be like. She hated the thoughts and pushed them away. It felt like she was somehow betraying Mark by envisioning a tiny casket and flowers to put on it. She almost couldn't bear the thoughts that bombarded her. How would she ever sleep at night?

"Honey, it's so late now. You need to rest. I . . . I guess I should get back home and try to sleep too. It's well after midnight. I want you to get better." Tom was rambling, but he didn't know what else to say or do. He wanted to go out of the hospital and breathe fresh air. That made him feel so guilty, as Dorothy was going to be stuck in here for several days yet. He wondered if he felt the need to escape because of what he was going to have to endure the next few days, all alone.

"You're right, Tom. You need rest. So do I. I'm so sorry. I'm so sorry." Dorothy began to cry again.

Tom wrapped her in his arms and rocked her again. "Shhh, shh. It's not your fault. Or mine. It just is." He held her for a few more minutes and felt himself becoming weary and drained.

"I'm going to go get Nurse Fern before I go, all right?" he finally said.

"Yes, yes, that's a good idea. I'm in a lot of pain," replied Dorothy, gingerly touching her belly.

Tom stood and walked to the door. He looked over his shoulder to see Dorothy struggling to get comfortable, and he stepped out in search of the nurse. He felt resolved to keep putting one foot in front of the other and keep going.

Nurse Fern was at the desk and stood as he approached. She smiled gently at him in anticipation.

"Hi. Dorothy says she is feeling some pain, and I'm getting ready to go home. Can you give her something?"

"Absolutely. I'll also be moving her to a private room, and I'll let you know the number tomorrow when you come. She should feel more comfortable there, and you'll be able to visit for as long as you like."

Tom nodded and said, "I'll just let her know and then be on my way."

"I'll be there in a few minutes. Dr. Brooks wants to examine her. Then he'll prescribe something for her pain."

"Thank you, Nurse Fern. You've been so helpful through all of this," Tom replied.

"I'm so sorry, Mr. Cornell. I'll do whatever I can to help you both," she said.

Tom went back to Dorothy and explained what was going to happen next and gave her a hug and kiss. He assured her he would be back after he met with Mr. Rans in the morning and said goodnight.

Dorothy watched as her husband left the room. All the air seemed to go with him, and she felt claustrophobic and alone.

Just as quickly as he left, Dr. Brooks and Nurse Fern stepped in. They smiled kindly at her, and she appreciated their genuine concern. She listened as they explained the next steps, and Dr. Brooks lifted her bandages to examine her stitches. Dorothy chose not to look and stared at the ceiling, allowing them to do what they needed to. He sent Nurse Fern off for some pain meds and rebandaged her incision.

Nurse Fern returned with a glass of water and a paper cup with pain pills in it. As Dorothy took the pills and drank the cool water, Nurse Fern pulled in a second gurney that Dorothy would be moved on to and then taken to a private room, away from this room filled with pain and stale air.

Chapter Ten

Tom once again found his way to the parking lot, feeling dazed and exhausted. Climbing into his car, he sighed and clicked the seat belt. Starting the car, he made the short journey home for the third time in less than twenty-four hours.

Pulling up to the house, his pulse quickened as he saw the light on in the nursery. For a split second, his mind told him that Dorothy and Mark were in there. Perhaps she was feeding him or changing his diaper, and he was simply returning home from work.

As quickly as the fantasy thought raced through his mind, it left him with the grim reality that he'd forgotten to turn out the light when he'd been home earlier to retrieve the sleeper to bury his son in.

Fresh tears simply ran unchecked down Tom's face. He didn't have to be strong for Dorothy right now. He could freely grieve and cry with no one to watch.

Parking his car, he drew his sleeve across his eyes and pulled his white linen hanky from his pocket. Blowing his nose, he just sat in his car for a few minutes.

Disjointed and broken thoughts bounced around in his brain as he tried to focus on his situation. His current reality. He didn't want to go inside the empty house alone. He knew he had to. He knew he had to find sleep to face the morning coming.

With one last sigh, he climbed out of his car and shut the door quietly. Walking into the dark kitchen, he snapped on a night light Dorothy had placed in the corner of the counter. Its soft glow was just enough. Tom's eyes burned and felt swollen from all the tears shed for so many hours. He knew he wasn't done with crying and didn't know—much less care—when he would be.

Slipping out of his suit jacket, he pulled off his tie and walked to his bedroom. There he went through the motions he always did to get ready for bed.

Not quite ready to lie down, he walked back to the kitchen. As exhausted as he was, he didn't think he could go to sleep just yet. He pulled a heavy glass from the cabinet and, from another, took down a bottle of cognac. Not much of a drinker, Tom wasn't sure if a shot of cognac would help him sleep, but he was so distraught, he didn't care. It always seemed to work in the movies when someone was upset or needed to sleep, so he poured himself a small shot in the glass.

Sniffing the alcohol, it stung his nose. He carefully took a small sip. The cognac burned his throat and hit his gut with a hot sensation that made him cringe. He set the glass on the counter, leaned over the sink, and spit the nasty taste out of his mouth. That, for sure, wasn't what he was looking for!

Instead, he settled on a glass of water and walked down the hall toward his bedroom. The nursery door was open, and the light was still on. Tom paused at the door but didn't go in. It was too painful. He looked at the furniture and blinked back tears. Shutting the light off, he pulled the door till it was almost shut. That was more he'd have to deal with in the coming days. But not right now.

Tom walked into their bedroom and sat on the edge of the bed. He took another sip of water and set the glass down on his nightstand table. He felt the need to talk to God and ask for peace, so he silently prayed. No instant relief surfaced, but he prayed anyway.

Finally, he lay down and pulled the sheet and blanket up. He thought of Dorothy in the hospital. He thought of Mr. Rans taking care of his son. As more tears slid down his face and into his pillow, he finally drifted off into a restless sleep.

Chapter Eleven

Morning dawned with bright sunshine that woke Tom with a vengeance. His eyes felt gritty, sore, and dry. He slowly sat up, remembering the nightmare from yesterday. The reality of it all was slowly sinking in. His thoughts immediately went to Dorothy, and he decided he would call her before heading to the funeral home. It was just eight o'clock, and he had time before he had to meet with Mr. Rans.

Quickly Tom showered and dressed in slacks and a sweater to ward off the early spring chill. The sun shining seemed like a cruel joke on what was a wrenching day for him and his wife.

Pouring a cup of coffee, he called the hospital from the kitchen phone. The nurse who answered wasn't Fern; he supposed her shift was over. The new nurse said that Dorothy was in room 212, and she connected him right away.

"Hello?" said a weary voice.

"Dottie, it's me. I wanted to call you before I left home this morning. How are you feeling?"

"Oh. Hi. Well, I'm tired and sore. How are you?" Her voice was almost devoid of feeling.

"I'm tired too, honey. I'll come and see you as soon as I can. I just wanted to tell you that I love you," he replied.

"OK. I love you too. See you later," Dorothy replied. She still sounded monotone.

Tom hung up the phone, anxious to be with her. She needed to heal and be strong. He needed to help her.

Gulping down his coffee, which seared his throat, Tom grabbed his keys off the counter. He set the cup down in the sink, next to the shot glass from last night, and went out the kitchen door. This time, he took a moment to lock the house and went over to his car and got in. He was glad there were no neighbors out that might ask him what was going on. He didn't think he could carry on a conversation.

He drove down the street and headed toward the funeral home across town. Midland wasn't very big, and it wasn't fifteen minutes before Tom was pulling into the driveway of the low-set building. Ware Smith Funeral Home was a tan brick building of a mid-century modern design.

Tom could see a hearse parked off to the side and a few other cars he assumed belonged to Mr. Rans and the staff. No other cars were around. He was glad of that. The fewer people he had to talk to, the better.

As Tom opened the door to the funeral home, Mr. Rans was walking toward him, buttoning his suit jacket.

"Mr. Cornell, thank you for coming," said Mr. Rans, holding out his right hand. Tom nodded and shook his hand, not really trusting himself to speak.

"Please, join me in my office where we can talk." Mr. Rans turned down a short hall to the left of a parlor that had French doors standing open. Tom could see chairs, and soft music was playing. He followed Mr. Rans into a well-appointed office and took a seat opposite a wide mahogany desk as Mr. Rans sat down.

"I'm so sorry for the loss of your son, Mr. Cornell. We are here to assist you with decisions and help you through this process." Kyle stated as he did to all the clients he served. This would be difficult, but he was professional enough to get through it without becoming personally involved.

Tom cleared his throat and looked around the elegant office. "Thank you. I don't really know where to begin, I guess." Tom held his hands up at a loss for words.

"Of course. This is something you don't often anticipate, but we are here to help. Would you like some coffee?"

Tom nodded, thinking he really didn't care if he had coffee or not, but it seemed like the proper response. He just felt numb and almost like he was watching this entire thing from another room! He couldn't really describe how he felt.

Kyle picked up his desk phone and asked his secretary to please bring coffee in. A few moments later, a woman of an indeterminate age appeared with a tray holding two coffee mugs with creamer and sugar bowls. She placed the tray on a credenza under the window, nodded to Kyle Rans, and left.

Kyle asked Tom how he took his coffee, and Tom responded with "Just black." Kyle placed a steaming white mug in front of Tom and then mixed sugar and creamer into a mug for himself and settled back down at his desk.

"OK, Mr. Cornell, let's talk about what kind of service you'd like to have for Mark."

Tom took a deep breath as he felt familiar tears prick his eyes. He didn't want a service at all. He wanted to be home with a newborn and his wife. How would he get through this? He took a small sip of coffee and cleared his throat.

"Well, I think I want something small. Private. Dorothy will be in the hospital for several more days yet. She can't even attend. I don't want to put her parents or mine through this. They shouldn't have to see their grandson like this." He still couldn't really say the word *dead*. It was too final, too cold.

Kyle nodded with understanding, but he also knew that families benefited from support of loved ones, so he spoke his next words very carefully.

"Tom, no one wants to face what you are facing. It's incredibly difficult to do this on your own. If your parents or Dorothy's are here, you'll have them for support. What about any siblings? Do either of you have any siblings?"

"Yes, I have a sister, and Dorothy has two sisters. However, they all live over two hours away and have their own lives and families. It would be a lot for them to find childcare for their own kids. I'm sure they wouldn't bring them to a service for a baby. Both of our parents are elderly, not in the best of health. This would be very difficult for them. I just don't think I could bear their grief, along with my own, especially with Dorothy not here. I think I just want it to be private. Just me. And, of course, our priest from Holy Family Episcopal."

"Oh yes, would that be Father Morgan, correct?"

"Yes, Father Morgan. I need to call him. I haven't called anyone. There hasn't been time. I . . . I need some time." Tom looked at the funeral director, and tears once again stung his eyes as he thought of all the calls he would have to make and all the responses he would hear.

"I understand. Let's move on to other topics, and we'll get back to phone calls. I can help you make a list of who you need to call." Kyle nodded as he spoke and made notes on his forms.

"OK, thank you," replied Tom, sounding weary.

"Next would be the cemetery. Where will interment take place?"

"Um, the town cemetery, I guess."

"OK. I know they have an area there just for children. I can contact them and set that up for you."

"OK," Tom said again. He couldn't bring himself to care much about what was going to happen. He kept thinking of Dorothy and how much he wanted to see her.

"Tom, the next thing we have to discuss is the casket. I understand how difficult this is, but I want you to choose a special casket for your son. Would you follow me please to the casket room?" Kyle Rans stood and buttoned his suit jacket. He had found it best to be professional during casket selection. It was incredibly painful for families to pick out the casket their loved one would spend eternity in and especially so when it was a baby or young child.

Tom slowly stood and followed as Kyle led the way out of his office and down another hall. Tom mindlessly filtered the soft music in the background that lulled him into a kind of numbness that seemed to allow him to continue putting one foot in front of the other.

Kyle turned into a side room, and Tom followed reluctantly. There were caskets set up all over the room in various colors and styles. Along one wall was a display of tiny caskets and ones that were too small for grown adults.

The lump in Tom's throat swelled once again. That there was even a need for these boxes simply broke his heart. He blinked away tears as he followed Kyle to the display. There were tiny pink and blue caskets. One was a light yellow, another green. A few were white. As he looked at the tiny boxes that were meant to hold remnants of lives never lived or cut short, he slowly shook his head and felt anger bubbling up inside. Why had this happened? What had they done to deserve this heartbreak? He swallowed hard and tucked those feelings deep inside. Now was not the time to fight with God. That would be later after all this was done and he had time to think about it and process it all—if he even could. He needed to be strong for his wife. His feelings would have to wait.

"Please take your time and ask me any questions you might have, Tom."

Tom tried to focus on the caskets in front of him. Again, the feeling of this being completely surreal overwhelmed him. He reached out a hand and touched a white casket. It felt cold and smooth. He thought about the layers of white Mark would be buried in. He turned to look at the blue casket. It had shades of light blue in the lining that looked like the sky. The tiny pillow was just a bit darker. The outside of the casket was the same baby blue as the lining. Tom liked baby blue. Dorothy's favorite color was blue. Maybe this was the right choice. He felt like perhaps Mark would feel loved, surrounded by his parents' favorite color.

There was a second blue one, nearly the same shade as the other. The handles on one were gold and silver on the other. Inside the lid of the silver-handled piece were three intertwined hearts that were sewn in silver thread. The words "God's Beloved" were embroidered below the hearts. Tom knew this was the one.

Turning to Kyle, Tom pointed at the tiny casket and nodded, not trusting himself to speak.

"OK, that's the one. I can take care of that for you. Let's head back to my office."

They made their way back to the office and settled back in their chairs.

The next order of business was writing the obituary. Tom listed all the family names of the survivors that would be printed on the paper. Of course, there would be no photograph since Mark had never lived.

It was Wednesday, so they decided to have the funeral the next day. There was no sense in waiting since Tom would be the only one attending. He needed to spend as much time as possible with Dorothy, and he just wanted this to be over with. Kyle understood, and he saw no reason to postpone it either.

They took time then to make a list of all the people Tom needed to call, starting with his parents and Dorothy's. He'd call his sister, but he'd let his in-laws tell their other daughters. He needed to call Father Morgan right away, too, to be sure he could do the service on such short notice.

Tom decided to call his neighbors and friends after the service to avoid as many questions as possible.

Kyle asked him about flowers. Tom hadn't thought of flowers. What was the point, really? He decided he would like three blue carnations and one white rose to bury with the baby. Kyle said he'd take care of the order.

Finally, they were finished with all the details, and Kyle stood up. He said he'd see Tom in the morning at ten o'clock at the cemetery. Tom didn't need or want a service here or at his church. Tom thanked him and shook his hands.

Kyle walked him to the door and said, "When we get to the cemetery tomorrow, I'll have the casket open so you can say goodbye and place the rose inside."

Tom just nodded, fresh tears brimming over his lashes.

Kyle squeezed his shoulder and held the door open. No words were needed.

Tom hurried to his car, anxious to get to the hospital and see Dorothy.

Chapter Twelve

The drive to the hospital was all too familiar. However, the parking spot Tom had used the day before had a car parked there, so he parked a bit further away. Shielding his eyes from the bright spring sunlight, he quickly made his way into the building and asked for directions to room 212.

He swiftly walked the halls until he came to Dorothy's room. The door was ajar, and he quietly poked his head inside in case she was asleep.

She wasn't asleep but sitting up in bed, looking out the window, a forlorn and sad expression on her face. She turned as she heard the door open and gave a wan smile to her husband.

Tom walked to her bed and sat on the edge. He gathered her cool hands in his and squeezed them gently.

"Hi. I hope you were able to get some rest last night. How are you feeling?" he asked her, searching her eyes.

"I'm OK, I guess. The pills helped with the pain. I think they helped me sleep too. I still feel so tired and weary, though," she replied.

"I imagine you'll need some time to recover from surgery. I'm tired too. We both are. This is so hard." Tom's sentence drifted off. They were both at a loss for words about the situation they seemed to be blindly navigating.

Dorothy cleared her throat and nodded. "How did it go with Mr. Rans?" she asked, her voice not much more than a monotone.

Tom again squeezed her hand. He told her about the blue casket and the simple flowers he had ordered. He let her know that Mr. Rans would let him see Mark one last time and put the white rose in the casket. He couldn't quite get all the words out without more tears slipping down his face.

For a while, he and Dorothy simply clung to each other, crying silent tears, shuddering with pain and emotion off and on.

Finally, Dorothy pulled away and wiped her eyes with the backs of her hands. Sniffling, she blinked hard and said, "OK, OK, we have to get through this, Tom. I've been thinking about all the things Dr. Brooks has told us about babies born like this. I do think it's a blessing that Mark didn't have to endure a short and painful life. I have to believe that there is something better in store for us later on. What do you think?" Her eyes searched his for support and confirmation that he might feel the same way.

Tom thought about it for a few minutes. The pain they were going through was incredibly heart-wrenching and seemingly non-ending. He knew rationally that as time passed, the pain would lessen. But he would never forget, and he didn't know if he could forgive—forgive himself for failing his wife. Or maybe he failed God in some way. He was wracked with guilt he didn't know where to place. Maybe Dorothy was right. Maybe there was a better plan coming later on that they simply couldn't know about yet. He finally sighed and said, "Maybe you're right. I just wish this pain would end for us. I can't bear to see you so hurt. I can't fix it. I feel so guilty!"

"Tom, it's not your fault. Please don't feel guilty. I feel guilty that I can't be with you tomorrow. I don't know how you will get through it, but I know you will. You're the strongest man I know. Are you sure you don't want anyone there with you since I can't be there?"

"No. I thought about it a lot. There's nothing our families can do. The situation is so sad and so personal, I think they would all feel so uncomfortable. I don't want to put them through that. It's hard enough being strong for each other. I can't stand the thought of having to comfort anyone else. Maybe that's selfish, but I don't care. I don't even know when I should make the calls to our parents. Should I call them all today or wait till it's over tomorrow?"

"I think we should wait. If we call them today, they'll insist on coming, and I know you don't want that. I'm sure they'll come at some point, but we can keep this just for us for now." She was the one rubbing his hands as his shoulders shook with more quiet sobs. Her heart was torn. The baby she had lost, she could no longer help. But she could help her husband, whom she loved so much. They had to be there for each other, or they would never heal.

Dorothy was tired of lying in the hospital bed, staring out the window and still mostly bare trees. Spring was always so fickle. One day the sun would shine bright, and the next, it might snow! She thought about tomorrow and hoped for a clear day for the burial and for Tom's sake.

Dr. Brooks appeared at the doorway and knocked gently. "Well, hello, Tom. It's good to see you this morning. I've been in to see Dorothy already, and she is healing nicely so far. The infections she has experienced are still there, but the medications we have her on are helping. Her fever is quite low this morning. If she continues to get better, I will release her in about three days."

Tom nodded and thanked the doctor for his help. Then he and Dorothy were alone again in the room.

"Are you hungry, Dot? Have you eaten anything?"

"Not very hungry. I did have some broth earlier, which seemed silly to eat at breakfast time, but it sounded good, and I've kept it down. They want me to eat more solid foods, but I'm just not hungry, and I don't care if I eat or not. Have you eaten?"

"Not really. It seems wrong that we can eat while our son never will. It's one of the things I feel guilty about. Why should I be allowed to enjoy anything when he can't and never will?"

"Tom, we have to stop thinking these things. I feel like that too. But I also know I want to be here for you, and I hope you want to be here for me. Our lives aren't over, even though it kind of feels like it. I'm going to heal and get out of here. I am going to spend time with you, and we're going to meet with Dr. Brooks and see what's next for us. I feel good about the future. I have to, to get through now."

Dorothy's words made sense, and Tom nodded as he slid his thumb across the back of her hand.

"OK, I'm on board with you, honey," said Tom.

Dorothy smiled and laid her head on his shoulder.

"So, would you like to try to eat something now? It's almost lunchtime," said Tom. If Dorothy was committed to getting better, he was going to give it his best too.

"Well, OK. I don't know what they want me to have for the noon meal," she replied.

"I'll go find out and see what I can come up with." Tom kissed her forehead and squeezed her hand. He knew they were both trying to be as brave as they could and looking for anything positive.

Walking to the nurses' station, he saw lunch trays being passed out. He inquired as to Dorothy's diet, and the nurse lifted the lid on a plate.

There was a chicken breast with gravy, a small salad, fresh fruit, and milk. It looked good, and Tom offered to take the tray to his wife. The nurse smiled and passed it to him and went on with her other meals.

Tom returned to the room and placed the tray on Dorothy's side table. "Looks like a pretty good lunch. I'll run to the cafeteria and see what I can get for myself and hurry back."

"OK, I'll just be waiting," Dorothy said with a small smile on her face. Tom's heart swelled with love and admiration for his wife's bravery.

Quickly he made his way to the cafeteria. It wasn't too busy, as there weren't a lot of patients in the hospital at this time. He selected a hamburger, side salad, cottage cheese, and chocolate pudding. He was hoping he could get Dorothy to eat some of it.

As soon as he got back to the room, he helped Dorothy to sit up in the bed and moved the tray table so that it was over the bed and in front of her.

He moved the bedside table and cleared it of anything he could so he could eat next to her. Then he uncovered her plate and opened the container of milk for her.

"Thanks, honey," said Dorothy, picking up her fork and knife. "It smells pretty good. I'm not really hungry, though."

"I know. Neither am I. But we have to eat so we can be strong." Tom put some mustard on his burger and bit into it. For hospital food, he found it to be quite good. Soon he'd finished the whole thing and started on his salad. He hadn't realized how hungry he really was. He watched as Dorothy ate a good bit of her food too and sipped at her milk. He knew she didn't like milk, but the doctor insisted that she had some.

Soon there was just the bowl of chocolate pudding left. Tom liked pudding, and he knew his Dottie did too. He'd purposely taken two spoons and handed one to her. She smiled and took it from him as Tom held the bowl up between them. They finished it off pretty quickly.

"My, I guess we were both hungrier than we realized!" Dorothy said, gently rubbing her now full belly.

"Yes, I guess so. I think we did really well. Here, let me gather this all up." Tom stood and made short order of the used dishes and utensils. He placed the tray out in the hall on a cart with some others.

Coming back inside the room, he watched as Dorothy stretched and yawned.

"I guess I'm kind of sleepy now. Later they are going to get me up and moving, they told me this morning. Maybe I'll take a nap now so I will be ready for that later," said Dorothy.

"That's a good idea, honey. I guess I should go home for a while. Check the mail and things." He didn't want to say out loud that he had planned to take the nursery apart. The reminders of what they were not meant to have were too much. He couldn't stand it.

"OK. That sounds like a good idea. Maybe you want to call your boss today and let them know what's going on."

"Yes, I need to. It's a good thing the office was having the carpets cleaned yesterday and today, so they let us have the days off, but they'll be expecting me tomorrow. I'm sure they'll understand why I won't be there. Maybe for a while." Tom nodded, making a mental note to call as soon as he got home.

"OK, dear. Well, I guess I'll sleep now then. Thank you for having lunch with me," Dorothy said, a smile playing on her lips.

"Oh, I plan to have a lot of meals with you." Tom kissed her forehead and hugged her. "I'll be back this evening for dinner, OK?"

"OK. I love you," replied Dorothy as she snuggled down under the white blanket.

"I love you too," said Tom as he quietly left the room, closing the door softly behind him.

He thought about how strong his wife was as he made the drive home once again. He was going to try to be just as strong as her for what he was going to do once he arrived home.

Chapter Thirteen

When Tom arrived home, he quickly went inside and locked the door. Most of his neighbors weren't around during the weekdays, but now and then, someone might drop by.

Tom needed privacy and time alone. He needed to make phone calls. He needed to undo the nursery he and Dorothy had spent so much time making just perfect for their baby.

He took a deep breath and stared at the olive-green phone on the counter. He thought if he called his boss first, calling his parents and then Dorothy's might not be quite as hard.

He stood at the counter after pouring himself a glass of water. He had his boss Mr. Kline's personal number. With the carpet cleaning being done, no one was at the office. It was a nice break for everyone to be off for a couple of workdays, but his break had turned into heartbreak.

Tom took a long drink of the ice water and dialed Mr. Kline's number. As the phone began to ring, Tom felt his heartbeat quicken. He wasn't even sure what he would say. Finally, the phone was answered by a woman.

"Hello, Kline residence."

Tom cleared his throat before speaking. "Um, hello? Mrs. Kline?"

"Yes, this is Mrs. Kline. To whom am I speaking?"

"Uh, this is Tom Cornell. I was wondering, ma'am, is Mr. Kline available?"

"Oh, Mr. Cornell. Hello. I hope you're well. Mr. Kline is just outside. Let me get him for you." With that, Tom heard Mrs. Kline lay the phone down. He was glad she didn't stay on the line too long and ask about Dorothy.

After a few moments, a voice came on the line. "Tom, hello. What can I do for you? Is everything with Dorothy OK?"

Tom felt the all-too-familiar tears prick at his eyes. He took a shaky breath and cleared his throat.

"Mr. Kline, I'm sorry to bother you at home, but no, things are not OK." He didn't know if he could get the words out without breaking down completely.

"Tom, are you all right?" Mr. Kline finally said after Tom was silent for several seconds.

"Mr. Kline, the baby, the baby didn't survive. He was stillborn yesterday." Tears ran down Tom's face, and he couldn't imagine having to call his parents and hers next. This was devastating him.

"Oh, Tom! I'm so, so sorry! I don't know what to say! What can I do for you?" replied a stunned Mr. Kline.

"Well, there isn't anything anyone can do, really. He had a condition. He wouldn't have survived no matter what. Um, I'm burying him tomorrow, and I was wondering if I could take the rest of the week off. Dorothy's in the hospital for a few days yet. I . . . I need some time to take care of things."

"Tom, you don't have to say another word. You take off as much time as you need. Do you want me to inform your secretary and staff?" asked Mr. Kline in a quiet voice.

"Yes, I don't think I can bear to make too many calls," Tom replied, thankful that he had such an understanding boss.

"Of course. Would you like me to come to the service? Can I help in any way at all?" he asked.

"No, no, Mr. Kline. I appreciate the offer, but I'm going to do this on my own. I can't see people just now. I hope you understand," Tom said, a catch in his voice.

"Certainly, Tom. Why don't you call me on Sunday? Let me know how you and Dorothy are. If you need a little more time off, I can arrange that for you. Please, please let me know if there is anything at all I can do for you. I'm so very, very sorry to hear your news. God bless you and Dorothy. I'll be praying for you," said Mr. Kline, his voice full of sincerity and concern.

"Thank you, Mr. Kline. I'll call you over the weekend," replied Tom.

As he hung up the phone, he took another shaky breath and downed the rest of the ice water. He needed a break from talking to people out loud about what had happened.

He walked slowly to the nursery and snapped on the light. The room was filled with a warm glow. The curtains were closed, and the sunlight wasn't very bright this afternoon.

Slowly he looked around the room, wondering what he should do first. Walking to the dressers, he opened the drawers. There weren't a lot of baby clothes in them, but he decided he should bag up the clothes first.

Walking back to the kitchen, Tom retrieved some paper bags from the grocery and took them back to the nursery. Carefully he folded the tiny clothes that would never be worn and carefully placed them into the paper bags. Next, he took the few outfits that hung in the closet and folded them into the bags as well. There were three bags full when he was done.

Tom took the bags down to the basement off the kitchen. There were two storage closets he'd built down there, and he decided to place the bags in there for now. Neither he nor Dorothy used the closets often, so it was a good place to store the clothes. It wouldn't be a constant reminder if they were tucked out of sight in there, he thought.

Next, he took each drawer out of the dresser and took them two at a time down to the basement as well. There were a couple of rooms in the basement he'd made for storage and entertaining. One held a ping-pong table and a bar. When he and Dorothy were a bit younger, they'd have friends over for ping-pong and drinks! Dorothy was one heck of a ping-pong player!

He placed the dresser drawers carefully in the smaller storage room and went back upstairs. Before tackling moving a dresser, he poured another glass of ice water and looked out the kitchen window.

The mid-spring afternoon was waning. He saw dark clouds moving in. He had no idea what tomorrow's weather would be but hoped for another sunny day.

Tom carefully maneuvered the dresser through the bedroom door and pushed it down the hallway. It slid pretty well on the linoleum, and he didn't have too much trouble getting it down the basement steps. He only ran into trouble, turning it at the bottom to go around the corner. He took his time, and several deep breaths later and with lots of patience, he managed to shove the dresser into the storage room. He replaced the drawers and stood looking at them for a minute.

The dresser looked completely out of place in a dark storage room in a basement. The light shone dully on the pink and blue drawers. He remembered how excited he was when he painted it. Shaking his head so as not to start crying again, he made his way upstairs and back to the nursery.

He did the same thing with the taller dresser, removing the drawers and hauling them downstairs, followed by the dresser. This one was a bit harder, as it was somewhat taller than the other one. He was able to get it into the storage room, though, and set it beside the first one.

Now for the crib. He went in search of the screwdriver and hammer he'd used to put it together and started taking it apart. He felt himself becoming angry and bitter about the whole situation. How was it fair that his baby was dead? Was this some kind of joke God was playing? Was He getting a kick out of watching Dorothy and him suffer like this? What was the point?

Tom almost started hitting the crib with the hammer but instead stopped and took a deep breath. Running his hands through his hair, he realized he shouldn't do anything stupid. There might be another baby at some point, and they'd need this crib. He momentarily felt guilty because this was Mark's crib, in a way, even though the baby would never sleep in it.

Tom was so frustrated. He just continued to dismantle the crib in a stiff manner, trying to shut his feelings off and just do what he needed to, to get it in the basement with the other items.

Finally, he finished and went back to the room again. There were a few pictures on the walls of baby animals they thought would suffice until they brought home either a son or a daughter and then they'd add to what they had already hung up.

A few baskets of toys were also there, patiently waiting for a child who'd never play with them. Tom carted it all to the basement storage room. He pulled the chain of the lightbulb and shut the door firmly behind him.

Once again in the nursery, he looked at the rocking chair and stool sitting forlornly in the corner. The rocker had belonged to Dorothy's mom. He didn't want to move it. It seemed like it should be there. He stroked the arm of the chair and wondered if his Dottie would ever hold a baby of her own in this rocker.

Glancing around one last time, Tom snapped off the light and left the room. He didn't shut the door all the way; he left it a crack open. It didn't seem right to shut the room off completely.

Tom walked slowly back to the kitchen and sat down at the dinette. He looked at the clock, surprised to see that it was after five. Suddenly he felt a little bit hungry and decided he'd eat to keep his strength up.

Looking in the fridge, he took inventory—eggs, cheese, milk, some ham sliced for luncheon meat, potatoes, and onions.

Hauling it all out, he made himself an omelet. He sliced and fried a potato to go with it and dished it up on a plate.

Setting the plate down on the table, he poured himself a glass of milk and sat down. He managed to eat most of his meal, his thoughts flitting from one thing to another so fast, he couldn't keep his thoughts straight.

He decided to make a list of people he needed to call and tasks he needed to do. Sitting back down, he ate a bit more and scrawled names of who he needed to call—his parents and hers. He'd already decided her parents could call Betty Jean and Phyllis. Tom would call his own sister. He didn't want his parents to have to tell her. They'd be upset enough.

Since he'd already called his boss, that was one name he could cross off the list. He decided he'd call a couple of friends and a few of the neighbors they were close to. But he wasn't going to call them until after the service.

Tom knew his parents and in-laws would want to come to the service, but he didn't want anyone there. He kept his decision to wait until tomorrow to call them and set the list aside. He couldn't think of much else he would need to do, as he'd already torn down the nursery.

Cleaning up his supper dishes, he decided to go see Dorothy before it got too late.

Chapter Fourteen

Tom arrived once again to a quiet hospital. He'd stopped on his way there and picked up a small container of mint chocolate chip ice cream at the City Dairy Ice Cream Parlor. It was his Dottie's favorite, and he wanted to try to cheer her up. He selected black cherry for himself.

Dorothy was sitting up in bed when he walked into her room. A nurse was just checking her vitals and taking her temperature. Dorothy gave him a weak smile as the nurse removed the thermometer and read it.

"Looks like your fever is nearly gone, Mrs. Cornell. That's very good. The rest of your vitals look good too. I'll be sure to let Dr. Brooks know how you're doing."

Dorothy thanked her and breathed a sigh of relief as the nurse left the room. Looking up at Tom, she noticed the paper bag in his hand. She recognized the City Dairy bag and gave him a small smile. She knew he was doing whatever he could to make her feel better, and she appreciated it, even though she didn't think she would ever really feel better.

"Hi, Dottie," said Tom, holding up the bag. "I brought your favorite." He gave her a slight grin and moved the tray table over to the bed, situating it so he could sit on the other side of it and they could have their dessert together.

"How did it go today, getting up and moving around?" he asked, busying himself with opening the ice cream containers and getting out napkins.

"Oh, it went all right. I'm pretty sore and weaker than I thought. I'll probably be here until the weekend. They said every day they will get me up more often and for longer periods of time. I'm glad. I need to get back in the swing of things."

Tom knew she meant that she wanted to get past this awful time and move forward. He nodded and handed her a spoon.

"What did you have for dinner tonight? I made myself an omelet," he said.

"You did? Well, that's great! I had meatloaf and sliced carrots. It wasn't too bad, actually. I was hungry, I guess, because they'd had me up and doing things."

"I imagine you're right. How's your mint chocolate chip?" Tom asked.

"Oh, it's perfect! Always been my favorite. So, what did you do today? Did you call Mr. Kline?"

Tom nodded as he had a mouthful of black cherry ice cream.

"Yes, I called him. He was very concerned. Sends his prayers. He said I can take off as much time as I need to. He said to please let him know if he can do anything for us. He's very sorry, of course."

"What else did you do? That can't have taken all day?" Dorothy asked. She had a feeling she knew exactly what he'd done, but she asked anyway.

"Oh, Dorothy," he said, hanging his head and blinking back tears.

"I . . . I put away the things from the nursery so you don't have to see them all when you come home. I put them all in the basement."

Dorothy nodded, and silent tears glittered in her eyes and rolled down her cheeks.

"I wondered if that's what you were doing. I appreciate that. I can imagine how hard that was for you, Tom. I love you so much, and I'm so thankful for you. I'm sure you're right. I don't need reminders when I come home," Dorothy replied and stroked the back of his hand.

"I left the rocker in there, though. It seemed, I don't know, like it should be left in there," he said, looking at the floor.

"I understand. That's OK, Tom."

They were both quiet for a bit, eating their ice cream, lost in their own thoughts and feelings.

"I will come up tomorrow, after, you know, after . . ." Tom's voice trailed off. Saying *funeral* made it very final that their son would be gone forever, and he didn't want to speak it out loud.

Dorothy put down her ice cream and reached for her husband. Tom moved the tray table away and put his arms around his wife. Together they cried and held on to each other, looking for strength and reasons as to why this had all happened.

Finally, Dorothy sat back and used her napkin to wipe her tears and reached up and dried Tom's tears as well. Her heart shattered that she couldn't be there with him tomorrow. She didn't know how he would get through it, and she didn't want him to worry about her while he was there and she wasn't. Her heart and mind were struggling to take each breath, but she was determined to be strong for her husband, who would be burying their child all alone.

"Tom, I know you can do this tomorrow. Do it for Mark since I can't be there. Surely he knows how much we love him."

Tom nodded and squeezed her hand. Dorothy hadn't seen the tiny casket, and he didn't want her to ever have to remember their son in it. He vowed never to burden her with any more pain.

"OK, OK. I will come as soon as I can afterward. I want to spend the day with you tomorrow," he said, looking into her brown eyes edged with green. She had a small black speck in the iris of her left eye that he'd always been fascinated by. He loved his Dottie so much.

"When you're here tomorrow, we can call our parents," Dorothy said. She knew Tom had planned to make those calls from home, but it wasn't fair to expect him to do everything connected to this heartache.

"Are you sure, Dorothy? I can call tomorrow evening after I leave here. I can do it," he said.

"No, Tom. You have done so much already, and you have to get through tomorrow. I'll call my parents, and you can call yours. We need to do this together," she said, tears again glistening.

Tom nodded and hugged her. "Well, I better head on home. You need your rest," he said, holding her gently.

"I suppose you're right. I am tired and kind of sore." Dorothy placed a hand on her belly where the stitches were. It was a nagging sort of pain that came in sharp jabs if she stretched too much.

Tom gathered the ice cream containers and threw them in the trash. Leaning over the bed, he kissed Dorothy, and she hugged him back. He could feel her love for him in her embrace and drew strength from it for the next day.

Chapter Fifteen

Once home, Tom got ready for bed, doing his normal evening routine, determined not to fall apart. After the late evening news, he fell into bed, hoping to sleep well. Of course, he spent a lot of time tossing and turning, disturbed by fractured dreams, and getting up for water a few times too.

Morning came, and he was almost glad of it in a way. The sooner the day started, the sooner it would be over, and he could concentrate fully on Dorothy and getting her home as soon as possible.

He showered quickly and dressed in a dark suit of charcoal gray. He wore a lighter-gray dress shirt and chose a tie of baby blue for Mark. He didn't know if that was the right thing to do, but he needed to do something to feel connected to his son if he could.

He made his way to the kitchen for coffee and a little something to eat. As the coffee brewed, Tom looked out the window. He was surprised to see raindrops splash against the glass intermittently. Of course, the weatherman had said to expect rain today off and on, but he'd been hopeful it would miss his area. Sighing, he looked up at the dark clouds hanging low in the sky. Off to the south, though, it looked a little lighter. He had a couple of hours before meeting Father Morgan at the cemetery, so maybe it would clear up.

Tom carried his black coffee and a toasted bagel with butter on it to the living room. He placed it all on the coffee table and walked to the television to turn it on. He found the morning news and sat down to have his coffee and meager breakfast.

The bagel tasted like dust, and the coffee wasn't strong enough, but he didn't care. He only knew he had to have something in his stomach to get through the morning.

Finishing his bagel, he took his plate and mug to the kitchen. Another cup of coffee sounded all right, so he poured some more and looked at the sky again.

A weak sun was trying its best to push through the clouds, and he prayed it would as he sipped the hot brew. This cup tasted somewhat better, so he stood at the sink awhile, drinking it and just looking out at the yard. Springtime birds were busy building nests, and he saw a robin pluck a worm out of a crack in the sidewalk.

He noted that the bird feeder needed to be filled and made a mental note to do that tomorrow. A bright-red cardinal picked that moment to alight upon the feeder, searching for food. As it bobbed around, pecking at the remnants left behind, Tom recalled reading somewhere that cardinals were loved ones visiting from heaven. At just that moment, the cardinal seemed to look him straight in the eye and suddenly flew off from the feeder.

Tom set his mug down, grabbed his raincoat from the hook next to the door, grabbed the bucket of seed they kept by the basement steps, and went out to fill the feeder. Rain be damned, if there was any truth to that saying, he was going to keep that feeder filled all the time. Logically, he knew it was silly to think spirits came in the form of cardinals to see people, but it made him feel better to do this simple thing. He and Dorothy loved birds and wildlife.

Shaking the raindrops off his coat, Tom slipped it off and hung it back on the hook. He still had about half an hour before he had to leave.

He topped off his coffee and sat back down in the living room. The news was still on, and he listened to it absently. They were talking about President Kennedy signing an order to create something called the Peace Corps. Tom had heard a little about it at work but not a lot.

The weatherman came on again and said to expect rain the rest of the day and into tomorrow. Spring in Michigan was dicey like that. Temperatures could range from upper seventies to below freezing with frost in March. It was even known to snow.

Tom sighed and stood up. It was time to get ready to leave. He took his coffee mug to the kitchen and finished drinking it quickly. Then he washed it out and set it on the drainboard to dry.

Making his way down the hall to the bathroom, he used the toilet, washed his hands, and checked his hair.

Walking back down the hall, he stopped momentarily and looked into the nursery. He decided it was just an empty bedroom now and pulled the door almost closed.

Back in the kitchen, he reached once again for his raincoat. Just as he was buttoning it, the phone rang, startling him. He walked to the counter and picked up the receiver.

"Hello, Tom. It's me," said Dorothy.

Tom's heart surged. "Hi, honey. How are you this morning?" He didn't know what else to say.

"Oh, you know . . . OK," she replied.

He could hear the shakiness of her breath, but he was so touched that she had called.

"I'm just getting ready to leave. I'm so glad you called before I left," Tom said.

"Me too. I just want you to know how much I'm thinking of you and how much I love you," Dorothy said.

"I know, honey. I love you too. I guess I better get going," Tom said quietly.

"OK, I'll see you after. I love you so much," Dorothy choked out.

"Me too," Tom replied, hanging up the phone.

Quickly he checked his pocket for a hanky and was relieved to find he had one in his coat pocket. Grabbing his keys, he flipped the light switch off in the kitchen and stepped out into the drizzling rain.

Chapter Sixteen

Climbing into his car, he made sure his umbrella was in the backseat and started the engine. Turning on the wipers, he made the drive across town to the cemetery. The rain was still not more than a drizzle when he pulled through the gates, following markers until he came to the Baby Land section, way in the back. He wondered why this section was way in the back. Was it because there weren't a lot of children to bury or because it was just so sad, they didn't want it to be seen from the street?

Tom slowly brought the car to a stop and shifted into Park. He could see Father Morgan standing on the far side of a hole, dirt piled next to it. A stand like a table was over the top of the grave, and there was the tiny blue casket that held the body of his son.

Off to the left, Tom could see two men, shovels in hand, standing under a tree. They were looking down, trying to give Tom his privacy, he assumed.

He felt the familiar sting of tears as he gazed at the tiny box on the stand. He could see three blue carnations and one white rose in a vase next to it, waiting to be placed on top of the casket, or the grave, whatever he decided to do.

Father Morgan had a Bible in one hand and a black umbrella in another. As Tom climbed out of the car, Father Morgan started toward him.

"It's OK, Father. I have an umbrella," said Tom as he leaned down into the back seat to retrieve it.

Father Morgan nodded and made his way back to the far side of the grave.

Tom opened the umbrella, as the rain was coming down a bit heavier now. Slowly he walked to the stand and looked at the tiny casket. He reached out and placed his hand on it. It was cold and wet from the rain, but he guessed that really didn't matter since it was going into the ground.

"Tom, are you ready to begin?" asked Father Morgan.

He looked up at the kindly priest who'd been in charge of his church for many years. He simply nodded and left his hand on the casket.

Father Morgan asked for blessings from God and that God receive the soul of Mark Thomas Cornell. He asked for healing for Tom and Dorothy and to trust that God's will was the right thing.

Tom was thinking that Mark's soul was already in heaven; it had never really been here. It comforted him to think that God was taking care of this baby and would perhaps bless them with another at some point.

He was glad Dorothy wasn't here to see this tiny casket. He didn't know if she would have been able to bear it. It was all he could do to wrap his mind around the reality of it.

He focused on what Father Morgan was saying as he made the sign of the cross and spoke the words, "Ashes to ashes, dust to dust. Amen."

"Tom, would you like to open the casket now and place the white rose inside with Mark?"

Tom took a deep breath and nodded. He blinked hard and hoped he would be able to get through this excruciating pain.

Father Morgan placed his Bible on the other side of the casket stand and put his umbrella on the ground. Quiet raindrops pelted his priest's clothing, but he didn't seem to care.

Carefully, he lifted the lid of the small casket and stood back, giving Tom his moment.

Tom opened his eyes, meeting Father Morgan's for a brief moment. The priest nodded and stepped back once more. Tom put his own umbrella on the ground, not caring how wet he would get.

Tom looked down at his tiny son. His skin was so dark against the white sleeper and blanket. The only color seemed to be the teddy bear placed by his side. Gently he stroked Mark's soft cheek. It was cold to his touch, and it made his heart ache. He took a few moments to gaze at the baby one last time, memorizing his features and sending silent "I love yous" to his baby.

Taking the white rose, he kissed it and then leaned down to kiss Mark once more. He placed the rose on his chest and let his hand linger there for a few seconds. Finally, he whispered to his son that he and his mommy would love him always and never forget.

Slowly Tom straightened and took the hanky from his pocket. Tears were sliding down his face, nearly out of his control, as he watched Father Morgan make the sign of the cross over his baby and quietly shut the lid of the casket for the last time.

Father Morgan retrieved his Bible and umbrella and walked to the opposite side of the stand where Tom stood, staring down at the casket.

"Tom, do you want some time alone here?" Father Morgan asked.

Tom looked up at the priest and nodded. "Yes, I need a little more time. Is that OK?" He glanced over at the gravediggers who still stood, waiting patiently.

"Yes, of course, take all the time you need. Would you like me to stay with you awhile?"

"No, that's OK, Father. I just want to be here for a little bit. Then I'm going to see Dorothy. We are going to call our families and let them know what happened. But can we call you if we need to?" Tom asked.

"Absolutely, you may call any time," replied Father Morgan. "I'll leave you to it then. I'm so very, very sorry." He shook Tom's hand and squeezed his shoulder before making his way to his own car, parked just down a nearby lane.

Tom heard the priest start his car and slowly drive off. But he couldn't seem to move. He stared at the casket. He had had so many hopes and dreams for this child. He and Dorothy had fantasized about family vacations and events. So many things, all never meant to be.

As Tom thought about all that wasn't to come, his tears ran unchecked, mixing with the rain that fell steadily now, nearly soaking him.

Finally, he took a breath. He needed to be with Dorothy. Nothing here would change, but he and his wife would need to change to cope with this enormous loss, and he needed to be with her.

As he looked up, his gaze met those of the gravediggers. He waved them over and picked up his umbrella.

"You fellas want to lower the casket down, and I'll put these flowers on top of it, OK?" Tom asked.

"Yes, sir. We are sorry for your loss, sir," replied one of the men.

Tom nodded thanks and stepped back so the men could move the stand and lower the tiny box into the ground.

Once it was placed down in the grave, Tom walked to the edge. Lifting the blue carnations out of the vase, he kissed each one and carefully leaned down to drop them on the casket lid. Miraculously, they all stayed on top and didn't slide down into the dirt. He took one last look and stood back. He thanked the men for their work and turned to go to his car.

His need to see Dorothy was almost overwhelming. The rain was coming down harder, and he thought he heard thunder in the distance.

He looked over at the two men as he climbed into his car and started it. He silently blessed them for doing a job that no one would really want to do and drove off down the lane to the street.

He took a deep breath as he turned once again on the roads that led to the hospital. He wanted to hold his wife and concentrate on her now.

Chapter Seventeen

Tom found a decent parking place, grabbed his umbrella, and quickly went into the hospital. He shrugged out of his wet raincoat as he walked down the hallway to room 212.

The door was slightly ajar, and he quietly stepped inside. Dorothy was looking out the window but immediately turned toward him when she heard the door open. She flung her arms wide, and Tom dropped both his coat and umbrella as he rushed to her bed and took her in his embrace.

Overwhelming emotion claimed them both as they rocked and cried together for what seemed to be the millionth time in just a couple of days.

After a bit, they pulled away from each other and dried their tears. Tom told her about the service in as much detail as he could. Her tears started again, but she pressed them away with a hanky.

"So I'm here now," Tom finished.

"I'm so glad you're here. I'm so sorry I wasn't able to be with you." She touched his hand.

"It's OK, Dottie. We need to get you well so you can come home. So we can get back on track," Tom said, trying to sound light.

"Yes, we do. I was up earlier, and it went better. They said later today we'll walk several halls."

"I'm going to stay and help you. We can have lunch, make our calls, and then tackle the hallways!" Tom was determined to help his wife with her recovery and hoped she would be all right.

"That sounds like a good idea. It's nearly lunchtime now. I heard it was chili today."

"Chili! Haven't had that in a while. It's cold out with the rain, so that will warm me up," Tom said as he ran his hand through his damp hair.

Dorothy smiled and brushed a wavy lock off his forehead. She nodded and agreed that chili would be good.

They spent some time going over what they would say to their parents on the phone. Tom said he would go first since he'd already been through it with his boss. That way, Dorothy could listen and decide exactly what she wanted to say to her parents.

Tom assured her that they could call Father Morgan at any time if they wanted or needed to when he saw how much Dorothy was struggling.

"I know. He's a good priest. I'm glad he's available for us. I'm more glad that you are here with me now, Tom."

A few minutes later, Dr. Brooks arrived to examine Dorothy. Tom stepped out into the hallway while the doctor was with her and watched as nurses were taking food trays into rooms. He quickly went to the cafeteria to get a meal for himself. They had plenty of chili, and he grabbed crackers and an ice tea to go with it.

By the time he got back to Dorothy's room, Dr. Brooks was just finishing up with his wife.

"Hello, Tom. Dorothy is healing up well. Her fever is gone now, but I want her here just another day to be sure all is well."

"That sounds good, Dr. Brooks. Thank you," replied Tom as he placed his tray on the bedside table.

"I'll leave you two to your lunch. Nursing will be in afterward to get her up and walking. I'll see you tomorrow," said Dr. Brooks.

Both Tom and Dorothy thanked him. As he left the room, a nurse came in with Dorothy's lunch tray and put it on the portable bedside table. Tom moved the items from the tray and handed the tray back to the nurse. Then he placed his meal on the table, too, and sat on the bed as had become his habit.

Tom and Dorothy took their time with the chili and crackers. They talked about lots of things, never staying too long on one subject. They knew they had to make their calls soon, so they kept their conversation as light as they could.

As they finished, Tom collected their bowls and set them on the cart in the hallway. Then he poured them each some ice water from the pitcher on the counter in Dorothy's room.

"Well, I guess we should get this over with and make the calls," Dorothy said.

Tom nodded and picked up the tan-colored phone that sat on the bedside table. It had a long cord so patients could move it onto their bed if they needed to.

This time, he settled in a chair next to the bed so he could more easily face his wife.

"OK, here goes." He lifted the receiver and dialed his parents' phone number. He listened as the phone sounded tones and clicks and finally started to ring. Glancing at the clock, he noted that it was only 1:00 p.m., and his folks should be home.

"Hello, Cornell residence," said a deep baritone voice.

"Dad, hi. It's Tom."

"Tom? What are you doing, calling in the middle of the week? Is something wrong?"

Tom and Dorothy always called their parents on Sunday evenings every week, so it was odd for his dad to hear his voice on the other end of the line.

"Yes, Dad. Can you go and get Mom? I've something to tell you," replied Tom evenly.

"She's just right here. Hold on," said Tom's dad, Cliff. Tom could hear the worry in his dad's voice and knew what he was about to tell them would break their hearts. Mark would have been their first grandchild.

"Jenny, come here. Tom's on the phone. Something's wrong." Tom heard his dad say. Then he heard his mom's voice but couldn't make out the words. Tears pricked his eyes, and Dorothy handed him a clean hanky.

"Tom, we're both here. What's the matter? Are you and Dorothy OK? Is it the baby?" His father practically yelled into the phone. Tom envisioned his parents huddled together by the phone in the kitchen, just as he and Dorothy were huddled on the bed, the receiver between them so they both could hear.

Clearing his throat, he glanced at his wife, who clasped his free hand. "Dad, Mom, I'm calling to tell you that the baby . . . the baby was stillborn."

"What? What do you mean, Tommy? What happened?" exclaimed Genevieve, known as Jenny to everyone.

"Well, the baby, it was a boy. He had a condition the doctors didn't know he had. He wasn't going to make it if he had been born alive, but he died before he was born."

"Oh my god!" Tom's dad, Cliff, said loudly.

"Tommy, when did this happen? Is Dorothy there with you? Where are you? Is she OK? What can we do?" Jenny's words tumbled out so quickly that Tom could hardly understand her, but it didn't matter; he knew all the questions she was asking.

Tom took his time and explained in detail about hydrocephalus and how it's almost always fatal. After explaining it all and answering their questions over and over, the line was silent for a few moments. He heard his mother sigh.

"Tommy, I wish you had let us know so we could have come to the service today. We would have been right there. Would you like us to come now or when Dottie gets home? We can help you with anything you need," said Tom's mom in earnest.

"No, Mom. We're OK. Besides, it's planting season. I know you're busy with that, Dad. And, Mom, you always help out too. We'll be OK. Really, there's nothing you can do anyway. But thank you."

Tom was glad, in a way, that it was raining today, so his dad was home and not out planting fields. The whole middle and southern part of Michigan was getting a lot of rain today, and his folks lived a couple of hours south of Midland.

"Son, you just let us know if we can come or help in any way. Dorothy, how are you feeling?" Tom's dad asked.

"Hi, Cliff, Jenny. I'm all right. Getting stronger every day. I'll probably be going home the day after tomorrow. Thank you for your support," replied Dorothy quietly.

Tom spoke a bit longer to his folks and explained that they had to call Dorothy's parents and had better get off the phone. He had wonderful parents who lived a simple farming life. He knew they'd respect his wishes and let him call his sister Joan, who was married to a farmer named Gale. He didn't want them to have to tell her. He promised he'd call her after they'd called Dorothy's parents.

After several "I love yous," Tom hung up the phone and looked at his wife. She leaned over and hugged him, and he hugged her back.

"Ooh, I need to stretch a minute after that," said Tom, standing up. He paced the room for a few minutes and sipped at his ice water.

"Are you ready to call your folks?" he asked Dorothy.

"Yes, I think so," Dorothy replied.

Tom resumed his spot in the chair next to the bed and slid the phone closer to his wife. Dorothy looked at him and picked up the receiver. She dialed the number to her parents' home, and her mother answered on the second ring.

"Mom, it's Dottie. I need to talk to you and dad." Dorothy jumped right out of the gate with her words. By her tone, her mother knew it was serious and said she'd go get her dad and be right back.

Once again, Tom envisioned a set of parents leaning over a phone so they both could hear what was being said.

They heard as Dorothy's father pulled out a kitchen chair and sat down.

"Dorothy, what is it? What's the matter?" her father, Emory, said.

"Mom, Dad, I'm calling to tell you that I had the baby, but . . . but it was stillborn." A gasp from her mother and a throat clearing from her father sounded from the other end of the line.

"Oh, Dorothy, what happened, dear?" asked her mother, her voice shaking with emotion.

Dorothy took her time explaining to her mother, Frances, what had happened with her son. She answered questions they both had over and over as they tried to understand what had happened to their grandson.

After many tears and silences, her parents also asked if they could come or help them. Dorothy was their youngest daughter who'd been childless for so long, so Emory and Frances had a special place for her in their hearts. They were very obviously crushed and heartbroken about the entire situation.

"It's OK, Mom. There's nothing anyone can do. Maybe in a few weeks, you can come visit. I would appreciate it, though, if you'd tell Betty Jean and Phyllis. I just can't . . . I just can't explain it all again.

I know it's not your responsibility, but that's what you can do for us," said Dorothy.

"Yes, Dorothy, we will let them know right away. I'm sure they will want to call you. How long did you say you'd be in the hospital?" asked Frances.

"I'll be here for two more days. But listen, Mom, I'm trying to heal and get out of here. I just don't have the energy to talk to them. I love them *so* much, but I'm so worn out, Mom. Please ask them not to call me. I'll call them both next week. I just need a little time, OK?" Dorothy pleaded.

"Of course, dear. Of course. We will explain it to them and let them know you'll call them. You know we would have come for the service if we had known. We love you both so much," said Frances. Emory concurred in the background.

"I know, Mom. We appreciate it so much. Listen, Tom's going to call his sister now, so I need to get off the phone. I'll be in touch," said Dorothy.

Hanging up the phone, she suddenly burst into tears. Tom understood all too well how she was feeling and shoved the phone out of the way to get to her and hold her in his arms. They clung to each other once again, letting the emotions happen, and more tears cleared their eyes.

"Just one more call to make. Joan will be heartbroken. I just want her to hear it from me," said Tom.

"I know. I know you and Joan are close. I understand," Dorothy said, squeezing his shoulder.

Picking up the phone again, Tom dialed his sister's number from memory. Gale wasn't in the field either with the rain pouring down and answered on the first ring. Tom knew that he would be playing solitaire at the kitchen table. Joan might be sewing or baking her famous homemade rolls. That thought made his mouth water a little bit, and he recalled past meals and hoped to see his family again soon. He needed their support.

"Gale, it's Tom and Dot. We need to speak to you and Joan. Is she around?" Tom asked.

"Oh, hi. Yes, she's just folding the laundry. Let me get her," replied Gale. Tom could hear the worry in his voice.

A few moments later, he heard Gale call out to Tom's sister, his wife of many years, and shortly he heard her voice.

"Tom, what's going on? Why are you calling in the middle of the day?" They, too, had standing Sunday evening phone calls.

"Hi, Joan, Gale. I have Dottie here too. We are calling to tell you that the baby was born, but he was stillborn. He passed away before he could be born."

He heard his sister gasp and what sounded like a fist pound on the table. He assumed that was Gale pounding out frustration. He and Joan had been unable to have children, and they were so looking forward to a little nephew or niece to show the farm to and teach them all about it.

"Oh no! What happened?" cried Joan.

Tom once again described the situation and explained everything as best he could. He answered their questions, and Dorothy spoke too.

They offered any support needed, as had everyone else, and soon, they hung up.

"I'm glad that is over with," said Tom quietly. "I don't think I can make any more calls today." He hung his head and sighed.

"Me neither. You did so well, Tom," said Dorothy.

They took a few moments, just sitting quietly on the bed, lost in their thoughts and thinking about what would come next.

Tom stood and moved the phone back to the nightstand.

"Do you want to nap before they have you walking?" he asked his wife.

"On no. I need to get up. I've sat here long enough. I need to move and get my emotions under control. I want to move around," Dorothy stated with vigor.

"OK then! That's what we'll do! I'll go get the nurse, and we can get you up and moving," Tom patted her leg and made his way to the nurses' station.

Chapter Eighteen

The nurses came and helped Dorothy out of bed, and after showing Tom what to do, they spent a couple of hours walking the halls and talking. They were both eager to get out of the hospital and hoped that Dorothy would be released Saturday. It was Thursday, and time seemed to be passing slowly.

Tom felt a little guilty, wanting her home, but he needed her, and she needed him too. They would have to tell their story several times to friends and neighbors, and they needed each other to lean on.

Dorothy felt guilty because Tom had to take on so much of it alone. Her body was trying to heal, but she wanted to be home. She planned to talk to Dr. Brooks in the morning and see if he would think about releasing her Saturday. She knew Tom would probably go back to work on Monday, and she just wanted to be back in her own house. She needed her familiar surroundings and friends and neighbors. She didn't want people to come see her at the hospital.

Before they knew it, it was time for dinner. Dorothy's menu included spaghetti with meatballs and a salad. Tom asked if he could get an order as well, so the nurse called the kitchen and arranged for him to have a meal along with her. He was tired of going to the cafeteria all the time.

Tom helped Dorothy clean up before the meals came, and the nurse helped him with details so he could assist her at home. They decided they'd show Dr. Brooks that they would get along just fine if he'd release Dorothy on Saturday.

Dinner arrived, and they took their time eating while talking about the future. They hoped to someday have a baby, but who knew what was in store?

Not long after dinner, Tom hugged and kissed his wife goodnight and headed home once again. The air in the house seemed stale and stuffy. He opened random windows and, after getting ready for bed, sat down to watch some TV. The late news was on, and he listened with half an ear, his thoughts focusing on the next day and starting to tell people what was going on.

After a while, Tom felt sleepy and stood up to stretch. He went to the kitchen for a glass of water before going to bed and gazed out the kitchen window. He knew tomorrow would come quickly, and after going to see Dorothy at the hospital, he planned to call a few friends and let the neighbors know what had happened. He didn't want the house descended on by everyone at once. He knew they'd all want to visit, offer condolences, and bring them food. The food he wouldn't mind! But everyone coming at once would just be too difficult.

Crawling into bed once again alone, Tom said some prayers for guidance, patience, and release from all the pain he and his Dottie were going through.

Chapter Nineteen

Morning dawned with a weak spring sun and cool wind. Tom dressed warmly and headed to the hospital shortly after having coffee and a small breakfast. Arriving at the hospital, he parked and quickly made his way to her room.

Dr. Brooks was at the nurses' station, and they walked to Dorothy's room together. He greeted Dorothy and said he'd read on her chart how well she was doing with walking.

He wanted to examine her and said he wanted Tom to stay so he could show him her incision and talk to him about helping her care for it. Summoning a nurse, Dr. Brooks had Dorothy recline on the bed.

The nurse arrived with a supply of topical ointment, bandages, and written instructions for Tom and Dorothy to follow to help her heal.

Dr. Brooks took his time explaining it all as his patient and her husband listened carefully and asked questions.

When he was finished, he said, "Dorothy, I know you're eager to get home, and I'm going to release you tomorrow morning. Think you two can handle the recovery care?" he asked with a slight grin, hoping to lighten the overall mood of the situation, as they were going home with no baby.

"Oh, yes, Dr. Brooks! Thank you. I've been walking and resting. I think I will be all right. Tom is going to be there too. I'm sure my parents or one of my sisters will come next week to help out as well if we ask them to," replied Dorothy, scrunching the sheet between her hands.

Nodding, Dr. Brooks said he'd write up the paperwork and see her in the morning before releasing her.

After he and the nurse left the room, Tom and Dorothy talked about her coming home and how hard that might be for her. She knew going home without a baby and having to tell everyone the story would be very difficult and taxing. Tom assured her that he would be making calls all afternoon and visiting with the neighbors.

It wasn't quite as hard on Tom as he wasn't the mother. He couldn't imagine the depth of his wife's loss. His own was tearing his heart apart. He squeezed her hand and kissed it.

"I'll be right there with you. And if you want me home all week next week, Mr. Kline said that'd be OK."

"We'll see. I mean, what can you do, really? I'm sure my parents or Phyllis will come if I call. I'd really just like to have private time, heal and figure out what to do next. I don't particularly want the distraction of visitors staying in the house," Dorothy replied, her eyebrows knitting together.

"That's fine, honey. We'll just take it as it comes and make decisions together. OK, it's getting close to lunchtime, so I'm going to head home, make a sandwich, and start calling folks. Later, I'll go see our close neighbors and tell them what happened. I'll leave it up to them to contact other people on our street if they want to. I'll request no visitors. I'm sure they'll understand. But I also think they'll start bringing food over right away so that we don't have to cook," Tom said with a small smile.

"I didn't think of that, but I bet you're right! I wouldn't mind not having to cook for a bit," said Dorothy.

"OK, honey, I'm going to go now. You just do what they ask, get some lunch, and do some walking. I'll call you later. Then I'll see you in the morning." Tom hugged and kissed his Dottie, and she hugged him back.

"OK, I can do this. We can get through this. I love you," she replied.

"I love you too," said Tom. He waved as he walked out the door and down the hall. He could smell fried chicken coming from the cafeteria and suddenly felt actual hunger for the first time since all this began. A slight grin lit his face as he left the hospital and drove home.

Chapter Twenty

Tom arrived home and let himself into the kitchen. Quickly he made a ham sandwich and added cottage cheese on the side. He drank a big glass of milk along with it and took a few moments to gather his thoughts before he started on phone calls.

Cleaning up his dishes, he poured another glass of milk and sat back down at the table. The cord for the phone was long enough so that he could sit there with a pad and pencil to cross names off and add names to his list.

Tom started with his boss, and Mr. Kline's secretary put him right through. Mr. Kline let Tom know that he informed Tom's staff and the other people who worked in the same department about the situation. Everyone was quite understanding, and a plan to cover for Tom was put in place if he decided to take the following week off to be with Dorothy.

Tom thanked his boss profusely and told him that unless Dorothy needed him, he'd be back at work on Monday. Mr. Kline was glad to hear it but insisted that Tom take off if he needed to.

Tom hung up the phone, impressed that he'd gotten through the call with no tears. His staff and coworkers were a good bunch of people, and he enjoyed working with them.

He took a drink of his milk and got out his hanky, just in case. He would now start calling other people who didn't already know, and he felt like he might not make it through the calls without shedding some tears.

Tom and Dorothy's closest friends were Rosemary and Larry Stein. Larry also worked at Dow but in a different department and only part-time. Tom hoped they'd both be home as he dialed the number he knew by heart.

"Hi, Ro, it's Tom," he said, his voice steady.

"Tom, hello! Are you off work early today? How's Dottie doing? She must be so ready to have that baby! Is that why you're calling? Did she have the baby? I'm so excited! Let me get Larry!" Rosemary was talking so fast, Tom just held the phone silently, waiting for his friend to come to the phone.

"Tom, Tom, Larry's here! OK! What's happening? Do we have a boy? A girl? I can't wait! Tell us, tell us," Rosemary stammered with excitement.

Tom hated that he was going to upset their dear friends, but he took a deep breath and plunged in. "I'm sorry to have to tell you, Ro, Larry. The baby was stillborn," Tom said again, quietly and reserved.

Silence met his ear for a few moments. He imagined the looks on their faces as he spoke the words out loud for the first of many times he'd have to today.

"Tom, *no!*" exclaimed Rosemary.

"Tom, I can't believe it! What happened?" asked Larry in the background.

Tom took another deep breath and went into the long explanation about what had happened with Mark.

When he finished, Rosemary asked, "When is the funeral? We want to be there. What can we bring you? When does Dottie come home?"

Her questions rattled off end over end, and Tom waited a heartbeat before responding. "Ro, I already had a service. It was just Father Morgan and myself. I couldn't bear the thought of anyone else being there. Besides, you don't ever want to see a baby's casket. I hope you both can understand. I had to do this alone. Dorothy would have been there, except she's still in the hospital until tomorrow."

Again, silence met his ears for a bit.

"I understand. I just wish we could have been there to support you both, Tom. I can't believe it. I'm so sorry. Would you like us to call anyone else for you?" asked Larry.

"You know, let me tell you who I plan to call, and then if you can think of other people, I'm fine with letting you make those calls. I don't want to have to go through this any more than I have to," replied Tom. Thankful for his dear friends who'd reacted just as he thought they would.

Tom read off a short list of friends and the names of neighbors he planned to tell later when people would be home from work.

Rosemary offered to let the bridge club ladies know. Some of them were teachers from the school where Dorothy taught. Tom figured she would want to let her principal know but didn't see the harm in having Rosemary share the news. It'd be easier for Dorothy the less she had to repeat it all.

After heartfelt sympathies, Tom hung up the phone and stood up to take a break. He was surprised to see that it was nearly 3:00 p.m., so he washed his milk glass, used the bathroom, and stepped out into his backyard.

He looked at the spots where he'd imagined a swing set and sandbox would go. It made the lump in his throat return again. Quickly he pushed those thoughts away, determined to believe that there would be another child there one day—maybe even more than one—who'd swing, slide, and build sandcastles.

He walked around the yard, inspecting the early spring flowers. Daffodils, crocuses, and small hyacinths were starting to shoot up and bloom. Soon the forsythia and lilacs would come. Tom loved to garden, and he knew Dorothy enjoyed the scent of fresh flowers.

Tom strolled over to his rose bed, where he grew all different types of roses in several colors. The leaves were coming on, and he could just see the start of the buds. By June, he'd have a lush rose garden with blooms he could cut and bring in for his Dottie. He hoped they'd make her smile.

As Tom walked the perimeter of his yard, he could see his next-door neighbor Ralph Wilson pushing his lawnmower through his own backyard. Ralph was retired, and his wife didn't work, so they were home a lot. He decided to wait just a few minutes, and then he'd walk over and let them know what was going on. The Wilsons had four kids of their own, and Tom knew this was going to be hard. He felt envious of the Wilsons at that moment. Here they had four healthy kids, and he lost the only one he never got to bring home.

He shook his head and tried to clear the negative thoughts out. Checking his pocket to be sure his hanky was close, he walked around the fence and bushes that partitioned the yards from one another.

Ralph was just pushing his lawnmower in Tom's direction and waved as he approached. He got to the end of the grass and shut the mower down.

"Well, hi, Tom! How are you? Hey, has that baby decided to finally come?" asked Ralph with a big smile.

When Tom didn't immediately answer and Ralph saw the sad look on his face, he cleared his throat and asked, "Is something wrong, Tom?"

Tom nodded and took a deep breath. He slowly explained what had happened. When he got to the part about the funeral having already happened, he had to put his hanky to his eyes.

Ralph placed his hand on Tom's shoulder and squeezed it. "Tom, I just can't believe it. I'm so very, very sorry. Can I have Beulah fix you something and bring it over? She's just inside."

"Oh no, that's OK. I mean, I ate a little bit ago. I will bring Dorothy home tomorrow. We decided that I'd make most of the calls and let people know. We aren't going to be much for company for a bit. I'm sure you can understand," Tom said, a weak smile crossing his face.

"I do understand, Tom. Nonetheless, you'll need to eat. Beulah makes great lasagna. I'll have her bring some over tomorrow for your dinner. She won't stay, I promise. What can we do for you?" Ralph asked.

"Well, you can tell the other neighbors if you'd like. I plan to go see Pat and Bill Norris and Don and Marianne May later. But you can tell the others if you'd like. If you don't, Dottie and I can start tomorrow," Tom replied wearily.

"Oh, now don't you worry. We'll get a hold of the other neighbors. They'll all want to help, I'm sure. Don't you worry. I'm so sorry, Tom. I'm so very sorry."

"Yes, well, I appreciate that, and so does Dot. I'm going to go home for a bit now. Didn't mean to interrupt your mowing," said Tom.

"Hey, don't worry about that. We'll take care of the other neighbors, and I'll see you tomorrow." Ralph squeezed Tom's shoulder once more and went inside his house to let his wife, Beulah, know what was going on.

Tom made his way back to his kitchen and sat down. He looked at his list of people he needed to let know and crossed several names off of it. Beulah would take care of them, and Tom would just go see the Mays and the Norrises. They had all been friends for years, and he wanted to tell them face-to-face.

Chapter Twenty One

Tom looked in the cupboard to see if there was anything he could make himself to eat later. He decided on a simple can of soup. Maybe he'd make a grilled cheese sandwich. He'd just have to see how he felt after he went to the neighbors' homes.

He still had a little time before his friends would be home from their jobs, so he took the time to get out clothes to wear for the next day—just a pair of slacks and a lightweight sweater.

Tom decided to walk the block to his neighbors' homes, as it wasn't too far, and the fresh air helped to clear his mind.

Donning a light windbreaker to ward off the late afternoon chill, he set out north down the street. He passed homes and waved greetings at anyone he saw, his heart feeling heavier with each passing step. He didn't think any of them knew yet, and he was glad of that.

The sunlight was waning as he walked up the driveway to the Norris household. He could see Bill's car in the driveway and was glad his friend was home.

Knocking on the back door, he stepped back and waited for someone to answer. Soon Pat Norris was at the door, holding it open.

"Well, Tom! What brings you here? Bill just got home. Did you want to see him?"

"Actually, I'm here to see both of you."

Pat's eyebrows knit as she sensed something was wrong, and she invited Tom in as she called out for her husband, Bill.

He joined Tom and Pat in the kitchen, and Pat offered Tom a seat and drink. Sitting down, Tom declined a drink and waited as the couple sat down at the table with him. Tom took a deep breath and started his story. Pat was in tears, and Bill rubbed her back and nodded at Tom with sympathy. Neither had the right words to say to their friend, but there weren't any right words to say anyway.

When Tom had nothing else to say, he stood up and told them he was going across the street to see Don and Marianne May. The Norrises reassured Tom that they would be in touch and come see them as soon as they wanted company. Tom thanked them and headed down their driveway and directly across the street to the Mays' house.

Don worked at Dow, but he was often transferred to other places for a couple of years at a time. Then the company would bring him back to Midland, and they'd stay awhile. They, too, were trying to start a family but weren't having any luck.

Don answered the door, surprised to see his friend Tom on the stoop.

"Well, hello, Tom! What's going on? Where's Dot?" He looked around Tom and down the street, but of course, she wasn't there.

"Hi, Don. Is Marianne home? I need to talk to you both."

"Oh, sure. She's here, just finishing up the dishes. Come on in. I'll get her," replied Don, the perplexed look on his face that Tom was beginning to expect.

Don motioned for Tom to have a seat on the couch while he went to get his wife, Marianne.

Marianne stepped into the room, wiping her hands on a dishtowel, a look of concern on her face, with Don following, holding a tray of ice waters.

They sat down in chairs facing Tom, expectant looks on their faces. "Tom, what's going on?" asked Marianne, her brown eyes searching his face.

"We lost the baby, Marianne. It was a boy. He was stillborn."

Tom told his story once again and watched the sorrow as it etched its way across the faces of his dear friends. He was so weary, he almost didn't have the energy to pick up the glass of ice water from the tray and take a much-needed gulp.

As the Norrises did before them, they offered any help they could give and condolences.

Finally, Tom stood, ready to get home and not have to talk anymore. The Mays said they'd let other mutual friends know and asked Tom to call them when he could.

After hugs goodbye, Tom made his way back down the street. The sun had nearly set, and he was glad it was near twilight as tears slipped down his face.

Finding himself at home once again, he decided to get ready for bed before calling Dorothy to say goodnight.

Settling down at the kitchen table in his pajamas, he dialed the hospital and was connected to Dorothy's room. He told her about letting people know, and they cried together over the phone line. He was glad this would be the last night he had to spend alone with his Dottie.

After they hung up, he had a drink of water and then fell into bed, exhausted and spent.

Chapter Twenty Two

Saturday dawned bright and sunny. Tom was thankful for that. At least he wouldn't be bringing his Dottie home in the rain. A sunny day was needed to make things just a tiny bit easier.

Dressing quickly, he poured some coffee and had some toast. He dialed the hospital and got a hold of Dorothy. He asked if she'd seen anyone yet about being released. She told him the paperwork was in progress and he could come to get her as soon as he was able.

Hanging up the phone, Tom picked up his coffee mug and walked through the house. He looked in again at the nursery. The old rocker and footstool looked lonely. He made his way to the window and opened it to let in some fresh air. He didn't linger in the room; it was too painful. He wondered how Dorothy would feel when she saw it. Shaking his head, he went back into the hall but still left the door open a bit.

Tom decided to change the sheets on the bed so it'd be fresh for Dorothy tonight. He threw the dirty sheets and his bath towel in the wash and quickly put clean sheets on the bed. Then he ran a dust rag over the furniture around the house and vacuumed too. He didn't want Dorothy to do a thing, and she wasn't cleared for housework at this point anyway. The last thing he wanted was for her to pull her stitches open or anything like that.

Once he finished straightening up the house and taking out the trash, he realized the washer had spun out. He tossed the clean wet things in the dryer and decided to go get Dorothy.

As he pulled out of his driveway, he saw Ralph Wilson outside, picking up his newspaper. They waved at each other, and Ralph nodded with a somber look on his face. Tom nodded back with a slight smile and headed toward the hospital once again.

Being a Saturday, the parking lot was nearly empty. He parked as close as he could to the door and didn't waste any time getting to Dorothy's room.

The nurse was just helping Dorothy get her shoes on when Tom walked in.

"Hey! Looks like I'm here right on time!" he exclaimed.

"Hello, Mr. Cornell. Yes, the paperwork is just done, and we're ready to get Dorothy a wheelchair to take her to your car."

"Hi, Tom. I'm so glad to see you," said Dorothy, a quiet smile on her lips.

"Hi, honey. I would have been here a little sooner, but I was straightening up at home," Tom said.

"Oh, you didn't have to do that, Tom."

"Well, I wanted to. Let me go see if there's anything I need to sign while they get you situated, and then I'll go get the car."

Dorothy nodded, and the nurse walked with Tom to the desk where he needed to sign the release forms. There was an appointment set with Dr. Brooks for the following Friday. Tom made a note to call his boss and ask for Friday off. He was sure it wouldn't be a problem.

The nurse explained again about bandages and any pain medication that Dorothy could take if she needed it. All the nurses expressed their sympathy to Tom and wished them well.

Tom nodded and thanked them for all their help, and then he went to get the car while the charge nurse took a wheelchair to collect Dorothy.

He drove his car up to the doors, under the concrete awning of the hospital, and went around to the passenger side and opened the door. The nurse was waiting there with Dorothy and helped her to stand up and then get seated in the car comfortably. She decided to forego the lap seat belt, as it would rest directly on her incision. They thanked the nurse, who waved goodbye to them as they drove off for home one last time.

On the way, Tom asked Dorothy if they'd told her about her appointment with Dr. Brooks for the following Friday. She said they had mentioned it, and he told her he would be taking her.

Soon they were home, and Dorothy sighed as they pulled into the driveway. She was glad to be home but so sad that there was no baby wrapped in her arms to bring into the house.

Tom parked and came around to help his wife get out of the car. He held her arm as she made her way up the two steps into the kitchen.

Dorothy sat down at the kitchen table to rest for a few minutes and adjust to being back home. She looked around her kitchen, taking in familiar sights and feeling like she hadn't been there in months instead of just a few days.

She appreciated that Tom had done some cleaning and laundry. She knew she wouldn't be up for that for a while, even though she knew her friends and neighbors would only be too happy to give her a hand. She felt her love for him surge with emotion, and her heart broke again, thinking of him at the cemetery alone.

Tom put his hand on Dorothy's shoulder. "Honey, can I get you anything? Would you be more comfortable in the living room, on the couch?"

Dorothy looked up at him with a wan smile. "Yes, that'd be nice. I'm kind of tired."

Tom helped her out of the chair and guided her to the sofa. Once she was reclined, he turned on the TV to the classic movie station. Something starring Grace Kelly was on. He wasn't sure what it was, but it gave some background noise that seemed comforting.

"I'm just going to get the laundry out of the dryer now . . . unless you need anything," said Tom.

"I'm fine, honey. Thank you so much. I'm going to rest awhile, and then I need to do some walking." Dorothy closed her eyes and almost immediately fell asleep.

Tom went about folding the sheets and putting them away. Then he made lunch for them both. He'd wake Dorothy when it was ready. He put together chicken noodle soup and grilled cheese sandwiches.

He placed it on the kitchen table, along with a basket of crackers for the soup. He poured them each some ice tea and then went to wake Dorothy.

Dorothy's eyes fluttered open when Tom quietly said her name. She took a moment to realize where she was and looked up at him with a soft smile.

"Hey there. I have lunch on the table. I'm hungry, and I thought you'd be too," he said.

"Oh, thank you. I guess I am. I didn't eat much breakfast. I was so anxious to come home. I think I need to go to the bathroom first, though," she replied.

Tom walked his wife to the bathroom and stood by in case she needed him. When she was done, she washed her hands and met him in the hall.

In the kitchen, they sat down for their lunch, and Dorothy smiled, thinking how nice it was that he had made lunch for the both of them.

As they ate, they talked about their families and whether or not they wanted any of them to come visit.

Dorothy thought about having her folks come for just a day, not even to spend the night. It was a lot for them now that they were older, but she could use a hug from her parents.

Tom agreed and said maybe the next visit could be to his parents. Then they'd talk about siblings coming.

Tom planned to go back to work Monday if Dorothy was OK with it. She said she thought she would be. After all, what could he do here? Nothing really. She would just be resting and walking around the house. They could do household work together, and Tom could get things from the store as needed.

Dorothy would contact the school where she worked and arrange to have the rest of the school year off. Spring break was about over, but there weren't that many weeks of school left. She didn't want to face the other teachers and kids who'd been so excited for her to have the baby and bring it to school. Everyone would just feel so awkward and uncomfortable. She didn't want to put them through that, and she didn't have the energy or heart to explain it all over and over again. She knew her principal would understand. She'd been there for several years and had time off accrued.

After lunch, Dorothy called her mom and dad. They decided they would come on Monday for the day. It was a two-hour drive from Grand Rapids, and that wasn't too far for them to go. They'd be there before lunch and stay for early dinner before going back home. Dorothy's mom wanted to stay a few days, but Dorothy insisted that just a day trip would be fine, noting again that there really wouldn't be that much for them to do.

Tom called his parents after that, and they decided they would come on Wednesday. Tom and Dorothy would have a day in between both sets of parents coming. Tom decided he'd ask for both Wednesday and Friday off. He knew his boss would be OK with it. Tom also knew that both sets of parents would want to go to the cemetery. He didn't know what Dorothy felt about that yet. He would talk to her about it later. Just now, they were on a somewhat positive note, talking to their families, and he didn't want to bring the reality of the grave up just yet.

After their phone calls, Dorothy said she felt like walking. First, she wanted to see the nursery. She knew Tom had emptied it, except for the rocker, but she wanted to see it anyway. He held her hand as he pushed the door open.

Dorothy stood in the silence, looking at the bare room. Her heart lurched in pain. Her hand instinctively went to her belly. She blinked back tears as she gazed at the empty spot where the crib had stood for so many months, waiting for a baby that never arrived. The spaces where the dressers had been were empty and bare. She glanced over at the closet. One door was partially open, but no tiny clothes hung on hooks. The walls were devoid of the baby-themed artwork they'd hung together.

Dorothy turned to Tom and buried her face into his shoulder. They shed quiet tears and clung to each other, each lost in their own painful thoughts.

Finally, Dorothy stood back and wiped her eyes. "OK, OK. I'm OK. It's just a room for right now. One day, one day, a child will have this room. I know it."

Giving Tom her best effort at a smile, he hugged her tight, and they walked out of the room and down the hall to their bedroom.

Dorothy thanked Tom again for changing the bed sheets and opened a window to let spring sunshine and fresh air in.

"Let's go outside, Tom. Show me your gardens! I can smell the grass, so I know blooms are coming soon, right?" Dorothy was doing her best to be upbeat, and Tom appreciated it.

"OK, let's go. I was out here yesterday, and things are definitely blooming and more on the way! The hyacinths are up, and I know they smell so good! The roses are thinking about it. They'll be full-on by June!" Tom smiled as he took his wife's hand and led her back through the house, out the kitchen door, and slowly into the backyard. He didn't want her to overdo it, but she looked strong, and her color was better than it had been.

"I just want to smell the hyacinths! Oh, look at the tiny crocuses! They are so pretty. The lilacs are starting to green up too! They are my favorite!" exclaimed Dorothy.

Tom knew this was all good for healing, not just for her but for him, too. They walked to the group of hyacinths and leaned down to smell their fragrant scent. It was funny how scents could take you to places in your memory.

Tom always thought of days on the farm when he was a kid. His mom had a beautiful flower garden across from the vegetable garden. He knew summer was coming when the hyacinths came up, along with the crocuses and other springtime blooms.

For Dorothy, it took her to her childhood home and lead crystal vases filled with hyacinths, lilacs and tulips, scenting the many rooms of her parents' large home. She preferred to leave the flowers to grow and not pick them, but her mom enjoyed them, so her dad often brought her flowers from the shop in town.

They walked around the yard, and Tom showed her the rose garden and pointed out other things coming into season.

Wiping their shoes off inside the kitchen door, Tom walked with Dorothy back to the living room. Dorothy took her spot back on the sofa while Tom sat across from her in the recliner.

"How are you feeling, Dottie?"

"I think I'm feeling all right. Maybe I'll have some hot tea. I don't really know what to do with myself. I'm used to being so busy, but now, there's not a lot to do. I guess I'll call the principal and see about getting the rest of the semester off."

"That's a good idea. After that, I'll call Mr. Kline and tell him I need Wednesday and Friday off. Oh, I spoke to Ralph Wilson next door yesterday. He insisted that Beulah would be bringing over lasagna for us tonight. He promised she wouldn't stay, just bring over the food. Is that all right with you?"

"I guess so. She doesn't have to do that, though."

"Oh, Dottie, I think lots of people are going to be bringing us food for a while," Tom said.

Dorothy thought about that for a minute. She supposed that's what people did. It was such an awful situation; she decided they didn't know what else to do, so bringing food would be the best thing for now. She nodded at Tom and said that'd be OK.

"I'll go make you some tea while you call the school." Tom got up and went to the kitchen to put the tea kettle on.

Dorothy reached for the phone on the end table and had a quick reminder that she had stitches in her belly. She gasped a little from the sharp pain, but it quickly went away.

She dialed the number of the school, and the secretary answered. Dorothy said who she was, and Miss Bowes put her right through to Principal Adams.

"Dorothy, how are you? I'm so very sorry. We all are. What can we do for you?"

"Hi, Mike. I'm OK. Thank you for asking. There really isn't much anyone can do. However, I would like to be off for the rest of the school year. I don't want to have to come back and explain to the kids and everyone about what has happened. I'm sure you understand." Dorothy spoke quickly to keep her emotions in check.

"Yes, of course. I'll do the paperwork. You don't need to worry about a thing. I hope you are all right and Tom too. I don't have the words to say to help. I'm sorry. We are all thinking of you both," replied the principal.

"Thanks, Mike. I'll be in at some point to clean up the room over the summer, get ready for fall."

"That's fine. Don't worry. Please call and check in so we know how you are. I won't call and bother you. You just get better, OK?"

"I will, Mike. Thank you." Dorothy hung up the phone just as Tom set a steaming mug of her favorite apple tea on a coaster.

"That sounded like it went well, honey," said Tom.

"It did. I'm glad to be off the phone, though. I guess it gets a little bit easier with each call, but I hate making these calls." She picked up her tea and blew on it to cool it down. She took a small sip, enjoying the crisp apple flavor.

"I'll call Mr. Kline now," said Tom.

He lifted the receiver and dialed his boss. As he anticipated, Mr. Kline was fully understanding of Tom taking off both days so he could see his parents. Mr. Kline again offered the whole week off to Tom, but Tom insisted on coming back Monday. There wasn't much sense in delaying it in his mind, and he knew there would be work piling up.

He hung up the phone and sat down in the chair across from Dorothy again. They sat in silence for a few minutes, each wondering what to do next!

"I don't know what to do with myself, Tom. Maybe I should call one of my sisters?" she asked.

"Well, that's not a bad idea. You can do that, and I can run to the store for a few groceries. How does that sound?"

"I guess that's a good idea. Do we need a lot of things?" Dorothy replied.

"I'll make a list. I know laundry soap is getting low! I'll get some basics and be back soon."

Tom stood up and went to the kitchen to write out a list. Dorothy sipped her tea and thought about calling her sisters. She was closer to Phyllis, as she was just a couple of years older. Betty Jean was a full eight years older than Dorothy, so they weren't as close.

Tom returned shortly, list in hand. "Can I get you anything or help you do anything before I go, honey?"

"Oh no, I'm fine. Thank you for the tea. I might make another cup in a bit. I'm going to call Phyllis. Thanks for going to the store."

Tom dropped a kiss on his wife's forehead and went out the kitchen door. The A & P wasn't far, so he didn't worry too much about leaving Dorothy home alone for an hour.

Dorothy watched as Tom pulled out of the driveway, heading to the store. She slowly stood up and made her way to the bathroom again. Once done, she stopped at the nursery door and poked her head in. Gazing at the empty rocker, she sighed and squeezed her eyes shut against threatening tears. She had to pull herself together and call her sister. She'd know what to say to help.

Chapter Twenty Three

Dorothy took her mug to the kitchen and turned on the stove to boil more water in the kettle. Another cup of tea would be comforting while she talked to her sister.

She moved the phone to the table and sat down with her fresh mug of tea once the water was ready and picked up the receiver. She dialed her sister's number by heart, and Phyllis answered on the second ring.

"Oh, Dottie! I'm so glad you called! I wanted to call you, but Mom said to give you some space. My heart is breaking! Red's too! We just feel so bad for you and Tom! Please let us come and take care of you. Anything you need!"

"Phyll, please, don't worry about that. Mom and Dad are coming tomorrow for the day. I just want to see them for a little bit. I'm not even letting them spend the night. I mean, really, what can anyone do? I'm healing well. It's just going to take a while. Tom is staying home Wednesday when his folks come for the day, and he's taking me to the doctor Friday. I'm sure the neighbors will stop by anytime we call, and truly, there isn't anything that anyone can really do. Just knowing you're there is enough for me. Maybe in a month or so, we can come see you, or you can come for the day."

"Dottie, you're so brave. I can't imagine what you've been through. And poor Tom! Aww, Dorothy, I just feel so terrible."

"I know, Phyll. I know. This is the hardest thing we've ever been through. I feel kind of numb. I don't know if it's all sunk in yet. I keep feeling scared, then angry, then sad. It's overwhelming."

"Oh, Dottie, you know we all love you two so much. We'd do just anything for you."

"I know, Phyll. I haven't called Betty Jean yet. I might later. I just wanted to hear your voice. Why don't you tell me what's new with you all? Get my mind on something else."

"Are you sure, Dot? I don't want to upset you, talking about kids and such."

"Oh, Phyllis, really! You have four wonderful kids! My nephews and nieces! Of course, I want to hear about them! I love them and you and Red so much. Please, catch me up on what's happening with my favorite redheads."

So Dorothy listened as her sister told her all that was new with each of her kids and how Red's job was and her job as a social worker. It was calming and normal to have a long chat with her sister and Dorothy felt herself relaxing and even smiling at some of the things Phyllis was telling her.

"Oh, Phyllis, it's so great to catch up. I hope we can get together this summer at Miller Lake." Phyllis and Red had a summer cabin on a lake near where they lived. Tom and Dorothy went a few times during the summer to fish, play ping-pong and mini golf, and spend the evenings playing cards and laughing. Those were some of Dorothy's fondest memories, and she really needed to make some more of them this summer.

Phyllis promised as many weekends as they could make it to come to the lake and visit. They ended their call with a promise to talk over the upcoming weekend, and Dorothy felt a lot better after having spoken with her sister.

Just as she hung up, she heard the car pull into the driveway. She stood and opened the kitchen door as Tom walked in with three bags of groceries.

"How was your talk with Phyllis?" Tom asked, setting down the bags.

"Oh, it was really good. I knew it would be. I'm feeling a bit better. I might call Betty Jean in a little while."

Together they put away the groceries, and Tom told her about the store, just for something to talk about.

Once everything was put away, they sat down at the kitchen table again. Neither could think of anything to say, so they were quiet for a bit.

"How are you feeling, Dot?" Tom finally asked.

"OK. I know you feel like you have to keep asking me, but really, I feel OK. I know I'll need help with changing the bandages tonight and maybe some help bathing in the morning. But really, I feel OK."

He nodded and patted her hand. "Well, it's almost dinnertime. I wonder if Beulah is going to show up with lasagna," he said with a smile.

"Oh, I bet she will. Any time now, actually," replied Dorothy with a smile of her own.

"I'm going to turn on the evening news. Do you want to watch with me?" asked Tom.

"Sure. I should catch up on what's going on, and I know you're interested in the weather forecast," she said, giving him another small smile.

They made their way into the living room, and Tom walked to the TV set and turned it on. Channel 5 was just broadcasting the weather. He knew they'd go over it again in a bit, so he wasn't concerned that he'd missed too much of it.

Dorothy settled on the couch, absently rubbing her belly. Tom noticed, and it made his heart sad. She had been doing that for several months, feeling the baby move, and now there was just an angry scar covered in stitches.

As the news anchor droned on, Dorothy felt the emptiness of her belly and wondered when she would stop feeling for the baby who was gone.

A knock at the kitchen door startled her from her thoughts, and Tom got up to go answer it.

Dorothy heard the quiet voice of her next-door neighbor Beulah Wilson. She could also hear the deeper voice of her husband, Ralph.

Tom popped his head around the door frame and said, "Dot, the Wilsons are here. Would you like to say hello?"

Dorothy gave him a nod and a small smile. She might as well start getting used to visitors.

Beulah and Ralph stepped into the living room. Beulah immediately walked to Dorothy and gave her a brief hug. They both said how sorry they were and let her and Tom know that they'd let other close-by neighbors know what had happened. Of course, everyone sent their condolences and was so very sad for the couple.

"Well, we'll be on our way. I brought you lasagna, salad, and green beans, dear. I hope that's OK," said Beulah, patting Dorothy's hand.

"That sounds just wonderful, Beulah. Thank you so much. I'll get your containers back to you tomorrow," replied Dorothy.

"Don't worry about that. No rush. You just call me when you're up for a little visit, and I'll come on over to see you."

"Thank you both for being such good neighbors. We appreciate it. Thank you for dinner. It smells delicious."

With that, Dorothy stood and walked with the couple through the kitchen. Tom strolled with them to the driveway and thanked them again for their generosity.

Back in the kitchen, Tom and Dorothy got out plates and sat down to a wonderful home-cooked meal that tasted delicious.

"Beulah is such a good cook," said Dorothy.

"Hey, so are you, but it's nice to not have to, isn't it?" Tom replied.

"Yes, I guess so. I just wish the reason was different," Dorothy said.

Patting her hand and giving it a little squeeze, Tom said, "I know, honey. I'm sorry." Tom didn't know what else to say to make it any better.

Dorothy shrugged and took a bite of the lasagna. It was really good, so she decided to enjoy it and let it help her body continue healing.

When they were done, they did the dishes together and put the leftovers in the refrigerator. Tom said he'd return Beulah's containers in the morning.

Dorothy decided to change her bandages, and with Tom's help, they followed the instructions the nurse had given them. The incision was healing, although here and there, the skin was still red and angry-looking. She gasped as Tom applied ointment to one of the sore spots.

Dr. Brooks had told her it'd take several weeks to heal, so she expected the pain. She was glad to have Tom's help, as it was hard for her to see where the gauze needed to be placed.

When they were done, Dorothy slipped on a loose nightgown, washed her face, and brushed her teeth.

Then Tom got ready for bed as well. He was happy to have Dorothy home with him, and together, they sat on the couch and watched a little TV.

Around 9:00 p.m., Dorothy said she was ready for bed. Tom checked the door locks and shut off the TV.

When he climbed into bed next to his wife, he held her for a little while, and they enjoyed the cool night breeze drifting in through the window.

Both slept soundly for the first time that week, and neither was plagued with nightmares for once.

Chapter Twenty Four

The next day dawned with weak sunlight and March winds. Tom and Dorothy had coffee and a light breakfast.

Since it was the weekend, Tom was around to help Dorothy with anything she needed. He ran to the hardware store for some things he needed to fix a broken step to the basement. He decided since he had the weekend and wanted to be home for Dorothy, he might as well catch up on things that needed attention.

Dorothy decided to shower and then call her oldest sister, Betty Jean. Betty Jean and her husband, Ray, had three children that were already adults and out on their own. Dorothy wasn't as close to her as she was to Phyllis because Betty Jean was eight years older than Dorothy, but she was a teacher as well, and they often shared school stories that made them chuckle.

Betty Jean and Ray were, of course, just heartbroken for Dorothy and Tom. Dorothy told the story once again, and both she and her sister shed tears over the phone. Betty Jean offered any help needed, as Dorothy knew she would. She reassured her that she and Tom were OK and were putting one foot in front of the other to muddle through.

After her phone call, Dorothy decided to see what Tom was up to. She found him in the garage, sorting through screwdrivers and hinges. She was glad she had a husband who was handy and could fix things around the house.

It was nearing lunchtime, and Dorothy asked him if he was hungry.

"I guess so. The toast we had for breakfast is long gone! What sounds good, Dot? I'm happy to make something."

Dorothy smiled and replied, "Hey, you're fixing stuff, and I need something to do. I'll go see what there is and get something going." She patted his arm and walked out of the garage. The wind had died down some, but it was still a chilly March.

Back in the kitchen, Dorothy rooted around in the fridge for something good. She found bacon, lettuce, and tomatoes. That would be perfect.

She set about making BLTs and got out plates and chips to go with them. Pouring glasses of ice tea, she set the kitchen table and then finished frying the bacon.

When it was ready, she poked her head out the door and called to Tom. He replied that he'd be right there, and she went back in to wash her hands.

During their lunch, Dorothy told Tom about her conversation with Betty Jean. He nodded while he chewed his sandwich.

They both felt that they'd get many of the same responses from everyone as the story spread and people contacted them. It wasn't any easier to tell, but knowing that people actually cared and wanted to help was comforting.

Dorothy decided to lie down for a while after lunch. Her stitches felt a little sore, and it was too windy to go for a walk.

Tom continued to putter in the garage and fix whatever needed fixing around the house.

Later in the afternoon, the phone rang. It was Father Morgan checking in. He said the church family was going to be making meals, and he would deliver them tomorrow evening. Father Morgan said the congregation, in unison, was so very sorry for them and praying for healing.

Tom let him know how much they appreciated that and told Dorothy when he got off the phone.

"I suppose we won't need to go to the grocery store any time soon, huh?" asked Dorothy.

"I guess not. Between the church and our neighbors, we'll have food for a while." Tom gave her a weak grin. It was kind of a catch-22. Free homemade meals, but no baby to love. He'd rather go hungry and eat noodles for a year than have his baby dead in the ground, but he didn't have that option. He was sure his Dottie felt the same way.

It was close to dinnertime, and the phone rang once again. This time, Dorothy answered to hear their neighbor Mrs. Thorne on the other end. She extended their condolences and said she was bringing over meatloaf with all the fixings. She said she'd be right over, and Dorothy thanked her and let Tom know. He went out the kitchen door and met Mrs. Thorne, helping her to carry the containers of food to the house.

Stepping into the kitchen, Mrs. Thorne put down the pan of meatloaf covered in foil and immediately went to Dorothy and hugged her. When she backed away, she had tears in her eyes.

"Dottie, I'm so sorry. We all are."

"Thank you, Sandy. We appreciate that very much. And the food, oh my goodness, thank you for that! You didn't have to do this."

"I didn't know what else to do, Dot." Sandy held up her hands in a questioning gesture.

"Well, I'm sure we'll enjoy this, and I'll get your containers back to you tomorrow," piped Tom. The smell of the meatloaf, potatoes, and vegetables was making his mouth water. He was glad neither he nor Dorothy had to cook. They probably wouldn't eat much at all if they were doing the cooking.

"You just take your time about that. And please enjoy it. Also, please call, or come down if you need any little thing! I'll get out of here now so you can eat while it's hot."

With that, she hugged Dorothy again and then Tom and stepped out the kitchen door. Tom followed behind, just to make sure she got to her house, just two doors down.

The Thornes were such nice people. Sandy and Mike had two sons in elementary school, and they had been good neighbors.

The meal Sandy had prepared for them was delicious, and both of them ate more than they thought they would.

Together they cleaned up and washed Sandy's dishes. Tom would return them tomorrow and thank her once again for her generosity.

As the evening wore on, a few neighbors and friends called with their sympathies and offers of help and food.

Tom and Dorothy knew they were blessed and thanked each person who thought of them. Dorothy wondered if she should be sending thank-you cards to everyone and asked Tom what he thought.

"I don't think anyone is expecting a thank you in the mail. They are truly sorry for us and just doing what they can for us."

"Maybe we can write a thank-you letter, and you can make copies, and we can just hand them to our neighbors," suggested Dot.

"That's a good idea. We sure do know some good people," replied Tom.

"Yes, we do," agreed Dorothy.

The rest of the evening was spent watching the news and just resting. With tomorrow being Sunday, Tom would mow the lawn if it wasn't raining. Dorothy would look at lesson plans she'd already made in anticipation of maternity leave and get them ready to send to school. Or maybe someone would pick them up. She didn't feel like driving anywhere yet, and her doctor hadn't cleared her to drive anyway.

When they went to bed, they held hands until sleep parted them.

Chapter Twenty Five

The weather on Sunday was fair but chilly. Nonetheless, Tom mowed the lawn, trimmed the bushes, and tended to his flower garden. Dorothy sorted her lesson plans and stacked them neatly to be taken to school. It felt good to be productive and somewhat busy.

When Tom was finished with the yard work, he checked in with Dorothy to see if she felt up to walking to the Thornes to return their containers. Dorothy nodded and went to get a sweater.

Strolling down the sidewalk, they looked about at the trees and grass. Here and there, early spring flowers were showing their colors. The grass greened up more each day, and leaves were beginning to come on the trees.

The Thornes weren't home, so they left the containers on the stoop of the side door. Dorothy was secretly OK with this, as she really didn't feel like talking to anyone.

They continued to walk down the street, listening to birds and watching squirrels scamper up and down the trees. Their neighborhood was pretty well established, and it was a quiet street with several families and young couples.

Usually, in the summer, there were a couple of block parties that everyone participated in. The Fourth of July one was always fun. They chatted about that and hoped the party would happen again this summer.

A few cars drove by, and they returned waves from drivers. When they got to the end of the street, they rested for a few moments and watched traffic on a crossroad go by.

Dorothy was ready to head back, so Tom grasped her hand, and they headed back up the street to their house. It was a nice ranch, with three bedrooms and one bathroom. Maybe someday they'd add on, make their bedroom bigger, and add another bathroom. For now, it was just right for the two of them. Tom had painted it a cool shade of dark green, with burgundy stained shutters at the windows. There was a railing that ran up the three steps to the front porch, although they almost always used the side door into the kitchen.

Dorothy loved their cozy home and was happy to be back inside after their walk. She went to the bathroom to check her bandages and noticed that her incision was a little red and inflamed. She asked Tom to help her with cleaning it and applying ointment and a fresh bandage. Then she relaxed on the couch for a while. She might have dozed off, for suddenly, she was opening her eyes, hearing voices coming from the kitchen.

Carefully she got up and walked into the kitchen to find Tom and Father Morgan talking as they carried in container after container of meals their church family had lovingly made for them!

Dorothy was amazed at the number of containers stacked on her kitchen counter!

"Oh my goodness! I can't believe this!" she exclaimed as Father Morgan set down three containers, and Tom followed in behind him with another two.

"I think that's all of it, Dorothy. Everyone was happy to cook for you two and are sending prayers as well," said Father Morgan.

"I'll clear space in the freezer, and we'll get it in there," said Tom.

"Father Morgan, we can't even begin to thank everyone. This is so very kind," said Dorothy.

"Oh now, Dorothy, you know you'd do the same for anyone else. Just enjoy it all. Everything is in containers you can keep or throw out, so don't worry about returning anything. You just eat, heal, and come back to church when you are ready," said the priest.

Father Morgan took the time to pray with the couple before he left, and they appreciated it very much.

"Tom, I'm getting tired of feeling so sad about all this. When is it going to get better?" asked Dorothy, a pleading look in her eyes.

"I don't know, honey. I'm tired of it too. It's such an awful thing that no one can fix. I guess we just have to keep moving on and hope we can feel somewhat normal again. Whatever that means. Maybe Dr. Brooks will have some suggestions on Friday when we go see him," Tom said.

"I hope so. I'm glad you're going back to work tomorrow. My folks will be here probably around ten or so. That will give me something to do, I guess," Dorothy said.

"Yes, that's true. I can stay home if you'd like," he said.

"Oh no, honey. I know you need to get back to work. Mom will pamper me and do laundry probably. Dad will run any errands that might need to be done. Do you have anything for him to do? He'll be looking for a project or something, I'm sure."

"Well, let's see. I fixed that broken step to the basement, but I could use help replacing the hinges on the side door to the garage. That's what I was looking for yesterday. I don't seem to have any in the right size."

"Oh, OK. I can send him to the hardware store, and he can get that done. Mom and I will do, I don't know, something!" Dorothy said, throwing her hands up. "I mean, what really is there they can do? Not much! I just would like to see them for a bit, though. Sometimes, I still need my parents. So I'm glad they're making the trip here," she mused.

Tom smiled at his wife. Sometimes she just spoke her thoughts out loud, and it made him smile. "Yes, dear, I know there isn't a lot for them to do here, but I know they want to see you as much as you want to see them. Then my folks come Wednesday. I hope that's not too much."

"I'm sure it will be fine. They have a bit of a further drive. I hope it isn't too much for them."

"Oh, they'll be all right. Dad's used to driving, being a farmer for so many years. They probably won't stay as many hours, though. Planting still isn't done, and he'll need to get up early Saturday to get back to it."

"I appreciate that they are coming. I know how important planting is," said Dorothy.

"Of course, they will come. They are heartbroken for us," said Tom quietly.

"So, what meal should we eat tonight?" asked Tom, rubbing his hands together.

"Oh my! Let's have a look through and pick one. It's still so odd to me to think that so many people have cooked for us. I'm so grateful."

They sorted through the containers and decided on chicken parmesan. Dorothy made a salad to go with it while Tom heated up the oven and put the chicken in a pan that could fit in it.

Soon the kitchen was filled with delicious scents, and the couple enjoyed another meal from people who cared about them. It was humbling and delicious too.

The evening was quiet and cozy—just the two of them watching the news, as was their habit, and early to bed.

Chapter Twenty Six

Tom didn't like the idea of leaving Dorothy Monday morning to head to work, but she insisted she was fine and her parents would be there mid-morning anyway.

He kissed her goodbye and held her in a hug a little longer than usual before heading out the door.

Dorothy waved goodbye and unconsciously rubbed her belly with her other hand. It made her instantly sad, as she suddenly realized this was a gesture she'd been doing for several months when he would leave for work.

Tom always left before she did, and waving goodbye was something she'd always done. Once she was pregnant, she would find her other hand gently rubbing her belly, excited to be a family of three. Now that that wasn't the case, Dorothy was sad and anxious to see her folks. She needed a hug from her mom, and that was all there was to it.

Dorothy puttered around the house and made a fresh pot of coffee. She loved the sound of the percolator as the coffee brewed. The scent always drew her in, and she looked forward to pouring a fresh cup with her mom and dad.

Reaching into the fridge, she pulled out a Bundt cake one of the parishioners had sent over with Father Morgan. Unwrapping it, she was delighted to catch the scent of lemon. There was a thick lemon glaze frosting covering it as well. Setting the oven on warm, Dorothy transferred the cake to a round pan to heat it up just a little.

As she busied herself getting ready for her parents' arrival, she thought about what she was going to say to them. She didn't want this to be a visit filled with crying. She needed hope and support. She knew there would be tears initially, but she didn't want that part to last long.

Gazing at the clock on the wall, she knew they'd be here very soon. She went into the living room and started watching the street. The coffee had just finished perking, and she hoped they'd arrive soon.

Just then, she saw her dad's 1959 black Cadillac. Dorothy's father was the vice president of Haskelite Manufacturing. They made plywood-coated trays, bowls, and utensils that were sold all over the country. Dorothy's mom never worked outside the home. She had been busy raising their three daughters.

Dorothy met her parents at the side door, not wanting to step outside in front of the neighbors. She was feeling so emotional, she needed her greeting to be private.

Her dad stepped out of the car, his gray felt hat with the black band a familiar sight to Dorothy. He gave her a small smile as he walked around the car to help his wife, Frances, with the door.

As soon as Dorothy saw her mother, tears began to flow down her cheeks. Frances and Emory hurried into the house to comfort their youngest daughter.

"Oh, Mom" was all Dorothy could say through her sobs. Her mother held her there in the kitchen while her father dug in his pockets for a handkerchief.

Frances rocked her daughter slightly in her arms, hushing her, and her dad rubbed her back. They were all trapped in sorrow, drawing comfort from one another.

Finally, Dorothy stood back and wiped her eyes with her dad's hanky. It smelled like his pipe tobacco, and she immediately pictured her childhood home, where all was safe and well and happy. It made her tear up again, and the lump in her throat threatened to choke her. She had to pull herself together. She was a grown and married woman who'd just lost a baby.

"I'm sorry. Please, take your coats off. I have a cake warming in the oven. I'll just get it, and we can go in the living room and talk," said Dorothy, trying to be brave and play the hostess part.

"Emory, why don't you take the coats, and I'll help Dottie in here?" said Frances, determined not to cry anymore and make her baby feel even worse. She had to be strong for her daughter.

Dorothy took her hot pads and drew the cake out of the warm oven. She shut the oven off and slid the cake onto a platter.

Meanwhile, Dorothy's mom, Frances, poured three mugs of coffee and placed them on a tray. She called Emory into the kitchen to carry it out for her, and she took the platter with the cake on it, following him into the living room.

Dorothy brought the cake slicer, forks, and spoons for coffee, along with some napkins. She was going to do her best to make this a positive visit, as much as it could be.

They settled on the couch and her dad in the chair, each fixing their coffee how they liked it. Dorothy sliced the lemon Bundt cake and slid pieces onto small dessert plates.

"My, that smells good, Dottie," said her mom.

"Oh, someone from church made it! Father Morgan brought over so much food yesterday, we won't have to cook for a long time!" said Dorothy, taking up her fork.

The cake was delicious, and she simply enjoyed being there with her mom and dad, having a moment where she could pretend all was well.

After they'd had some cake, Dorothy's mom turned to her with a faint smile. "Dottie, you can tell us whatever you want, however you want. I know you've been made to tell your story several times already, and I'm sure you're tired of repeating yourself. We're just here for you, for whatever you need. We are so very sorry."

"Thanks, Mom," Dorothy said. Her gaze slid to her dad. He nodded and smiled slightly in agreement.

Dorothy told her parents the entire story, as she felt they deserved and needed to know it firsthand. There were tears and hugs, but she got through it.

Frances poured them all more coffee when Dorothy finished her story and said, "Honey, we just want you to know that we love you both, and you can call us anytime, come visit, have us here, whatever works for you and Tom." Frances was very good at being matter-of-fact. She was direct but loving. Emory usually went along with whatever Frances said, and this time was no different.

"I'm so thankful that you came to see us. Tom went to work today, but he'll be home at lunch to say hello. If you don't mind, I need to put together a sandwich for him real quick. He'll be here in about half an hour."

Frances stood and helped Dorothy take the coffees back to the kitchen. Emory took the platter of cake, picking at a few crumbs left behind.

"Dad, Tom had a couple of things he thought you might like to do today." Dorothy looked at her dad, eyebrows waved.

"Certainly, dear. I'm here to do whatever," he replied.

"I'll just have him show you when he gets here. How does that sound?"

"That's fine, Dot. Since there's time, I'll just take the car to the filling station for gas so we don't have to stop on the way home. I'll be back soon." He kissed his wife and daughter and slipped out the kitchen door.

"You and Dad are the best blessings. I love having you here. Thank you so much," said Dorothy, tears in her eyes.

Frances looked at her youngest daughter, her arms covered in soap suds and nodded. Her eyes stung with tears as well. She hated that her daughter was living this nightmare.

They finished the dishes, and Dorothy quickly made an egg salad sandwich for Tom, along with a pickle and cottage cheese. She put it on the kitchen table and poured a glass of ice water.

Just then, her dad drove back up the driveway, and Tom pulled in right behind him. It was perfect timing.

Emory stepped into the kitchen and held the door open for Tom. They shook hands, and Emory squeezed Tom's shoulder. He told him how sorry he and Frances were.

Tom nodded, not trusting his voice. As in-laws went, he had pretty good ones.

"Hi, honey. I just made you a sandwich. How . . . how are things at the office?"

Tom kissed his wife on the cheek and thanked her for lunch. He washed his hands at the sink, and all four of them sat down at the kitchen table. "Well, the office was a little tough, but I managed to get through the morning. People don't really know what to say, and I keep telling them not to worry about what to say. I knew how they felt and appreciated their concern. I have work to catch up on, but it's keeping my mind occupied, so it's good. Frances, Emory, thank you so much for coming. Dot and I have needed you. My folks are coming on Wednesday for a few hours too. The neighbors and our church families have been wonderful. We have so much food and offers for help."

"Yes, Dottie was telling us. We're so glad you have people close by. We're always just a phone call away too," said Frances, squeezing her daughter's hand.

"Oh, Tom, Dottie said you had a little project for me to do! What can I help you with?" asked Emory.

"Oh yes, I have a door that needs hinges replaced in the garage. The little side door. After I eat, I'll show you and explain more." Tom dug into his lunch and chatted with his father-in-law about the door. It was nice to talk about something other than the baby.

Frances and Dorothy talked about Dorothy's sisters and how they were all doing. When Tom was done, he and Emory went out to the garage, and Frances dried the dishes after Dorothy washed them.

"So, Dot, what's become of the nursery?" asked Frances quietly.

"Oh. Well, Tom put everything away. Just the rocker and stool are in there now. We are leaving the door a little open. We don't want to shut it off completely. Does that make sense? He was so brave to come home and move everything into the basement while I was still in the hospital."

"Oh, honey, I just don't know what to say. We were wondering and a little unsure how to ask about it."

"I know, Mom. It's such an unexpected situation. No one really knows what to say or do. I see the doctor on Friday, and we'll find out more, I guess."

"You know, Mom, Tom has been so wonderful. He's so strong. I don't know if I could have done the things he has this week."

"Dottie, you had the baby. That's the strongest thing," she replied.

"You know, Mom, I don't know about that. Yes, it was horrible to know that my baby had died inside of me. But I was under anesthesia for the birth, and then I just lay in the hospital. Tom was the one who put away the nursery, and he was the one who buried our child. I think that's harder."

Nodding, Frances had to partially agree with her. But because Dorothy was her daughter and her youngest at that, she had so much sympathy and empathy for her. She prayed that this would never again happen and Dorothy would heal and another baby would come one day.

Tom and Emory came back into the kitchen, Emory holding a piece of paper he'd written the size of the hinges needed. Tom was just finishing his explanation of what he needed done, and Emory was nodding with understanding.

"Well, I've got to get back to the office. Emory, I sure do appreciate you taking care of this door for us. I've just been so busy lately. Thank you so much for coming and spending the day."

Emory and Frances told Tom they were happy to do it, and they all hugged goodbye. Tom kissed Dorothy and said he'd see her after work.

Once he'd left, Emory got in his car again and left for the hardware store to get what he needed to fix the door.

Frances helped Dorothy get some laundry going, and they sat in the living room and chatted more about just anything that came to mind.

When Emory came back, both Dorothy and Frances went to the garage to see if they could help at all with the door. He had them hold it while he removed the old hinges and leaned it against a wall.

Dorothy and Frances folded the laundry while they waited on Emory to finish and then had a glass of ice tea.

"Well," said Emory as he came through the kitchen door, "that's done, honey."

"Thanks, Dad. I really appreciate it, and I know Tom does too."

Her folks then got ready for their drive back to Grand Rapids, and promises were made for phone calls and scheduling another visit.

Dorothy spent the remainder of the afternoon doing some light housework and stretching like the nurse told her to do.

Chapter Twenty Seven

Tom arrived home after work, and Dorothy was just taking a casserole out of the oven. It was something with chicken and noodles in it, from what she could tell!

"Mmm, that smells good!" said Tom, kissing Dorothy on the cheek.

"It's from one of our church friends. I don't know who, but yes, it smells good. We are so blessed to have so many good friends."

"Yes, we are. Let me wash my hands, and I'll help you."

"Oh, there's nothing left to do but eat! It's all ready, and I got out plates before."

They settled at the kitchen table and enjoyed another home-cooked meal, counting their blessings, even though the reason for all the food gifts was covered in sorrow.

Tom filled her in on the rest of his day, and she related highlights from the rest of her parents' visit. She told him her dad had finished the door with the new hinges. Tom went to check it out when they were done eating. Emory had done a great job, and he was happy.

They talked about Dorothy being home the next day by herself. She assured Tom that she would be fine. She planned to write letters to people who'd sent baby gifts previously and explain what had happened. She thought it'd be easier to just write than to make heart-wrenching phone calls. She knew people had no idea what to say, and neither did she, frankly.

Tuesday passed in a blur as they each tried to find a new normal, new routines. So different from what they'd been planning for all these months.

Tom was looking forward to seeing his folks Wednesday and had left notes and instructions for his team at the office.

When his folks arrived, he helped his mother bring in several containers of food. He'd told her that the church members had loaded them down with meals that'd last for months, but being the wonderful mom and farm wife that she was, she couldn't stop herself from bringing her son's favorites.

The aroma of still warm, fresh fried chicken, rolls his sister had sent, green beans, and cherry pie were the comfort food Tom longed for without realizing it.

"Now, Dottie, you just sit. Let us get this all on the table. You rest, dear," said Genevieve. Dorothy loved her mother-in-law and her sturdy country roots. Even though she was feeling better, she let her mother-in-law fuss over her. Her father-in-law was quiet. He never really did talk much. He hugged her when they came in but was settled at the table now, happy to eat while the others spoke.

What had happened was the first topic they covered. Jenny, as Genevieve sometimes went by, shed some tears, recalling miscarriages of her own many years before. She'd never had a full-term baby that was born dead, but she had had a few miscarriages. She could understand some of Dorothy and Tom's pain, but not like this.

She patted Dorothy's hand several times and squeezed her son's shoulder. She knew they would get through this, and there would probably be other babies. It was just navigating this heartbreak that was going to take a long time.

After a bit, the talk turned to farming. The subject of the baby had been thoroughly discussed, and Tom wanted to lighten the mood. Plus, he wanted his dad in on the conversation! He knew bringing up farming would get him talking.

His dad became animated about planting season. What had been done, and how much there was left to do. Crops, tractors, fertilizer, the conversation could have lasted for days!

Dorothy was glad to have the distraction as well—anything to keep the sad thoughts at bay. She'd written several letters yesterday, reliving the week each time she wrote to another person in her address book. It was exhausting.

The food was amazing, and Dorothy knew she couldn't keep eating like this every day, or she'd never get back in shape and heal up! She'd be too tired to walk and exercise! But her mother-in-law's food and her sister-in-law's rolls were a wonderful treat, and she indulged. She told herself she'd be more mindful after today.

Tom filled his parents in on his job. They had been farmers for generations in their family, so it was hard for them to understand Tom's choice of office work. Nonetheless, he described his job and the people whom he worked with while they enjoyed the cherry pie with vanilla ice cream.

As the afternoon waned, Tom's parents insisted on washing all the dishes and gathering up their containers to take home.

They hugged Dorothy and told her to call anytime, and she promised she would. Tom walked his folks to their car and helped his mom get in.

Shutting the door, he leaned down to kiss her cheek and reached across to shake his dad's hand.

"Now, Tommy, you and Dorothy will get through this. Remember, you have so many people who love you, and the Lord will bless you. Don't you worry now," said Tom's mom, her hazel eyes searching her son's brown ones. She was determined not to cry and determined to help her son feel strong.

"Thanks, Mom. Dad, you be careful driving home now. Thank you for coming."

His dad nodded and slid the car into reverse. Tom waited in the driveway and waved goodbye as his parents drove off down the street. He felt his heart tug as he watched them go. Life was so precious. He loved his parents very much.

Back inside, Dorothy was finishing cleaning up the kitchen. "Well, we sure don't need anymore to eat today!" she said, a small smile on her face.

"We most certainly do not! Would you like to go for a walk before it gets dark?" Tom asked.

"You know, that's a great idea. Here, let me get our jackets," Dorothy said, walking to the closet.

Tom helped her put on a windbreaker and slid his arms into his. A nice walk with his Dottie was just what he needed.

The sun was dipping low in the west, as it was still mid-March. The breeze was light, though, and the temperature was not too cold.

They talked about the visits with both sets of parents and how thankful they were to have such support.

"You know, Tom, no one has asked . . . has asked . . . to go to the cemetery." Dorothy could barely get the words out. Saying it made it all so final.

"I noticed that too. I'm sure at some point, they'll want to go. But right now, they don't want us to hurt any more than we already do," he replied.

"I'm sure you're right. I don't know if I want to go there or not. Part of me never wants to see, because then it is so real. But part of me longs to be where he is," said Dorothy, wiping a tear from her eye.

Tom squeezed his wife's hand. "I know, honey. I know."

They walked the rest of the block in silence, each lost in their own thoughts.

Arriving back home, they hung up their jackets and got ready for bed. Thursday would be another "new normal" sort of day for them both. Then Friday, they would go see Dr. Brooks.

Thursday brought warmer temperatures but light rain as well. Dorothy spent some time knitting dishcloths as her mom had taught her. She did her stretching and paced around the house for exercise. She managed to do a load of laundry and put it away before she dug inside the freezer for another meal!

This time she found meatloaf and carrots. She would warm up the leftover rolls from yesterday to go with it. She set the table and then made herself a cup of tea and watched a little TV, waiting for Tom to get home.

Tom got home at his usual five-thirty from work and took off his jacket and tie.

"Smells like another good meal!" he said.

"Meatloaf and carrots this time. And Joan's rolls from yesterday." Dorothy handed Tom a glass of ice tea, and they sat down in their cozy kitchen and ate another wonderful dinner.

Tom helped Dorothy dress her incision before bed, and they talked about their appointment with Dr. Brooks tomorrow and wondered what he would have to say.

Drifting in and out of restless sleep, Dorothy kept hearing a baby's cry. She gave up around 5:00 a.m. and got up to shower.

Tom awoke to find Dorothy's pillow cold and empty. His heart panged with sadness. He knew she hadn't slept well. He got up, too, and joined her for coffee in the kitchen.

"Hi. How are you doing?" he asked, sipping from the proffered mug.

"I'm OK. Just didn't sleep. Kept dreaming of a baby crying. Probably normal for me to do that, huh?" she stated.

Tom sighed and squeezed her shoulder. He hoped Dr. Brooks would have good advice for them.

They got ready to go to the doctor's office, and Dorothy was actually looking forward to seeing Dr. Brooks and talking to him.

Chapter Twenty Eight

They arrived at Dr. Brooks's office at 10:15 a.m., a little early for their appointment. There was some paperwork to fill out anyway, so they had plenty of time.

Dorothy was thankful that there were only a couple of other people in the waiting room and it wasn't full of patients. She didn't know how long they would have the doctor's attention, but she hoped for a while.

One woman, quite visibly pregnant, was called in while they were waiting. Dorothy's hand drifted to her empty belly, and the familiar lump rose in her throat.

Noticing, Tom wrapped his arm around her shoulders and squeezed. "It will be OK, honey," he said, hoping his words would be true someday.

A few minutes later, Dorothy and Tom were called to the back, and he held the door open for his wife. They followed the nurse down the hallway to a room on the left.

The nurse had Dorothy step on the scale. She'd lost nearly thirty pounds since the baby had been born. She was quite astonished to see she'd lost that much; she still felt so big and awkward.

The nurse took her vitals and left her a hospital gown to change into. She said Dr. Brooks would be in soon.

Tom helped Dorothy to undress and get up on the table. He sat in a chair next to her and held her hand, waiting for the doctor.

A few minutes later, there was a knock at the door, and Dr. Brooks came in with a chart in his hand.

He greeted the couple, patting Tom on the shoulder and squeezing Dorothy's hand.

"Hi, folks. I'm glad to see you. Now, Dot, tell me how you're feeling."

Dorothy took a deep breath and told Dr. Brooks how she'd been feeling and thought she was healing well.

Then he had her lie back, and he examined her incision and the stitches. He said they could come out in another week.

"Now, Dorothy, Tom, I don't want to discourage you about having children. However, I'd like you to wait at least a year before you try again, if you're planning to. And I'd like to see how you're doing before another pregnancy happens."

Dorothy nodded, and so did Tom. They hadn't even discussed trying again yet. It was too soon, too painful, and somehow felt like a betrayal to Mark. Dorothy was very afraid that something bad might happen again and asked Dr. Brooks if there was any way to know about that.

Dr. Brooks explained that a baby having hydrocephalus was, in general, pretty rare. But he wanted to do blood work and see if there might be anything else out of sorts with both Tom and Dorothy before they pursued another pregnancy.

After the appointment, both Tom and Dorothy felt better about things and decided to take a drive. The sun was shining, and the air was fresh with spring scents and blooming trees all around.

"Tom, should we, I don't know, go to the cemetery?" Dorothy asked in a small voice.

"Do you want to? We can if you want to," he replied.

"I think yes, maybe. Let's drive around a little more and see where the road takes us," she said.

"OK, we can do that."

Tom drove through town and down to a local park. There were some people about, walking dogs, watching little ones on the swings. Next, he drove through the shopping area of town and noticed the plant nursery had flowering plants outside.

"I think that's our sign, Dot. See those blooming plants? I think Mark would like that."

Dorothy looked to her right and saw row upon row of blooming plants outside the large nursery. She nodded and brushed away tears at the same time.

Tom pulled in and parked. He helped Dorothy out of the car, and together, they walked the rows of potted plants. Some had blooms; others didn't yet. The smell of freshly turned dirt and the sight of occasional butterflies were calming to both of them.

Finally, they chose a tulip plant. It had yellow blooms, just starting to open. Tom then selected a small trowel to dig a hole with and a small bag of dirt. The checker gave them a plastic cup so they could fill it with water at the cemetery and water the plant after they explained what they were buying it for.

Back in the car, Dorothy held the plant, and Tom drove the few blocks down to the cemetery.

Pulling in, they noticed a few cars there and people pulling weeds and putting out fresh and artificial flowers of their own.

He wound his way back to Baby Land and pulled over. He could see the slight mound of dirt, still raised up from the grave where his baby son rested. He shut off the car and looked over at his wife. She was staring out the window, silent tears running down her face. He knew how hard this was going to be for them both.

Walking to the passenger side of the car, Tom opened Dorothy's door and took the tulip plant from her. She took his other hand and stood up.

They walked slowly to the grave, careful not to step on others they passed. Dorothy's free hand was on her belly, and she held on to Tom's hand tighter.

They stood looking down at the ground. There wasn't a headstone yet. They needed to order one. Tom bent down and put the tulip plant next to the freshly packed dirt. Then he put his arm around his wife.

Neither spoke as they remembered their little baby. Both cried, and Tom got out his hanky.

"I'll go get the trowel and dirt. Will you be OK for a minute?" he asked Dorothy.

She glanced at him, nodding and looked back down. The tears left tracks on her cheeks, and she rubbed her eyes.

Tom returned with the trowel, dirt, and cup. He squatted down and started to dig a shallow hole. Dorothy took the cup to the spigot at the end of the lane and carefully filled it with water. She took it back and held it until Tom had the tulip plant in the ground and dirt packed loosely around it.

Carefully she poured the water on the tulips and handed the cup to her husband.

Sighing, she rubbed her belly and whispered to Mark that she would always love him. Tom squeezed her hand, and they turned and went back to the car.

The ride home was quiet as they each dealt with the bitter reality of their loss.

Back at home, Tom tinkered in the garage while Dorothy dusted the living room and thought about life.

The day passed quietly, and they had another lovely dinner from a church friend.

"That was really hard," said Dorothy.

"I know. I know. We can get him a real nice headstone whenever you're ready," he replied.

Dorothy just nodded, staring at him with heartbreak in her eyes.

Chapter Twenty Nine

The weekend was upon them, and they talked about going to church on Sunday. Dorothy felt like they should go and thank the congregation for all the meals and prayers. Tom said he didn't feel ready to face all the people and retell their story yet again.

They talked about it over dinner Saturday, and Dorothy ended up agreeing with Tom. She knew their church family would understand their need for grieving and privacy for a while.

In the end, they called Father Morgan to let him know they'd come back eventually but just needed time for now. He said he understood and would speak to the congregation, just to let them know the Cornells were all right but taking time to adjust. Father Morgan reminded them that church was a place of love and support. They knew he was right, but they decided to still wait a bit before returning.

On Sunday, they took another walk around the neighborhood. The weather was perfect, sunny and close to seventy degrees. Many of their neighbors were out, and they stopped to chat whenever they saw someone they knew. They figured the sooner they got more used to letting people know what happened, the easier it would be when they did go back to church, Dorothy back to work and just life in general. They knew they had to be able to move forward and come to terms with what they had lost and what was meant to be or not to be.

The weeks began to pass as they fell into a sort of new routine. Dorothy's body was nearly healed; Tom was more focused at work.

Dorothy's sisters and then Tom's sister came to visit at different times. Just short visits, but still filled with love and support.

Tom and Dorothy took time to go visit their parents a couple of times on weekends. It was nice to get out of Midland and just be away.

The weekend of their anniversary in August, they drove up north to Traverse City and spent three days in a small hotel on a lake. It was restful and healing. They began to reconnect and look forward to the future.

Sometimes Tom would observe Dorothy rub her belly. He didn't know if her scar bothered her or if she was remembering the baby. He'd often hug her for no reason, and they'd have moments of quiet sadness.

The weekend in Traverse City was spent fishing, walking on the beach, exploring wooded trails, and having meals at cozy restaurants. It was just what they needed. They had been married now for ten years. Of course, their family life hadn't gone as they'd mapped it out in their minds, but they were finding their way, nonetheless.

Dorothy started back at school just after the Labor Day weekend. Tom had helped her decorate her classroom a week before school started. He wanted her to know he was there for her, and she appreciated it.

Tom was promoted at work and was glad to have the distraction of learning new tasks to keep his mind occupied.

Time moved on, and because it did, it forced them to as well. They did take the time to order a headstone for Mark's grave and went to see it once it was put up.

"Tom, do you think it will look nice? I want it to be nice for him," Dorothy asked anxiously on the day they drove to the cemetery. They didn't go often as it still made them too sad.

"I think it will be very nice, honey," Tom replied, his heart low at the thought of seeing his child's grave again. He had mixed feelings when he was at the cemetery. On the one hand, he felt closer to Mark when he was there. On the other hand, it only reminded him of the empty nursery and their empty arms.

Parking again where he had before, he helped Dorothy get out of the car. They'd brought some fall mums in a rusty burgundy color to replace the tulip plant that had long ago died.

Dorothy carried the mums as Tom gathered the gardening tools. They walked to Mark's grave and looked at the new headstone that had just been put in that week.

It read, "Mark Cornell, Forever an Angel, March 15, 1961." That's all it needed to say, as there was no separate birth and death date. The stone was a tall gray marble cross. It wasn't shiny, but bits of sparkle reflected from the sunlight dappling through the big maple trees surrounding Baby Land.

"See, I told you it would look nice, honey," said Tom. He set the gardening tools down and squeezed her hand.

Dorothy leaned forward and traced Mark's name with her finger. A single tear slid down her face. She said nothing but wiped her tear and set the mum plant down next to the tools.

"I'll go fill the watering can, Tom," she simply said and turned away.

Tom hoped she would be OK and set about digging a small hole for the new plant.

Dorothy came back with the watering can and patiently waited for Tom to finish putting the mums into the ground in front of the cross.

She stared at the new cross and thought it looked very old. She decided she liked that. It gave it an austere look that she admired. It was simple and yet lovely.

Tom placed the mum into the hole and covered it loosely. Dorothy gave it a good watering, and then they just stood there, holding hands, lost in thoughts about what might have been.

After that day, things once again fell into routines. Dorothy's school year was going well; she had nineteen kids in her class, and they were inquisitive and kept her focused.

Tom's work was ever-changing, and he enjoyed learning new things. He still found time to collect stamps from other countries and kept them in a binder on his desk. Maybe one day they'd have a child he could share them with.

Chapter Thirty

As fall moved toward the holiday season, Tom and Dorothy started going back to church. People were gracious and didn't ask a lot of questions, and they were thankful for that.

Thanksgiving took them to the farm of Tom's parents. The food was outstanding, and Joan and Gale were there too. Tom relished Thanksgiving with his parents and sister.

They always stayed in his old room across the hall from his mom and dad. It felt secure and safe. He didn't admit out loud that he was a grown man needing to feel those things, but he felt them just the same.

Dorothy enjoyed visiting with her in-laws and practiced crocheting with her sister-in-law.

It was a good time to be away from Midland once again, and they had plans to spend Christmas at Dorothy's folks' place.

Soon enough, it was time for their three-day visit to Grand Rapids. Dorothy's parents' house was packed, with all three of their daughters, spouses, and seven grandkids.

Tom and Dorothy felt like they were on the outside looking in, especially when the kids opened their many gifts under the Christmas tree.

Tom held Dorothy's hand as she tried hard not to cry, thinking about how this would have been Mark's very first Christmas.

Dorothy's family was gracious and kept things at an even keel for the couple who'd lost so much. They sent the kids off on adventures and errands with some of the other adults so they could take turns spending time with Tom and Dorothy, catching up and just spending time.

Christmas was over quickly, and Tom and Dorothy found themselves back in Midland to start 1962. They spent New Year's Eve at a neighbor's house who was having a small get-together. It was a lovely evening filled with card games, fancy dishes to try, and champagne at midnight.

Soon school started back up for Dorothy, and Tom was back to work for a harrowing first quarter. His office was always the busiest in January, but he didn't mind. It kept him occupied.

The couple had celebrated Dorothy's birthday on January 2, and she wondered to herself how many years she had left to try to have another baby. As she blew out her candles, she made a silent wish for another child.

Before they knew it, March arrived. It came in like the proverbial lion, with snow, wind, and dark clouds.

Tom wondered if it would be better by the 15th. It would still be a bit cold to plant anything there, and the ground would still be frozen with the cold March they'd had so far. He'd think of something else to take to Mark's grave.

"Tom, can we leave something at Mark's grave on the 15th? I know it's far too cold to plant anything, but I hate to leave nothing," Dorothy said a few days before the date. Neither of them referred to March 15 as Mark's birthday since he'd never taken a breath.

"I've been thinking about that, Dot. Why don't we see if we can find a small statue or maybe a wind chime?"

"I like the idea of a small statue. I don't like wind chimes," Dorothy replied, thinking about what might look nice with the gray cross.

They went the next day to the local nursery and looked at what was available. They found a small concrete angel that was kneeling with beautifully spread wings hovering over its shoulders. It looked perfect as if it was watching over someone.

Tom wrapped it in a blanket and loaded it into the trunk of his car. They still had a few days before the 15th, but he knew it wouldn't break.

The 15th fell on a Wednesday. As soon as Tom got home from work, he and Dorothy headed to the cemetery. It would be dark relatively soon, so they didn't want to waste any time.

Dorothy brushed old snow off the arms of the cross marking their son's grave, while Tom scraped snow away from the base where the angel would sit.

Tom unwrapped the concrete angel and placed it carefully at the base of the cross. It was white and shone brightly in front of the gray cross.

He stood and held hands with Dorothy. They both had tears as they remembered this day a year before. It seemed like yesterday and years ago at the same time.

After a few minutes, they each touched the cross, and then they walked back to their car.

"I wonder if we should try again, Tom. Dr. Brooks said after a year, we could. What do you think? I've been thinking about it, and I would like to try," said Dorothy quietly.

Tom was silent as he started the car and fastened his seat belt. He'd been thinking about trying again too. He didn't want to upset Dorothy by asking her nor somehow disrespect the son they'd had. He didn't want to replace Mark, but he didn't want to be childless. They'd wanted a family for years, and he didn't want to give up.

"I think it's a good idea. How about if we meet with Dr. Brooks and see what he has to say?" replied Tom as he drove the few miles home in the gathering night.

"OK. I can call his office and make an appointment. I feel fine now. I haven't felt any pain in months, and my scar has healed well," Dorothy said, rubbing her belly.

They ate dinner when they arrived home and spent the evening talking more about the possibility of another baby.

When they went to bed, they both felt a bit lighter, optimistic, and healed—for the most part, anyway. Mark would always be their first baby and always be in their hearts, but they felt they were meant to be parents and wanted to move forward with that goal.

Chapter Thirty One

Dorothy made an appointment at Dr. Brooks's office for the following week while school was on spring break. Tom made arrangements to have the day off work so he could go with her.

Dr. Brooks was happy to see the couple and glad they'd been working through their grief and healing. He knew from having other patients that had lost babies that the grief never fully left, but other children would come to assuage it, and they would be all right.

Dr. Brooks examined Dorothy and gave them the go-ahead to try to get pregnant again. They talked about the effects of having another child after losing one, and both Tom and Dorothy assured him that they had made peace with losing Mark. They still wanted to be parents and wished to try again.

Later that day, they talked more about becoming parents and what they would do if they lost another. For the first time, the topic of adoption came up.

Another teacher at school had lost a baby, and she and her husband decided to adopt. Dorothy had listened to the conversation in the teachers' break room as the young woman shared her story about her and her husband receiving a baby boy through adoption. She'd mulled it over off and on for months but hadn't said anything to Tom about it until now.

"I don't know, Dot. I've never thought about adoption. Do you think you could do it?"

"Well, I don't know. Mrs. Levy and her husband said they didn't have a lot of trouble adopting a baby, and they are very happy with their son. They knew it was the only way they could be parents after she'd had a miscarriage," said Dorothy, reflecting on the conversation.

They decided to think about that, should they not be able to get pregnant again or if something unexpected happened yet again.

Dorothy called Dr. Brooks's office the next day to ask if they had any information about adoption, and the nurse referred her to the Lutheran Social Services Agency. She said that several of Dr. Brooks's patients had become parents by adopting through that agency.

Dorothy made herself some tea before making the call to the agency. She wasn't sure if she wanted to make the call. But she wanted options in case she didn't become pregnant again or if they lost another baby.

Finally, she sat down at the table and lifted the phone receiver. She dialed the number and was surprised to feel her heart beating fast. She didn't know why she was nervous. She really didn't think she'd ever need an adoption agency. She was sure she would get pregnant again soon.

A pleasant voice answered the line, greeting her with "Lutheran Social Services, this is Trudy. How may I help you?"

Clearing her throat, Dorothy stated her name and asked for information regarding adoption. Trudy Belvins explained a bit of their process and asked Dorothy questions about her family. Dorothy shared that she had had a stillborn and might be interested in adopting, should they not be able to have a baby on their own.

Trudy had heard this story many times, and lots of times, it had worked out for couples to adopt a baby or young child through the agency. Patiently, she told Dorothy about their services, programs, and requirements. Then she said she'd mail Dorothy some information she and her husband could look over.

Dorothy thanked Trudy for her time and hung up. She was surprised her tea had gone cold and, looking at the clock, was startled to discover she'd been on the phone for close to an hour with Ms. Belvins. She thought about adoption off and on the rest of the day and was eager to speak to Tom about it when he arrived home from work.

Of course, she hoped she and Tom would conceive on their own, but she was still scared after what they'd already been through. Adoption sounded like something they should investigate.

Over dinner, she told Tom about her discussion with Trudy Belvins. He was hesitant, but the more she told him, the more at ease he became with it. They both hoped they would have a baby of their own, though, and soon the conversation turned to other topics.

Dorothy asked Mrs. Levy at school more about their adoption process. This was Mrs. Levy's first year at the school where Dorothy taught, and so she wasn't aware that Dorothy had had a stillborn child the previous year.

Dorothy felt bad, causing Mrs. Levy to feel uncomfortable about her having lost Mark, but she reassured the woman that she was doing better and that if she and her husband couldn't have a child, they'd be interested in adopting.

Mrs. Levy and Dorothy spent several lunch breaks over the next few weeks talking about the dynamics of adoption. Dorothy then relayed what she'd learned to Tom over dinners. They decided to put the topic on the back burner and try to get pregnant again on their own, but it was good to have the information from someone who'd already been through adopting a baby.

Chapter Thirty Two

School was out for summer, and Tom and Dorothy planned a getaway over the Fourth Of July holiday to Torch Lake, up in Antrim. It was a beautiful lake. The waters were as blue and crystal clear as the Caribbean! They'd never been but had been told by friends that it was a great place to visit.

Tom had rented a cabin right on the edge of the eastern shore of the lake for three days. He couldn't wait to spend the time with Dorothy and go fishing, sailing, exploring, and doing whatever else came to mind.

Dorothy took care in packing a variety of clothes, as it did get cold at night on Torch Lake. In the end, they had three suitcases packed in the trunk the day they left Midland and headed northwest to Antrim.

The cabin was easy to find, nestled in a grove of tall jack pine trees, with a view to rival any place they'd ever been to.

There were six cabins and a main lodge at Torch Pines, and the owner gave Tom a skeleton key for the door when he registered.

He drove the short distance to cabin number 3 and parked the car next to it on a small gravel space.

He and Dorothy carried their bags in and set them in the bedroom before taking time to explore their little getaway.

There were two bedrooms and one nice bathroom between them. The kitchen and living room were all one space, and there was a deck that faced the lake with big glass doors to simply walk through to get outside.

Tom slid the door open, and Dorothy walked out before him onto the deck. There was nice furniture there to relax on, and a walkway cleared down to the beach. There was a long dock that stretched out far into the lake from the beach.

Sliding off their shoes, they walked hand-in-hand to the shore of Torch Lake. Their cabin was set a bit apart from the others, and it was very private.

The waves quietly sounded against white sand that was warm to the touch. Seagulls called overhead, and the water was as clear as the sky, as far as they could see.

"Oh, Tom! This is wonderful! I'm so excited to be here!" said Dorothy, squeezing his hand.

"It is great, isn't it? Come on, let's walk along the shore!"

Hand in hand, they walked south along the shoreline, dipping their toes into the chilly water, collecting tiny shells and enjoying the afternoon sun.

After about a mile, they sat on a tree log that had fallen down from the edge of the woods near the shore. They gazed at the lake, just enjoying the waves splashing against the shore that was more rocky in this spot.

Dorothy looked over into the woods and heard several birds. The leaves were bright green, and high summer surrounded them. She was very happy, and it felt good to just relax and not have much in the way of responsibility for a few days.

Tom was thinking about fishing and asked Dorothy if she'd like to rent a pontoon the next day, and they could putter about the lake and maybe fish.

Dorothy said that would be wonderful, and shortly, they wandered back to their cabin so Tom could go make inquiries.

Dorothy unpacked their suitcases while Tom found the cabin owner and made arrangements to rent a pontoon and fishing gear for the next day. He also asked where they should go to dinner that night and pick up a few groceries to have in the cabin.

Tom and Dorothy got cleaned up and headed toward town. Making a quick stop at a general store, they bought coffee, eggs and bacon for breakfast. Then they drove to Central Lake Tavern on the advice of the cabin owner and weren't disappointed!

The restaurant overlooked the lake, and it was still light out, so they could see the clear blue water of the lake. Soon, twinkling lights came on as they sat at a table outside on an enormous deck. Soft music played in the background, and the atmosphere was romantic and cozy.

Their meal was fresh seafood and pasta that was so good, Dorothy didn't think she'd ever eaten anything as delicious as long as she lived! She was grateful to Tom for planning this getaway for them. They wanted to start their family, and this was a perfect way to begin.

Arriving back at the cabin, Tom turned on the old record player in the living room, and they danced to some of their favorite tunes before bed. They carried their romantic evening late into the night, and it was well after midnight before they drifted off to sleep.

The next day was the Fourth, and they were excited to get out on the lake with other tourists and see what Torch was all about!

Tom took the pontoon keys from Mr. Smith, the cabin owner, and he walked the couple to the pontoon tied up at the dock. He explained how it all worked and gave them fishing poles, bait, and life jackets. Then he asked that they be back before dark. There was a gas station for boats, right on the water across the lake he said they could go to if they needed fuel. He also pointed out a couple of bistros they could access from docks dotted along the shores surrounding the huge lake.

Tom quickly figured out the mechanics of driving the pontoon, and they were off to explore! It was a glorious day filled with bright sunshine, and the temperature soared into the eighties.

Cruising across the lake, they soaked up the sun, and Dorothy felt the breeze ruffle her brown hair and gazed lovingly at Tom. He looked so smart, driving the boat with ease.

They maneuvered to an area filled with other boaters, and they all waved at one another. It was fun to see other people out, enjoying the holiday weekend as well.

Hungry, Tom looked for a bistro, like Mr. Smith said they should easily find. Soon, they came across one that looked interesting with multi-colored umbrellas at high-topped tables on a large deck.

Tom carefully pulled the pontoon up to the dock, and Dorothy reached out for the pylon and threw the anchor rope around it. Tom helped tie off and climbed out of the boat. He reached down and helped Dorothy climb out, and hand-in-hand, they walked up the dock to the bistro.

Scents of hamburger and fish wafted across the dock, and they both felt their bellies growl with hunger!

A hostess sat them at a table with a bright orange umbrella, and Tom ordered a beer for him and a glass of white wine for Dorothy.

They looked around, nodding at other guests, trying to see what people were ordering. Tom ended up asking for a cheeseburger with everything and fries, while Dorothy got roasted chicken with coleslaw.

Their food was excellent, and Tom shared his fries with Dorothy. They each had another drink and enjoyed casual conversation with another vacationing couple at the table next to them.

After paying the check, they walked back to the pontoon and carefully climbed back on board.

Tom took his time, motoring along the shore, not too far out but enough so that they could admire the view of beautiful homes and other businesses that covered the shores of this beautiful lake.

Eventually, they arrived at an area that wasn't too populated, and many trees reached out over the water. Tom dropped anchor, hoping it'd be a good place to catch some fish.

Baiting her own hook, as Dorothy didn't mind doing, Tom found some music on the boat radio to play softly in the background. He didn't think it'd scare off the fish, but he really didn't care. He was truly enjoying spending time with his Dottie, just relaxing and having fun.

He cast his line on the opposite side of the boat from Dorothy's and settled on the bench, facing her. He looked at the concentration on her face as she stood and cast out her line deep into the lake.

Dorothy saw him watching her out of the corner of her eye as she cast her line, and it made her heart swell. She was having such a good time, and she loved her husband.

Dorothy took a seat near Tom, carefully set her pole in the fishing pole cup, and smiled at him.

"Are you having fun, Tom? I sure am. I hope we catch some fish! Lunch was great, by the way."

"Yes, I'm having fun. I think you are too! If we catch anything, we might have to eat it!" Tom laughed.

He leaned over into a cooler and pulled out two Cokes. He grabbed the bottle opener and opened them, handed one to Dorothy and took a drink of his own. It was going to be a good afternoon.

They talked about random things, like the weather, work, summertime, the lake—just anything that came to mind.

Suddenly, Tom's line went taut, and he grabbed his pole! Standing up, he started reeling in his line and felt a hard tug pull it back out.

"Tom! You've got something!" exclaimed Dorothy. She reeled in her line in case she needed to use the net to pull up whatever Tom might have on his hook.

Carefully Tom worked the line, and finally, a flash of pink and green splashed out of the water! It was a huge rainbow trout! Dorothy quickly grabbed the net and got close to the railing of the pontoon. Tom looked at her and nodded as he gave a big pull on his fishing pole.

The huge fish came up out of the water, and Dorothy snagged it up in the net as neat as could be!

"Well, look there! We have dinner!" said Tom with a big smile. He unhooked the fish and put it in the well at the back end of the boat. It was easily five pounds and nicely colored.

"OK, I've done my job! Now it's your turn!" said Tom with a laugh as he plopped the fishing well lid down.

"Oh, I think that'll feed us both, but just in case, I'm going to try anyway!" replied Dorothy with a laugh.

It wasn't long before she had a tug on her line, and Tom grabbed the net this time! Dorothy pulled in a steelhead trout, not quite as big as Tom's rainbow, but she was proud of it anyway!

Dumping it in the well with the rainbow, Tom stowed their gear, and he hauled up the anchor.

Motoring along the shore for a bit, they marveled at beautiful cottages and long docks reaching far out into the lake.

"Hey, let's go swimming tomorrow!" said Dorothy.

"OK, I'm game! I saw a floating dock out past our cabin. Did you notice it? It has a ladder we can climb up and sit on the dock."

"Oh yes! I did see that! It'll be perfect!" she responded.

Tom took his time steering the pontoon, and they found a drive-up gas station. He filled the tank to replace what they used, and they each used the restroom inside. There were trinkets and T-shirts for sale, and Tom bought Dorothy a brightly painted wooden fish that stood on a piece of driftwood to remember their trip by.

He handed her the wooden fish when she came out of the restroom, and he was happy to hear her giggle and see her eyes light up.

Back on the pontoon, he drove it to the dock near their cottage. Mr. Smith saw them and came to see how they did. Tom handed him the fishing gear and life jackets while Dorothy filled him in on their adventures. Mr. Smith had a bucket in the shed and brought it to them to fill with water and put their fish in it.

Leaving the fish in the bucket, Tom put it in the sink, and they quickly rubbed the sand off their feet, slipped on sandals, and drove to town for a few groceries.

The local grocery was just a few minutes away, and Tom was able to find a good parking place near the doors. He and Dorothy took a basket and wound their way through the aisles, exploring what was available. They selected a couple of fresh lemons, some rice, fresh peppers and mushrooms to sauté with their fish, and a French baguette bread that had just been baked that day.

"Hey, should we get some wine or something?" asked Tom.

"That sounds good! White?" Dorothy replied.

They looked at the selections and finally settled on a soft white wine from a local vineyard. Tom usually drank beer, but he was feeling romantic, and wine seemed to fit the bill.

"How do you feel about key lime pie for dessert?" asked Dorothy, looking into a cooler filled with delicious-looking desserts.

"Well, that sounds good!" said Tom, laughing.

Dorothy reached in for the pie, and Tom placed the bottle of wine in the basket. They grabbed some spices for their fish, coffee and bagels for breakfast, and some lunch food for the next day while they were there.

Back at the cabin, Tom cleaned the fish while Dorothy put away the groceries and helped prep for dinner. She set the table while Tom grilled the fish on a small grill out behind the cabin.

The sun was beginning to set, and here and there, fireflies lit the evening sky. They could hear the waves splashing against the shore, and it was all quite romantic.

Deciding to eat on the deck, Dorothy pulled the chairs up to the table in the center. She found some pillar candles in a kitchen drawer that were probably meant to be used should the power go out, but she took them to the table outside and lit them anyway. Their fresh-caught dinner turned out to be wonderful and maybe even more so because they had cooked it together.

When they were done, they took slices of the key lime pie and walked out on the dock. The moon was up, and stars filled the sky. Carefully they set their plates down on the dock and sat down, legs dangling over the edge, and enjoyed the homemade treat.

"Well, this certainly is how it's done, isn't it, Dot?" asked Tom, a glint in his eye.

"Oh yes, this is so perfect. I'm so glad we are here. I could spend days and days at this place!"

Tom laughed and agreed. They tossed some pie crumbs into the water and watched as tiny perch swam to grab the morsels before they disappeared into the water.

Soon they heard the booming sounds of fireworks as the breeze carried the sounds across the lake toward them. The sky lit up with a huge display of white-and-gold fireworks, and Dorothy gasped at their beauty!

They continued to sit on the dock, watching as, over and over, the sky lit up with brilliant colors, each one more beautiful than the last!

Finally, the show was about to end, and they held hands as a cacophony of fireworks went off one after another and then simultaneously! It was perfect, and they shared a kiss when the last of the fireworks fizzled out.

Back in the cabin, they washed up their dishes while listening to jazz on the stereo. As Dorothy put the last of the dishes in the cupboard, Tom took her by the arm and swung her into a twirl in time to the music.

Dorothy laughed and fell into dancing with her husband, just the two of them in the softly lit cabin on a beautiful lake, surrounded by nature and more romance than they'd experienced in many years.

The next morning, Dorothy awoke to the scent of freshly brewed coffee and stretched in bed. She sighed and sat up, swinging her legs over the side of the bed. Memories of last night brought a smile to her lips, and she stood and made her way to the kitchen.

Tom had just flipped the eggs over in the sizzling fat from the bacon in the frying pan when Dorothy came in for some coffee.

"Hi, sleepyhead! I was just going to wake you! Ready for breakfast?" he said, pulling out her chair and waving his arm in a flourish.

"Thank you, sir. I believe I will!" Dorothy laughed, kissed Tom on the cheek, and sat down to enjoy breakfast.

"I'm excited to swim today! But I bet that water is cold till much later on!" Dorothy said, taking a bite of crunchy bacon dipped in egg yolk.

"I know that's true! So what should we do until the afternoon? Maybe I can ask Mr. Smith if he knows of a good activity."

"That's a good idea! Maybe there are some events going on or a flea market or a boat show. Who knows? But I'm excited to find out!" said Dorothy.

"Me too. Right after breakfast, I'll go see what I can find out," replied Tom, finishing his eggs.

Dorothy showered after she ate and slipped on a sundress of ice blue. It was light cotton and perfect for this hot sunny day.

Tom found Mr. Smith and was excited to find out that there was a holiday festival in town that included some carnival rides, artisan vendors, and lots and lots of food!

Mr. Smith gave them directions to the festival area on the north end of the lake and said it would be easier to drive there instead of boating. He advised them where to park and told them to enjoy themselves!

Tom and Dorothy took their time driving around the lake, and it was easy to see where all the happenings were going on! There were throngs of people in the late morning sun, all seemingly having a great time, and they couldn't wait to join in the fun!

Tom parked and held Dorothy's door open. Hand in hand, they wandered through the booths of handmade items for sale. Dorothy lingered by a photograph of fireworks over Torch Lake that a local photographer had taken and framed in a frame of hammered silver.

"Ah, looks like last night, doesn't it?" said Tom, a gleam in his eye.

Dorothy smiled and nodded, tracing the line of the firework across the glass.

"I took that last year!" the vendor said. "I always have the previous year's firework photos done for the next year, framed and all."

Tom could tell that Dorothy wanted this memento of their trip and happily parted with some cash for it. The vendor wrapped it carefully in brown paper and tied it with string. They weren't too far from the car, so they walked to the car and placed it in the trunk.

Next, they checked out the carnival rides. Some looked a little fast, but the Ferris wheel looked slow and safe enough!

Tom bought some tickets and handed some to Dorothy. They waited in line, and finally, it was their turn to board the giant wheel.

The attendant snapped the bar across their laps, and off they went high into the sky! The view of Torch Lake was incredible from such a height, and they forgot to be nervous as they enjoyed the views, the fresh air, and the cool lake breeze! The sun was riding high in the sky, and it was a perfect day!

They decided to take a turn at the bumper cars and handed over a few more tickets. They felt young and free for a while that day, all their cares and sadness held at bay for once.

"Hey, want to get something here to eat for our dinner?" Tom asked.

"All the food certainly does smell good, doesn't it?" asked Dorothy, sniffing the air. It was heavily scented with the delicious smell of fried things, like chicken, French fries and onion rings!

They walked around, checking out all the food booths, and settled on shaved steak sandwiches with pickle spears on the side, delicious French fries, and sherbet for dessert.

They walked along the midway, and both tried their hand at games, like throwing a ping-pong bottle in a vase with a goldfish in it. Tom threw darts, and Dorothy tossed a ball at a net that was clearly too small for the ball to go in!

Neither ended up winning anything, but they had a wonderful time trying anyway. Deciding they were ready to head back to the cabin to swim, they passed a cotton candy vendor, and Dorothy asked to get a big cone of pink cotton candy! She loved how it instantly melted on her tongue.

Tom laughed as he paid the man for it, declining to get any for himself. He could take it or leave it, but it was fun to watch Dorothy savor the fast-melting spun sugar.

Back at the cabin, they changed into swimsuits and grabbed some towels.

At the end of the dock, they set the towels down for later. The sun was moving toward the western horizon, but the water felt pretty warm on their toes.

"Race you to the float!" Dorothy suddenly yelled and dived into the blue water! She surfaced, moving swiftly, doing a side stroke, and laughing at her husband!

Tom dived right in, quickly passing her with strong overhead strokes! He reached the float ladder just seconds before Dorothy, and they were both laughing and shivering as the water was a lot colder under the surface!

They climbed up on the floating dock and carefully walked around it. It pitched and swayed with their weight and the current of the lake, but not so much as to toss them off.

They sat down and observed the lake from their vantage point. There were countless boats on the far side of the lake, sailboats everywhere and even a few water skiers! They chatted and let the sun warm them up, their hair and swimsuits quickly drying under the rays. They watched as small fish swam by the float. Seagulls careened overhead, their white feathers bright against the crystal blue sky.

Dorothy sighed. "This has just been the best time, Tom. Thank you for bringing me here."

"Hey, I've loved it too. I'm glad we were able to come. It was just what we needed. So tonight's our last evening. I'm still full from earlier, but maybe we could go to the Tastee Freeze for a bit of ice cream?" Tom waggled his eyebrows at her. She knew how much he loved his black cherry ice cream. She was almost done in from the rich fair food, along with the sweet cotton candy, but she couldn't tell him no!

"You're on! Should we go clean up and head to town?" she asked, standing up.

"Sure! Are we racing back to the dock?" As Tom asked, Dorothy dived into the lake, taking off at a fast arm-over-arm pace!

Tom laughed and gave her a few more seconds, as he knew he could easily beat her there again.

Dorothy reached the ladder of the dock and climbed up, just as Tom got to the ladder.

"OK, you beat me! I guess you're first in the shower!"

Dorothy laughed as she towel-dried her hair and then wrapped the yellow-and-white-striped towel around herself.

Tom shook his head and dried his body off, watching as Dorothy slid into flip-flops and headed up the dock toward the cabin. He hoped so much that this little getaway would help them to heal and move forward. Maybe another baby would come along soon after this.

Cleaned up and dressed in shorts and a T-shirt, Tom smiled to see Dorothy in pedal pushers and a mint-green blouse. She always looked just right to him, and he loved her so much.

The drive to the Tastee Freeze only took a few minutes, and they decided to have their ice cream there, as there was outdoor seating near the water.

Lots of other tourists and locals were enjoying the warm summer night with frozen treats as well. There were Japanese lantern lights strung over a deck with ice cream parlor chairs and tables. They could hear music coming from somewhere. People were laughing, and kids were running all around.

Dorothy thought that it would be so much fun to bring a family here, and her hand passed over her belly. Maybe one day that would happen for them.

Tom stuck with his black cherry ice cream, ordering it in a big sugar waffle cone. Dorothy settled on a small chocolate malt with a red-and-white-striped straw! There was a red cherry on top that she popped in her mouth, and it tasted like candy!

They chatted with a few other tourists and watched as children messily ate their treats but having a lot of fun anyway.

When they were done, they took a stroll on the street there, as there were many businesses open late on summer evenings. They peered at souvenirs in shop windows, and Tom bought them each a T-shirt to remember their fun weekend by.

Tom held Dorothy's door open, and she slid into the seat. He handed her the T-shirts and went around and got behind the wheel.

It was a lovely night to drive with the windows open with soft music on the radio. They enjoyed seeing fireflies light their way, and soon, they were pulling back in under the pines. The fireflies were thick here, and Dorothy thought they added a special ambiance to the clearing around the cabins.

Tom parked the car, and he and Dorothy walked hand in hand to the cabin. Dorothy carefully folded the T-shirts that said "Torch Lake" in black letters on an aqua-blue shirt that matched the color of the lake. She would always remember this wonderful holiday weekend.

They sat out on the deck one more time, enjoying the night sky with its twinkling stars and bright-yellow moon. The waves lapped at the shore and lulled them into a comfortable silence.

After a bit, Tom took Dorothy's hand, and they headed to the bedroom for their final night at Torch Lake.

Chapter Thirty Three

The next morning greeted them with some low-hanging clouds. It reflected Dorothy's melancholy mood to have to leave the cozy cabin and head back to Midland. She and Tom had some coffee and eggs along with their bagels. They showered and packed their things, getting ready for the long drive home.

Tom loaded the suitcases into the car, and Dorothy climbed in while Tom returned the cabin key to Mr. Smith. He told the cabin owner how much they had enjoyed their stay, and Mr. Smith said he hoped they'd come back again sometime.

The drive home was uneventful, except for some rain showers off and on. Back at home, they unpacked, and Dorothy started the laundry.

Tom would be back at work tomorrow, and Dorothy would start thinking about the upcoming school year. Even though school didn't start for the kids until right after Labor Day, she was always welcome to visit her classroom over the summer to decorate and fill it with supplies for the new school year. She decided to write down tasks she wanted to complete in her classroom to keep herself busy and occupy her mind.

Soon they were back into their routines, although they did take time to go out to dinner, the occasional movie, and a walk through the neighborhood now and then.

Some neighbors moved away, and new families moved in. Tom and Dorothy would take welcome meals to new people and introduce themselves. It was a wonderful block to live on, and the Cornells were thankful to have good people around them.

School started, and September was rolling by. She had twenty-one kids in her class and was enjoying getting to know her new students.

One day, Dorothy's friend Rosemary Stein called to tell her that she and Larry were adopting a baby boy! Dorothy was so happy for her friends and couldn't wait to hear all about it.

She and Tom went to dinner at Rosemary and Larry's, and they explained how the process was working for them, and they were hoping to have a baby boy sometime soon!

That night, Dorothy approached the subject of adoption again with Tom. It sounded like something she would be interested in if they never got pregnant on their own again. Tom had given adoption consideration, and he wasn't opposed to it but did wonder if he could love another's child as if it were his own.

As Rosemary and Larry's experience progressed with adoption, Dorothy noticed that she'd missed her period in late August. She didn't want to say anything to Tom yet but made an appointment with Dr. Brooks. She felt her belly, and it felt smooth and a bit swollen. She was nervous but hopeful that she might be pregnant.

Dr. Brooks finished his examination and performed a pregnancy test. He felt quite sure that Dorothy was pregnant but wouldn't know for sure for a few days yet. He told her it would be fine to let Tom know.

Dorothy was excited, yet in the back of her mind, she was once again terrified that something bad would happen. She spent the afternoon thinking about how she felt and how she wanted to tell Tom. She thought about calling him at work but decided against it, as she wasn't entirely sure she was pregnant, and he'd been working on a big project with his team.

When he arrived home that evening, Dorothy had spaghetti and meatballs on the table, garlic bread ready to come out of the oven, and a small salad they could share.

"Hi, honey. How was your day?" she asked, taking the bread from the oven and laying it on a long cutting board.

"Hi, babe. It was busy! The project is coming along well, but it's taking longer than we originally thought. Dinner smells great. Do you need any help? I'll just wash up," he replied.

"Nope, all done! Just buttering the bread, and it's ready!" Dorothy replied with a smile.

Once seated, they filled their plates, and Dorothy poured dressing on the salad.

"So, how was your day?" Tom asked before a forkful of spaghetti.

"Oh, it was good. I went to see Dr. Brooks."

Tom swallowed his food and wiped his mouth with his napkin. "Oh? Are you all right?"

"Oh yes. I'm all right," Dorothy said, a nervous smile on her lips. "Tom, the doctor thinks I might be pregnant! He gave me a test, but it won't be back for a few days. But from what he can tell, he thinks I am."

"Oh, Dot! That's . . . that's wonderful! How do you feel?" Tom asked, grabbing her hand.

"I feel good. A little queasy. I missed my period in August, and it occurred to me that just maybe I might be pregnant."

"Well, I hope you are. I'm sure it will be OK this time!" Tom said optimistically. He wasn't sure if he believed his own words, but he wasn't going to be negative about this in any way.

"I hope so, Tom. I hope so," Dorothy replied, rubbing her belly.

"When will we know for sure?" Tom asked, getting back to his eating.

"Um, by the end of the week, I think," she said, taking a bite of the warm garlic bread.

They talked some more about the possibility of Dorothy being pregnant and decided they would just keep it to themselves if she was.

Chapter Thirty Four

The week dragged by, and Dorothy was glad school kept her busy and her mind off the phone call she was waiting for. On Friday afternoon, she arrived home around 3:30 p.m. and just as she was setting down her bag, the phone rang.

Quickly she grabbed the receiver, her heart beating fast. "Hello?" she said breathlessly.

"Mrs. Cornell? This is Dr. Brooks's office."

"Yes, this is she."

"Mrs. Cornell, I'm calling to congratulate you. You're pregnant!" said the voice on the other end.

Dorothy was so excited, tears sprang to her eyes. "Oh, thank you!" she exclaimed.

"Now, we're going to need to see you in about a month. Do you have a calendar ready so I can give you an appointment?" the receptionist asked.

"Oh yes, let me just get it," Dorothy laid the receiver down and rooted through her bag. The receptionist gave her a date in mid-October to see Dr. Brooks but told her if she had any problems, to call, and they would get her in.

Dorothy thanked her and hung up the phone. She placed both hands on her belly, feeling the tightness of it. Her emotions ran the gamut, and she was excited for Tom to get home. She was too wound up to even cook and hoped he was in the mood to go out!

She heard the car in the driveway and met Tom at the kitchen door. He knew the moment his eyes met hers that they were once again expecting a baby! Tom took his wife into his arms and hugged her close, kissed her lips, and smiled. She didn't even have to tell him the news.

"I go to the doctor in October, but they said to call if I needed to see them before then. Also, I didn't make anything for dinner! I'm too excited! Do you want to go out?" Dorothy's words all ran together with her excitement.

Tom laughed and hugged her again. "Sure, let's go to the diner."

Tom helped her into a sweater. He hadn't taken off his coat, so they walked right out the door. The diner was just a few blocks away and not very crowded.

They took a booth near the end of the aisle and ordered baked chicken with vegetables and rice. It was simple and delicious. They talked about when this baby might be due and wondered if it'd be a boy or a girl.

"Tom, I think . . . I think Mark would be happy if we had a baby. Don't you?" Dorothy suddenly asked.

Tom looked at his wife, her eyebrows knit with worry. "Yes, of course, he would be happy. Since he couldn't stay, he'd want us to have the chance to love another child. It's OK, honey." Tom patted her hand and smiled.

They enjoyed the rest of their meal and split a piece of chocolate cake for dessert.

Back at home, they got ready for bed and sat on the couch for a bit. They talked again about when the baby might be due and thought maybe in April. Tom was glad it would be after March.

The weekend was filled with yard work and getting ready for winter, and Dorothy did the grocery shopping for the upcoming week. They both were in lightened moods with their secret news, and they kept it between themselves.

Tom's work project finished, and he and his team were assigned another one. He went at it with gusto, engaging his team with new challenges.

Dorothy's students were getting excited about the holidays coming soon. She had them start planning what they all wanted to be for Halloween! The kids loved the fun holiday, and Dorothy was always amazed at the costumes the students came up with each year!

Time passed quickly, and soon, they were into October. The students had a four-day weekend coming, and Dorothy was starting to really feel her pregnancy. She was able to conceal her belly with loose fall sweaters, but she didn't know for how much longer.

The kids would be off Friday and Monday, so Dorothy planned to go shopping for some maternity clothes over the long weekend.

Wednesday night, she talked to Tom about where she planned to go. He wasn't able to get off work to go with her, but she was happy to go alone and enjoy herself.

The next day graced them with sunshine and warmth in the autumn sun. Dorothy looked at the leaves turning color and watched as the breeze blew them across the streets after she dropped Tom off at his office and headed to the neighboring town that had a maternity shop. She was glad the town was a ways from Midland, as she didn't want to announce her pregnancy yet.

Arriving in Freeland, she parked in the lot behind the Mother's Love shop and made her way around the front of the building to the door. Stepping inside, she was happy to see that there wasn't anyone there she knew. A clerk approached her and asked how she could be of service.

Dorothy explained that she was due in probably April and just wanted to get a couple of items just now. The clerk smiled and took her to an area offering fall tunics and slacks. Dorothy looked through the racks, feeling the fabrics, and chose a couple of patterns she felt wouldn't draw attention to her belly.

The clerk set her up in a dressing room, and Dorothy quickly tried on the outfits. As she turned this way and that in the mirror, she suddenly felt a sharp pain low in her belly. She gasped and immediately sat down in the chair in the corner of the dressing room.

The clerk knocked on the door and asked her if she was all right. Dorothy took some slow breaths and finally said she was fine, just excited about the clothes. But Dorothy was not fine. She felt her belly cramping and her skin warming quickly.

Waiting for the spasm to pass, Dorothy finally got her own clothes back on and left the dressing room. She explained to the clerk that she was late for an appointment she'd forgotten and left the store.

Spying a pay phone on the corner, she walked carefully to the booth. Lifting the receiver, she pushed a dime into the slot and dialed Dr. Brooks's number. She'd called there so many times, she knew the number by heart.

She told the receptionist what was going on, and the lady told her to come in right away. Dorothy explained that she was in Freeland but would head to the office right away.

Dorothy made her way back to the car and headed to Midland. She felt the cramping coming on again and had to pull over twice, as she could barely breathe.

She knew in her heart that she was losing this baby as well, and tears began streaming down her face. She wanted Tom, but he was at work, and she had the car anyway. By the time she parked the car at Dr. Brooks's office, she could feel wetness in her underwear. She knew without a doubt that the baby was lost.

Carefully she walked into the building and over to the desk. She told the receptionist what she felt, and the nurse standing there came to get her immediately and take her to a room.

The nurse helped Dorothy disrobe, and they were both upset to see blood in Dorothy's underwear. The nurse got Dorothy settled on the table and ran to get Dr. Brooks. He came in immediately to examine Dorothy. She could tell by the look on his face that what she knew was what was true. The baby was gone.

Dr. Brooks explained that her body was aborting the baby, but he couldn't know the reason why. He told her what to expect over the next few days and gave her a prescription for pain pills. He asked if she wanted to call Tom.

"No, no, that's OK. I have the car, and I'll have to pick him up from work anyway. I took the day to go shopping . . . shopping for maternity clothes," she choked out the words, gripping her belly, and unchecked tears rolled down her face.

Dr. Brooks handed her several tissues and patted her back. He knew no words would be helpful, so he just stayed with her and nodded at the nurse to help Dorothy to get dressed. Dr. Brooks said he'd be back with her prescription and that the nurse would help her clean up and dress.

The nurse said comforting words that Dorothy didn't hear. She was reliving what she'd already been through once. At least this time, there wasn't a fully formed baby they would have to bury. This was just like having a really bad period, she thought.

When Dr. Brooks came back in, he handed her the prescription and said he wanted to see her in a week to be sure she was all right. Dorothy nodded and took the slip of paper from him. The nurse made sure Dorothy was cleaned up and gave her several pads to use.

Dorothy slowly walked to the front desk and made her appointment for the following week. When she walked out, she saw a few women, pregnant as could be, and her heart wrenched as she wondered why she couldn't be one of them.

Dorothy went to the drug store and gave the prescription to the pharmacist. She then wandered about the store, placing random items in her basket. When they called her name, she took her basket to the counter and waited while the clerk rang up her medicine, toothpaste, and tissues.

Arriving back home, Dorothy cleaned herself up again. Dr. Brooks had told her to expect to keep bleeding for a few days like she would during her period.

Glancing at the clock, she saw that it was finally time to go pick up Tom from the office. She knew she would start sobbing the moment she saw him and took several hankies with her. She had spent the afternoon with her teeth gritting, angry and sad all at once.

Tom came out of the office door at 5:05 p.m., just as she expected him to. He smiled and waved at her when he saw her pull up to the door.

Climbing in, he said, "Hi there, Mama! How was shopping?" He was buckling his seat belt and hadn't seen the look on his wife's face yet.

Dorothy pulled over into a nearby parking spot and shifted into Park. Turning toward her, he was alarmed to see tears flowing down her cheeks! Immediately he knew what had happened, but he didn't want to ask her. She simply nodded at him, and he unbuckled his seat belt, slid over, and took his wife into his arms.

"Shh, shh, it's OK. It's OK," Tom said even though it was pretty far from OK.

Dorothy just sobbed and clung to her husband. Soon, she felt his shoulders begin to shake, and he was crying right along with her.

How could this be happening to them again? What had they done so wrong that they lost not one baby but two?

They stayed in the car, clinging to each other and crying for several minutes. No one was parked nearby, so they hadn't drawn any attention, and Tom was glad of that.

"Honey, let me drive home. Here, you scoot over, and I'll go around," Tom said.

Climbing out of the car, he reached back and held her hand as she carefully made her way to the passenger seat.

Tom practically ran to the other side of the car and got in. He held Dorothy's hand as he drove home as quickly as he could, safely.

Once home, Dorothy related to Tom about all that had happened. He listened as he rubbed her back and she held his hand. Many times she reached for tissues as fresh tears continued to fall over and over again. Tom used his hanky for his own tears, trying hard to be strong for his wife but crumbling inside.

After her story was done, Tom helped her to the bathroom to clean up again. She told him the doctor said this would go on for a couple of days but not to be alarmed. Neither was hungry, but Tom opened a can of soup, and they each forced down a few spoonfuls.

Tom helped Dorothy get to bed and settled. Then he told her he was going to call Mr. Kline and ask for the next day off. He didn't plan to tell his boss what had happened; it was simply too private.

Mr. Kline took Tom's explanation that he wasn't feeling well without question and told him he hoped he'd feel better by Monday. Tom carefully lay in bed next to Dorothy and made her promise to wake him if she needed him. The night passed with both of them restless, and neither slept very well.

Chapter Thirty Five

Dorothy awoke the next morning feeling like something was wrong, and then she remembered what had happened. The pain in her heart rivaled that of her body. She rolled over and touched Tom on the shoulder. He instantly awoke, and when he saw the tears in Dorothy's eyes, he, too, was vividly brought to the reality of losing yet another baby.

They lay in bed, just listening to the rain falling outside on the cold October day. Dorothy finally sighed and said she had better get to the bathroom to clean up. Tom helped her and made sure she was all right before going to the kitchen to brew some coffee. He looked out the window, watching as leaves fell, swirling about in the fall wind and rain. It felt like that inside his heart. Everything was dying, wet and cold.

Dorothy came into the kitchen, dressed in pajamas and a robe. She didn't have a reason to put on clothes, and she simply didn't care.

Tom poured them each a mug of coffee, and they sat down at the kitchen table. He laid his hand on hers and gently rubbed the back side of her palm. She looked at him with sorrow and took a sip of the steaming-hot coffee. It felt good on her throat.

"I'm glad we didn't tell anyone, Tom. We would have to go through it all again with everyone. So I'm glad we kept it to ourselves," she said in a monotone.

Tom nodded and agreed. He asked her how she was doing, and she explained that her body was still expelling what was left, but she felt all right. Just tired.

Tom said he was going to the store to get ingredients to make soup. His mother had taught him to make chicken noodle soup, and he always felt better when someone made it for him when he was sick. He knew it wasn't much to do to ease Dorothy's pain, but it was the best he could come up with. He, too, was facing the reality that a baby just might not be in their future—at least not in the usual way.

Dorothy nodded at Tom's offer to make soup. He'd made it for her before, and it was always very good. She didn't care much if she ate or not. She was consumed with thoughts that she was not meant to be a mother and that she had failed once again to bring a baby into the world. Her body just wasn't good enough. Or maybe she simply wasn't good enough. The guilt was eating her alive, and she felt the need to blame herself for two innocent lives lost.

Dorothy didn't know how to explain these feelings to Tom, so she just didn't say anything. She had no way of knowing that Tom was busy blaming himself and berating himself for getting her pregnant again. He felt that it must be his fault because, after all, both of Dorothy's sisters had had babies with no problems whatsoever.

Tom left for the store, and Dorothy poured herself a little more coffee and went to sit on the couch. She just stared out the window, watching the drizzling rain. She felt dark and empty inside and wondered about the future. All she and Tom had wanted for so long was to be parents, but it felt like it was not meant to be.

Dorothy rubbed her belly, empty once again of a baby. She wondered if Dr. Brooks would tell them not to ever try again. She was certain she didn't want to try again anyway. This was much too painful.

Tom got back from town and brought in a few bags of groceries. The rain had lessened to a light sprinkle, but the clouds were still dark, and the wind was picking up. They'd probably not seen the last of the storm for the day.

Dorothy asked Tom if she could help a little with the soup to keep herself occupied, if nothing else. He was reluctant to let her do anything, as he wanted her to rest, but seeing her need to keep busy, he had her dice carrots and mushrooms.

Soon the aroma of chicken and vegetables filled the air of the small kitchen. If Dorothy tried hard enough, she could almost believe they were just making a cozy meal to share on a dark and rainy Saturday.

Tom attempted to make his sister's rolls to have with the soup. It went a little better than he expected, save for them looking like uneven lumps instead of the uniform curved rolls his sister created every time she made them!

Dorothy was touched that he'd done so much work, rolling out the dough and kneading it to make the delicious rolls. She said she didn't care how they looked; they still tasted wonderful!

While the soup was simmering, the couple sat down on the couch and talked about their situation. Neither wanted to try to get pregnant again, but they both agreed that they wanted a baby. Adoption came up over and over during their chat.

Tom had a lot of questions, but he felt that maybe it was the right thing for them. Dorothy went to her desk in the corner of the living room and pulled out the envelope that Trudy Belvins had sent from the adoption agency. It had arrived just before they'd gone to Torch Lake. Dorothy had put it in her desk drawer, not wanting to really look at it in case it turned out that she would never need to. But now, she wanted to read about it and show Tom as well.

Their friends, the Steins, were very close to the arrival of their son. In fact, there was going to be a baby shower next Saturday for Rosemary. Dorothy was excited for her friend, even though she was going through another heartbreak of her own. She suddenly had so many questions for them, but for now, she and Tom would look over the information Trudy had sent.

Tom opened the packet and read out loud to Dorothy about how the program worked for adoption. They seemed to meet all the criteria requested by the agency. They looked at the forms that were to be filled out and talked about what they were really feeling.

Dorothy was concerned about getting a healthy baby. How would they know if it was healthy? Tom wondered if birth parents could get their babies back once they had been adopted by other people.

They spent a few hours writing down questions and talking about possibilities of things that could go right and things that could go wrong. Before they knew it, it was time to bake the rolls and fill their bowls with steaming hot soup.

Dorothy used the bathroom and was relieved to see that there was hardly any blood left at all. She was feeling better, as the doctor said she would, and she told Tom that when she came back into the kitchen.

He was glad to know that Dorothy was recovering rather quickly. He felt her forehead for fever but found nothing, and that made them both smile. Tom took the rolls out of the oven while Dorothy filled their soup bowls. It smelled wonderful, and they both were surprised to find that they were actually hungry.

They talked more about adoption as they ate and agreed that they should sleep on it and think about it for a while before making any calls. Dorothy would go to Rosemary's shower next week and talk to Mrs. Levy some more at school.

The rest of the weekend passed with Dorothy feeling a lot better by Monday morning. She had the rest of the day to get ready for school on Tuesday and felt she would be fine to go in the morning.

Chapter Thirty Six

Surprisingly, the week was passing quickly, and Dorothy was back at Dr. Brooks's office on Friday for her checkup. Dr. Brooks examined her and gave her a clean bill of health. He asked how she was feeling, and she said she was a little tired but assumed that was normal. He assured her that it was.

Dorothy told the doctor that she and Tom had decided not to try for any more babies but still wanted a family. She let him know they were interested in adoption, and he was quite pleased to hear this. He knew how much they wanted to be parents, and as a doctor, he had delivered many babies to women that weren't able to raise them and had given them up for adoption.

She told him she'd contacted Lutheran Social Services for information, and she knew two women who'd gotten babies from them and had been in contact with them both. Dr. Brooks felt that Dorothy and Tom were on the right track and encouraged her to continue investigating the possibility of adopting.

Dorothy filled Tom in on her appointment over dinner that evening. They went to the Elks' Club for the weekly Friday-night fish fry. The food was always good, and they always saw people they knew. It was nice to get out and see people, but they kept their conversation quiet.

The next day was Rosemary's baby shower. Dorothy had chosen a tiny outfit in navy blue for the baby boy they were expecting. She adored baby blue, but it brought too many memories of Mark along with it, so she opted for a tiny navy sailor suit with little white booties and a sailor cap with a red ribbon. She also had purchased a rattle, some nice baby bottles, and a stack of cloth diapers with pins. She wrapped it all in a large basket that Rosemary could surely use for something.

Dorothy had on a green dress that brought out the green flecks in her brown eyes. It was a nice shirt dress with a narrow belt at the waist. Observing herself in the mirror, she thought she looked like she always did, and no one would be the wiser that she'd just had a miscarriage. Even though her heart hurt, she knew that both her babies were in heaven and she was going to have a family in another way.

Tom had his Saturday chores and puttering around to do, so she took the car when it was time to go to the shower. Several ladies were there when Dorothy arrived, a gift in hand. Rosemary was so happy, and everyone was smiling. Dorothy felt a sudden burst of anxiety, placing her hand on her belly, and had to blink back threatening tears. She quickly recovered, reminding herself that this was Rosemary's day.

Larry, Rosemary's husband, had made himself scarce! Even though he was about to be a father, he didn't want to spend his afternoon with a bunch of women, oohing and ahhing over baby clothes!

Cake and refreshments were served as the ladies played a few baby shower games. There were blue balloons and ribbons strung about the room and music on the stereo.

Soon Rosemary began to open all the gifts, and Dorothy was given the task of recording what each gift was and who brought it! She was amazed to see the wonderful things Rosemary received and was happy to record them all for her friend.

After it was all done, guests took their leave. Dorothy stayed to help Rosemary straighten up and look at the gifts once again, double-checking her recording.

"Oh, Dottie! I'm so excited to get our baby soon! I think it'll be just another week or so, according to the adoption agency!" Rosemary exclaimed, fingering tiny outfits and toys strewn about her living room.

"You know, Rosemary, I was kind of wanting to ask you about that. You two are using Lutheran Social Services, right?"

"Yes! They are so good!" she replied, folding tiny sleepers and booties.

"Well, Tom and I are considering adopting, maybe. What can you tell me about your and Larry's decision to go that way?" Dorothy asked, checking off names that went with cards and gifts.

"Oh well, you know, we weren't able to have any babies on our own. We tried and tried, and once, I did get pregnant but lost it right away. Within a month, actually. We hadn't even told anyone. Then we decided we were going to adopt. We just can't wait. We're so excited," Rosemary told her.

Dorothy thought about it and then told Rosemary about her miscarriage and yet still wanting to have a baby. Rosemary consoled her friend and told her she understood. Then she gave Dorothy the name of someone at the agency and encouraged her to call about it.

Dorothy went home feeling much better and was glad she'd told Rosemary about their loss. She hadn't known Rosemary had also had a miscarriage, so they had each other to lean on. Now Dorothy was more excited than ever to explore adoption.

Tom had just finished raking leaves and burning them by the side of the street. The smoke wasn't unpleasant, and Dorothy suddenly found refreshment in the autumn feel even though so many things were dying for the winter.

"How was the shower?" Tom asked while washing his hands at the kitchen sink. He was glad to see Dorothy, her cheeks flushed, a smile on her face.

"It was really nice, Tom. Rosemary has lots of things for the baby! Then we talked about adoption. She shared with me that she had a miscarriage too! I told her about ours, and we both felt better for sharing. She gave me more information about adoption, and I think we should research some more. What do you think?"

"I think this might be the way we are meant to become parents," replied Tom, hugging his wife.

Dorothy told Tom more about what Rosemary told her as she put a meatloaf together for dinner. Tom helped by heating up a can of corn in a saucepan. He enjoyed cooking with his wife.

As heartbroken as he was over the loss of two babies, Tom was feeling better about the possibility of adoption by watching his wife heal right before his eyes. They enjoyed their meal in the living room while watching the evening news and then cleaned up the dishes after.

Sunday passed with church and gearing up for the upcoming week.

Chapter Thirty Seven

As the month drew to a close, Dorothy's students celebrated Halloween at the end of the school day, and she and Tom passed out candy that night on their front porch. They laughed at witches, goblins, and ghosts that came, holding out sacks to be filled with candy.

Dorothy had had several conversations with Mrs. Levy about adoption over the weeks and was more convinced that she and Tom should apply to the agency and see where it went.

Rosemary and Larry received their son just a few days before Thanksgiving, and Tom and Dorothy were among the first to be invited over to meet the tiny baby!

As Dorothy held the tiny baby in her arms, she thought of Mark and sent a loving blessing to heaven. Rosemary and Larry had chosen the name Christian for their little boy, and he looked like an angel! Fair-haired and light-eyed, he was soft and smelled good!

Tom carefully held the baby and felt the lump rise in his throat as it did when he thought of Mark and the other baby they had lost. But the joy of holding this newborn eclipsed the sadness, and he, too, thought adoption would be their way to become parents.

November came to an end with a vengeance of early snow and cold winds! Tom and Dorothy finished filling out the forms and sent them to the agency. Dorothy called after a few days to make sure that they had been received.

Trudy Belvins was happy that they had decided to apply to adopt. There were many babies just waiting for homes, and she was sure that Tom and Dorothy Cornell would be approved as potential parents.

Tom and Dorothy spent many hours talking about adoption and wondering when they'd hear from Lutheran Social Services. They met with Father Morgan for counseling, and he was helpful and positive, encouraging them to follow where God was leading them.

They even went to the Levy's house and met their son, who was nearing the toddler stage and very active. Both Mr. and Mrs. Levy said they felt they were John's parents in every way. They said that the adoption records were forever sealed and that the birth parents could never lay claim to their baby. That made Tom and Dorothy feel better, as that was a concern. What if the birth parents decided they wanted their baby back?

The adoption agency also assured them that once an adoption was finalized in a court of law, the birth parents had no rights at all to the child, and the child would become the legal offspring of the adoptive parents.

As Christmas neared and they bought a tree for the living room, Dorothy thought maybe this would be the last Christmas with just the two of them. Tom agreed as he placed an angel on top of the tree.

Dorothy placed the gifts she had bought for Tom under the tree the next day while he was at work. She had found him a few new ties for work that would go nicely with his suits and brown eyes and a nice new fedora for winter. He looked dashing in hats, she thought. She also had found a toolbox that would hold all the screwdrivers, pliers, nails, and screws in separate compartments she thought he'd enjoy.

Tom grinned when he saw the gifts under the tree that evening, and after Dorothy went to bed, he slipped her gifts under the tree by his. He'd gotten her a new perfume she had admired when they were out one day, a set of knitting needles and new yarns, and a necklace with a small garnet on it, her birthstone.

The next morning was Christmas Eve Day, and Tom and Dorothy were going to see his parents for the day and go to church for the early service. They could be back home by 10:00 p.m., so they had decided to go there instead of having his parents drive all the way to Midland.

As they made the two-hour drive to the farm in Charlotte, Tom and Dorothy talked about how they would tell his parents and sister that they were going to adopt a baby. Tom wasn't sure how his folks would feel about it, as they had never known anyone who had adopted before.

The atmosphere was cozy and jovial when Tom and Dorothy arrived at the farm. Joan and Gale were there already. Gale was helping Tom's dad with lights on the tree and putting a star on top. Joan was just taking her famous rolls out of the oven! They looked a lot better than the ones Tom had made, but they smelled just the same and his mouth watered as he thought about how good they would taste.

Tom kissed his mom on the cheek and gave her a quick hug before heading to the living room to help with the tree. Dorothy stayed in the kitchen and helped set the table. She'd brought an apple pie she'd baked and set it on the stovetop to warm from underneath. The family soon settled down to eat their midday Christmas meal of ham, rolls, green beans, corn casserole, mashed potatoes, and apple pie. There would be leftovers for days!

Tom broached the subject of adoption once everyone had their plates full. He and Dorothy had discussed telling his folks about the miscarriage and agreed that if they knew, they might be a bit more receptive to the possibility of their son and his wife adopting a child from someone else. They were quite conservative people, and adoption seemed foreign to them.

They took their time explaining the process, and by the end of the meal, they thought perhaps Tom's parents understood a little bit about what they were planning to do.

Bundling up, they headed to the country church a few miles away. Tom and Dorothy took their own car, as they would be heading home after the service. The sermon was focused on the birth of Christ, of course, but also focused on loving one another and helping when you can. Tom and Dorothy took this to mean that they were to help out birth parents that could not care for their baby. They felt good after the service, and there were hugs and Christmas wishes all around.

Light snow fell during their ride home, and Tom took time to drive through Midland so they could see Christmas lights glowing from homes up and down the streets. Their own tree lights were twinkling as they pulled into the driveway.

They were tired out from the long day and just spent some time chatting on the couch before bed. Christmas Day met them with sunshine, but there was an inch of fresh snow on the ground from the night before.

They enjoyed coffee and cinnamon rolls as they opened the gifts they'd gotten for each other. They talked about the strong possibility that this would be their last Christmas as a couple and that hopefully next year, there'd be a little one to tear open presents from Santa!

The week passed with visits from friends and neighbors. School was out for the holiday break, and it was quiet at Tom's office. Dorothy was anxious to hear from the adoption agency, but she would patiently wait until after New Year's to call and ask.

Chapter Thirty Eight

January 1963 rolled in with sunshine and a mild temperature! Dorothy took this as a good sign for the year! Her birthday was the next day, January 2. She would be thirty-two years old. Tom would be thirty-eight in May. She prayed they would become parents this year, and she planned to call Lutheran Social Services the next day. She still had the rest of the week off from school, so she had plenty of time to make the call she had been anticipating for a long time.

Tom was getting back into the swing of things at his office. Two new projects awaited him and his team. He was looking forward to Dorothy's birthday tomorrow. He planned to take her to dinner at a fancy restaurant called Justine's. He'd heard it was very good French food! It was a new restaurant, and he'd made reservations days ago.

Wednesday arrived, and Tom wished Dorothy a happy birthday as soon as they woke up that morning. Dorothy smiled and kissed him. Tom told her to put on her best dress and be ready to go to a surprise dinner that night! Dorothy was excited and hoped that he was taking her to Justine's! She'd heard about it at school, and people said it was very good and the atmosphere was elegant!

Searching her closet, she selected a dress of silver gray that came to her knees and had a boat neckline with three-quarter sleeves. There was a wide belt with a shiny silver buckle. She got out her new black pumps and matching evening bag to wear with it. For her jewelry, she chose a strand of pearls her mother had given her with matching earrings. To complete her look, she pinned her grandmother's cameo pin on the side of the neckline. She laid out all the items on the bed and then got ready to call the adoption agency. She hoped she'd have good news to share with Tom tonight to make their dinner even more special.

Settling at the kitchen table with the phone and a fresh mug of coffee, Dorothy made the call to Lutheran Social Services. Trudy Belvins answered and was glad to hear from Dorothy.

Trudy let her know that their application was being processed and that a social worker would be contacting them soon. The social worker would come to their house to meet with them face-to-face and get to know them. She also said there would be competency tests to be sure that Tom and Dorothy knew basic information, such as reading, current events, simple math, and social skills! Trudy explained that the social worker would also inspect their home to ensure that it was suitable for an infant, and then, at another time, there would be a surprise visit to be sure that the prospective parents were serious about adopting.

Dorothy took notes as Trudy spoke and became more and more excited about the thought that they might soon become parents! She asked Trudy how long it all might take. Trudy said that depended on how the visits went and the availability of babies.

Dorothy hung up, feeling positive and excited. She read her notes and thought about their home. Maybe she and Tom should redecorate the nursery again so the social worker would see how serious they were.

Dorothy got up and went down the hall to the nursery. Pushing open the door, she flicked on the light switch. She hadn't been in here in a while, and the air felt stale. Walking to the window, she opened it a few inches and felt the cold January air push its way in, fluttering the curtain.

She walked over to the closet and slid the door open. There were still tiny hangers there from when they were preparing the room for Mark. She touched one and silently sent a prayer to heaven, asking for the blessing of a baby to come soon. Closing the window, she left the room, leaving the door ajar as usual.

Later that morning, both of her sisters called and wished her a happy birthday. It was fun to catch up with them and hear about what they were all up to.

Then her mom and dad called, and she had a nice talk with them. She told them Tom was taking her out for a nice dinner, and they were excited for her.

After a light lunch, Dorothy wrapped a blanket around her shoulders and went out to get the mail. The air was cold, but the sun was shining, so it wasn't too bad!

There were cards from her sisters, parents, and in-laws in the mail. She opened each one and placed them on the counter. She felt very loved by her and Tom's family and hoped that soon, their love would extend to a new baby in their home!

Dorothy took her time getting ready for her dinner date with Tom and styled her hair a little differently. She felt pretty and was so excited to celebrate and share all she had learned with Tom from the adoption agency.

Tom arrived at 5:30 p.m. with a bouquet of red roses in hand and told her how beautiful she looked. Selecting a cut crystal vase from her china cabinet, Dorothy snipped the ends of the roses and arranged them in the sparkling vase! Their heady scent filled the kitchen as she placed the vase on the table.

Tom helped her with her coat, and they left to go to dinner. Dorothy was thrilled when Tom pulled into the lot at Justine's. Helping her out of the car, Tom tucked her hand under his elbow, and they walked quickly to the restaurant door.

A hostess opened the door, ushering them into the softly lit restaurant. They could hear music playing and took in a room full of small tables with little lamps in the center, glowing with a warm light. The hostess led them to a table off to the side and held their chairs out as they sat down. Dorothy was thoroughly impressed and said so as Tom smiled and wished her a happy birthday.

Momentarily, a waiter arrived with large menus that had gold tassels hanging on the bottom. He asked if they'd like a cocktail, and Tom ordered champagne to celebrate Dorothy's birthday. The waiter nodded and went off to fetch a bottle, ice bucket, and glasses.

Tom and Dorothy started looking over the menu, and when the waiter returned, he recited the specials as he popped the cork on the champagne and filled their glasses.

Tom ordered some escargot as an appetizer, and they said they'd take a few more minutes to decide on their meals.

"Ooh, escargot? That sounds interesting!" said Dorothy.

"You know that's actually snails, don't you, honey?" Tom said with a laugh.

"Yes, I know, and I like them! But if I call them 'escargot,' it doesn't sound so icky!" Dorothy said, laughing back.

They touched glasses, and Tom wished her a happy birthday again. The champagne tickled Dorothy's nose, and she smiled as she sipped the sweet, bubbly drink.

Tom looked at the menu again and decided he would try the chicken Provençal with olives and tomatoes. Dorothy selected the French cassoulet, which sounded like a casserole filled with sausage, chicken, and beans. They agreed to share their entrées as they enjoyed a crisp salad and a baguette of warm bread with warm butter.

The waiter refilled their champagne glasses when their main courses arrived, and they dug in with gusto, splitting their meals in half to share with each other!

As they ate, Dorothy filled Tom in on her conversation with Trudy Belvins. He became as excited as she was. They were really going to adopt a baby! Tom wasn't worried about them passing inspection. In fact, he was excited to redecorate the nursery. Dorothy asked him what he thought about it, and he said he'd bring the dressers up from the basement over the weekend. Dorothy would mop the floor in the room and help with the crib too.

Conversation about what would happen as the weeks unfolded dominated the conversation all through dinner. When the waiter came to inquire about dessert, they were both pretty full, but as it was Dorothy's birthday, they ordered cheesecake and coffee anyway.

The waiter brought back a large slice of chocolate cheesecake with a birthday candle flickering on top of it and two dessert forks. He wished Dorothy a very happy birthday and left them to enjoy their dessert after pouring them each a coffee.

Dorothy made her wish, and Tom was pretty sure he knew what it was. She blew out the candle, and they took turns eating the cheesecake until it was gone!

After they finished their coffee, Tom paid the bill and helped Dorothy with her coat. Dorothy stayed in the lobby while Tom went for the car, as the January evening had turned into a pretty cold night.

Back at home, the scent of the red roses still encased the kitchen, and Dorothy took a deep breath, enjoying it. Tom hung up their coats and then asked Dorothy to come into the living room. He turned on the stereo and put on their favorite song, "At Last" by Etta James. Tom took Dorothy in his arms, and they slowly danced in the living room, eyes closed, thinking about roses, babies, and family.

Chapter Thirty Nine

Both Tom and Dorothy were anxious to hear from the adoption agency, and as January continued, they redecorated the nursery. They brought the dressers and crib back up from the basement and rearranged the room a little differently than it had been set up for Mark. They couldn't erase him from their lives and, of course, didn't want to.

This time, they put the crib under the window instead of the wall opposite the closet. Tom moved the rocker next to one dresser and put the other where the rocker had been. He got out the pink and blue paints and gave each dresser a fresh coat.

Dorothy hung some child-themed photos on two walls, leaving a long wall blank for pictures of their new family that would happen soon.

About a week and a half into January, a letter arrived in the mail, stating that a Mr. Will Seeba would be coming to meet with them and look at their home. He listed the day and time for Friday, January 18, at 10:00 a.m. Dorothy couldn't wait to tell Tom that Mr. Seeba would be there in just two days.

Tom asked for the day off, and Mr. Kline was happy to oblige when Tom told him the reason. Mr. Kline was glad to know that Tom and Dorothy were trying to adopt a baby.

Dorothy arranged for a substitute teacher for the day and wrote out the lesson plan for her. Then she spent Thursday evening cleaning the house to make sure everything was in tiptop shape.

Tom made sure the sidewalk and driveway were clear of snow and ice. January was tricky that way! Sun would melt the snow, but then the night cold would freeze it into a layer of ice on the concrete.

Friday morning, Dorothy had coffee brewed and a coffee cake warming in the oven. They were both very nervous but so excited to meet the social worker.

Promptly at 10:00 a.m., a green sedan pulled into their driveway, and a gentleman wearing a heavy gray topcoat and matching fedora stepped out of the car, carrying a folder. Tom opened the kitchen door and invited Mr. Seeba into the kitchen. Dorothy took the man's hat and coat as introductions were made.

"Please, please, sit down. I have coffee and coffee cake if you'd like," said Dorothy with a nervous smile.

"Well, thank you, ma'am. That does sound good! It's a cold one out there, and I didn't spare time for breakfast! It's a little bit of a drive for me to get here!" said Mr. Seeba, opening his folder of papers.

Tom poured coffee while Dorothy served up the warm cinnamon coffee cake slathered in white icing. It smelled divine, and she hoped Mr. Seeba would approve of it and them!

"OK, Mr. and Mrs. Cornell, this is all the paperwork that I have to go through with you regarding adoption from the standpoint of the social worker and, therefore, the court. First, I will inspect your home and then go over any issues I may find. Then I'll be speaking to you both about any knowledge you have of babies and children. I'll also be quizzing you both separately to see how you each answer questions about common knowledge and things in general. I can already tell how eager you are to become parents. You have a lovely home, and I'm looking forward to your showing me all around. But first, I'd like to hear a little bit about both of you. Mr. Cornell, why don't you start?" Mr. Seeba then added creamer to his coffee and bit into the coffee cake, waiting for Tom to tell his story.

Clearing his throat, Tom looked at Dorothy, then at Mr. Seeba. "Well, I'm from Charlotte. I grew up on a farm. I have a sister. I didn't want to be a farmer, so I went to stenography school in Chicago. Then, well, I went into the Navy and traveled all over during World War II, then the Korean conflict as well. Dot and I have been married ten years. We had a stillborn, then a miscarriage.

We very much wish to be parents, and we decided adoption would be the right thing for us to do." Then he smiled at Mr. Seeba, hoping he'd said the right things. He didn't want to talk too much but also didn't want to be vague. He was nervous and had talked fast.

Mr. Seeba made notes on the forms and then turned to Dorothy. "That was informative, Mr. Cornell. So now, Mrs. Cornell, what about you?" he asked with raised eyebrows.

"First of all, please call us Tom and Dorothy. You don't need to be so formal," Dorothy said to ease her tense mood. She took a deep breath and continued.

"I'm from Grand Rapids. I have two older sisters, both of whom are married. One has three children, and the other has four. My dad is a professional, and my mother has always stayed at home. I've been a teacher since graduating from Michigan State, and I just love kids. I've always wanted to be a mother. Tom and I both want very much to be parents. As he said, I had a stillborn and then a miscarriage. My doctor advised us to not try again to have a baby naturally. I know some families who've adopted, and we've spoken to them and visited. We sure would like this to work out for us, Mr. Seeba." Dorothy quickly sipped her coffee, clearing her throat, hoping she'd done well. She watched as Mr. Seeba took notes.

"Tell me again, Mr. . . . I mean, Tom, what is it you do for work now? I don't believe you mentioned it before."

Tom realized he hadn't told Mr. Seeba his job and hoped it wouldn't be held against him! "Oh, I'm sorry! I work at Dow Chemical in the patent department. I have a team of people I supervise, and we help with approving patents from around the world."

"Oh, that does sound interesting. I must say, as prospective parents, you're doing quite well with this background and discovery check, both educated with steady, long-term employment. Your being a veteran, Tom, helps as well. Whenever you're ready, I'd like to tour your home now," said Mr. Seeba, finishing his coffee.

"Of course!" said Dorothy, standing quickly. Her eyes darted around, looking for anything out of place, although she knew she'd done her usual thorough job of cleaning. Her sisters had often teased her for being so neat and organized all the time. But Dorothy couldn't stand to have things out of place or messy!

Dorothy led the way into the living room, and Mr. Seeba had a checklist with him. He looked at the furniture and inspected it to be sure it was sturdy. Then Tom walked down the hallway to the nursery. He pushed the door open and ushered Mr. Seeba and Dorothy inside.

Both Tom and Dorothy watched closely as Mr. Seeba looked at the nursery. He opened the drawers of the dressers and looked in the closet. Then he inspected the crib to be sure it was well constructed and had safety locks in place.

"I think this is a fine nursery, although I would see about bolting the dressers to the wall. Small children, at some point, will pull out those drawers and climb up them to get on top of the dresser!"

Dorothy's hand flew to her mouth! She'd never considered that a child would do that, but it did make sense.

Tom led the way to the other bedroom, their bedroom and the bathroom. Mr. Seeba made short notes as he inspected the bathroom, making sure the tub functioned and that they had a rubber mat inside of it.

Back in the living room, Mr. Seeba spoke to them about the rather sharp-edged coffee table, reminding them once again that babies become toddlers and toddlers like to run, play, jump, and climb! Tom assured Mr. Seeba that they would replace the coffee table right away that weekend.

Back in the kitchen, Mr. Seeba finished writing his notes and then said he would conduct the test portion of his paperwork. Dorothy said she would go to the basement and start on some laundry so that she wouldn't be able to hear what was going on.

Mr. Seeba thanked her, and Tom sat down at the table, wiping his hands nervously on his slacks.

"OK, Tom. Don't be nervous. Really, this is just a basic set of questions that I'm sure you'll answer just fine!"

Tom nodded and placed his hands on the table, ready for the first question.

"OK, here we go. Can you tell me who the president is?" said Mr. Seeba.

"Sure, that's John F. Kennedy!" Tom replied, thinking that this was an easy test.

"OK, can you tell me what six times three is?"

"Eighteen!" said Tom, tapping his hand on the table.

"Very good! Can you tell me what color you get if you mix green and yellow together?"

Tom thought for a few minutes on that one. Then he said, "I think a lighter green?" He was unsure, then got very nervous. He knew kids liked to paint. What if he failed this question?

"That's pretty true, Tom! It can be a lighter shade of green or yellow, depending on how much green you mix in! You see, these questions are just basic and simple! We want to be sure that you have common sense and are responsible adults, that's all! OK, the next question is, what makes your relationship strong with Dorothy?"

Tom smiled as he thought about all the reasons he had a good marriage. Then he took a deep breath and said, "Dottie is my best friend! We've always had a lot in common and enjoy many of the same activities. We like to spend time with both of our families. We like to be outdoors, fishing, gardening, and taking walks. We both like our careers and support each other if we want to take on something new. And most of all, we not only like each other—we love each other. We want to share that with a child and make a family." Tom felt good about his answer, as that's how he felt.

"OK, Tom, that's real good!" said Mr. Seeba with a smile. "Would you like to go get Dorothy now, and I'll ask her some questions too."

"Sure thing. Thank you, Mr. Seeba."

Tom stood and went to the basement steps. He made his way halfway down and called out to Dorothy. He didn't want to go all the way down and cause Mr. Seeba to think he was telling Dorothy about the test.

Dorothy came to the stairs with a laundry basket in her arms. Tom took it from her, and she followed him up the stairs into the kitchen.

"Mr. Seeba, would you like some more coffee?" she said, holding onto the back of the kitchen chair.

"Certainly, that would be nice. Your coffee cake is delicious too!" he replied with a smile.

Dorothy poured him another mug of coffee and sliced a piece of cake. Tom said he'd go out to the garage and take care of a few things that needed attention to give them some privacy. Dorothy settled in the chair and looked at Mr. Seeba, so anxious to get the test done.

"OK, Dorothy, as you could tell, Tom was done with the questions rather quickly, and I'm sure you will be as well! I'm just going to ask you a few things, and you tell me what you think!"

"OK. I can do that," said Dorothy, folding her hands in front of her.

"My first question is, what is the capital of Michigan?"

"Oh, that's easy! Lansing!" said Dorothy, immediately relaxing.

"Yes, that's right! OK, next, tell me the correct pronunciation of this sentence. Would you say, 'I seen them people,' or would you say, 'I saw those people'?"

Dorothy laughed. "Of course, 'I saw those people.' I'm a teacher, and English is my specialty!"

"I knew that'd be an easy one for you! OK, tell me some of the reasons you'd like to be a mother."

Dorothy smiled and thought for a moment or two. "I've always had a special place in my heart for children. I was always the 'mother hen' with my friends growing up. I like to share knowledge with children, which is why I became a teacher. There's so much to learn in life. I love seeing delight in the kids' eyes when they learn something new or experience things they've never done before. I love Tom so much, and we've wanted a family for so long."

Stopping for a minute, she bowed her head and swallowed. "When I lost our son, I didn't know if I would be able to have another baby. The doctor told us it was something that just happened. It wasn't anyone's fault. But then I had a miscarriage, and I think we are meant to adopt. I truly do."

"OK, Dorothy, thank you for sharing that with me. I've read your application and am aware of the complications you had with your pregnancies. I know it wasn't any fault of yours or Tom's. But I appreciate you telling me about it. If you want to go and get Tom, I'm about done here."

Dorothy nodded and stood up. She grabbed her sweater and went out to the garage to get Tom. He was sorting nails into little containers.

"Hey, Mr. Seeba is done. He's asked that you come back in."

"Great! How'd it go?" asked Tom.

"Really well, I think. You?" she replied.

"Good, I think! OK, come on!" Tom held the doors, and they were back in the kitchen quickly.

Mr. Seeba was organizing his papers and smiling. Tom and Dorothy took seats at the table and looked at Mr. Seeba.

"Well, folks, I think you've both done fine on the questions, and with a few adjustments, your home is well suited for a baby. My next step is to turn in the paperwork with my report, and then the directors will make a decision. Then sometime after that, there will be an unannounced visit, just to see what it's like when you aren't expecting company."

"How, how long does that take?" Dorothy asked, her forehead creased with anxiety.

"Oh, not too long. Another week or so. Today's Friday, so no reports will go in until Monday. Then they have to review it and have a meeting. So probably the week after next. I know that seems like a long time, but I promise it will go faster than you think. I can tell you that I have no concerns, and my report will be all positive." Mr. Seeba stood and shook both their hands. He gathered his papers, and Tom walked him to the door.

After he left, he hugged Dorothy tightly. "I think we might get to be parents!"

"Oh, Tom! I just don't want to get too excited, but I'm so very excited!" said Dorothy, hugging him back.

Over dinner, they compared stories about their quizzes, and they were pretty sure they both did the best they could and were happy with their answers.

The very next day, they went to the local furniture store, Waltz, and bought an oval-shaped coffee table. They took the rectangle one out to the garage. Tom would find a use for it out there. Then he took his drill and bolted the dressers to the walls in the nursery. He didn't want anything to go wrong with their application or for the baby!

Chapter Forty

Dorothy was quieter than usual at school. It was hard not to share her news with her coworkers, some of whom were very dear to her. But she didn't want to announce the adoption any time before she had her baby in her arms and official papers from court!

Tom spoke to his boss, Mr. Kline, about it, simply because he felt like it! He was excited, and he knew his boss wanted the best for him and Dorothy. Mr. Kline assured him he could take time off once the baby came.

Dorothy excitedly awaited for the unannounced visit to happen. Mr. Seeba had noted that they wouldn't be home until late afternoon each weekday, so every time a car came down the street after Tom arrived home, Dorothy would look out the window to see if it was pulling into their driveway.

After nearly two weeks of waiting, she wasn't quite as excited as she was anxious. What could be taking so long? Did the superiors not like Mr. Seeba's report? Did they fail at something? Were there no babies to be adopted? She couldn't think of much else, stressing about the visit they were waiting for.

Tom did his best to concentrate on his work but often found himself recalling some of the questions Mr. Seeba had asked him. He started to second-guess his answers and wondered if Mr. Seeba was only telling them they did well so that he wouldn't have to be the one to tell them they were being turned down as adoptive parents.

Into the third week, which was also into February, the front doorbell rang one evening as Tom and Dorothy were eating lamb chops in the kitchen. Looking at each other, they knew exactly who was at their door.

Tom quickly got up and, wiping his hands on his napkin, headed to the front door. Dorothy was a step behind him.

Opening the door, Tom said hello to a younger-looking woman with golden-blonde hair and bright-blue eyes. She smiled and introduced herself as Amanda Brynley from Lutheran Social Services.

"Please, please come in, Miss Brynley," said Tom.

"We were just eating dinner. Would you care to join us? I have plenty," offered Dorothy.

"Oh, I didn't mean to interrupt your dinner. It's hard to plan unannounced visits when the clients work all day. I was hoping to be earlier or later than you ate! I surely don't want to take you away from your meal," she said.

"Oh really, it's no trouble!" said Dorothy, touching Miss Brynley's arm and leading her toward the kitchen.

Miss Brynley could smell wonderful food, and she was hungry. She thought for a moment and then said, "I do have some paperwork to go over with you. So, I suppose I could have a bite, and we could go over it." She looked back and forth at Tom and Dorothy. It would be interesting to see how they'd handle something unexpected because once you have a baby in the mix, unexpected things happen all the time, including drop-in visitors.

"Absolutely! Please have a seat right here," said Dorothy.

Tom quickly got out a plate and filled it with a couple of lamb chops, mashed potatoes, and peas. Dorothy poured her a glass of ice tea and offered her sugar and lemon. Miss Brynley said it was fine just as it was and thanked them for their generosity.

"This is just lovely, Mr. and Mrs. Cornell, and I appreciate your hospitality!" said Miss Brynley.

"Oh, you are most welcome. Please, call us Tom and Dot. We aren't formal here!" said Dorothy. She was so nervous, she lost her appetite, but she didn't want to just sit there, not eating, so she ate small bites and drank a lot of tea.

"OK, Mr. Seeba turned in his reports and the managers and other staff met and went over everything. There was an issue of bolting dressers to the walls. Has that been done?" Miss Brynley looked back and forth between both Tom and Dorothy.

"Oh yes! I took care of that the day after Mr. Seeba was here. We'll be happy to show you after dinner," said Tom with excitement in his voice.

"Wonderful! The only other thing was the coffee table in the living room."

"We replaced that the next day as well. We now have an oval one," said Dorothy.

"That's great! There were no other issues in the report, and you've been cleared and approved to adopt! So now, we simply have to wait until a baby becomes available," said Miss Brynley, enjoying the delicious lamb chops and side dishes. It wasn't often that prospective parents fed her a meal, but now and then, it happened. She enjoyed almost all of the clients she met, with the exception of a few that just didn't seem to be parent material.

"Do all the babies come from the same hospital?" asked Dorothy.

"Well, not always. It depends on the circumstances of each client. Most come from one in particular in the Detroit area," shared Miss Brynley.

"We wondered if birth parents ever try to get their babies back once they are adopted, or if they are able to find them somehow. I can't imagine being given a child and then losing it again to the birth parents," said Tom, his eyebrows raised with anxiety.

"I get these questions frequently, Mr. . . . er, Tom. Please don't worry about a birth mother or father ever coming to get the baby back. They must sign off all parental rights, and the court records it, and the baby legally becomes yours. They also are never told who adopted their baby or where the baby is going to be living. So you have nothing to fear, truly," said Miss Brynley with a smile.

"Dorothy, these lamb chops are amazing! I don't know when I've had such a wonderful home-cooked meal! Thank you so much again for including me!" said Miss Brynley to lighten the mood and get their minds off the worst that could happen. In all the years that Miss Brynley had been a social worker, not once had any birth parents ever tried to get their baby back.

"Well, thank you for the compliments, Miss Brynley! We both enjoy cooking and take turns. Tonight was my turn, and I hadn't made lamb chops in a very long time. We're happy to share!" Dorothy replied. She was quite anxious to show Miss Brynley their improvements so that her paperwork could get turned in and the wait for a baby would be even less!

Tom helped Dorothy clear the table when they had finished eating and then toured the house with Miss Brynley. She took notes, just as Mr. Seeba did, and Tom and Dorothy exchanged nervous glances. Noticing this, Miss Brynley assured them that she was just doing the checklist and everything was in order.

Miss Brynley hoped a baby would come to these folks real soon. They were excellent candidates to adopt a baby, and she'd be turning her paperwork in first thing in the morning.

"Well, thank you once again for dinner and the tour. Your house is in perfect order, and now it's just a waiting game!" said Miss Brynley, her hand on the front doorknob.

"You are most welcome. Thank you for coming and for answering all our questions," said Dorothy.

Once Miss Brynley left, Tom and Dorothy hugged, feeling quite positive that soon they would have a baby to call their very own.

"Tom, do you think we'll get a boy or a girl?" asked Dorothy once they'd gotten ready for bed and settled on the couch to watch a little TV.

"Well, I don't know. On the one hand, it'd be nice to have a little boy. Not that I'd be trying to replace Mark in any way. He'll always be the first. Then again, a little girl would be wonderful too! I don't know. I know we said either would be fine when we applied. I guess we will see!" said Tom, squeezing Dorothy's hand.

Dorothy nodded in agreement. She really didn't know if she wanted a boy or a girl. Replacing Mark was not at all what either of them wanted; they simply wanted a family.

They both slept soundly that night, feeling confident that a baby would one day soon be theirs.

Chapter Forty One

February proved to be a strong winter month! Bitter cold temperatures and lots of snow allowed for a few snow days called at school. Dorothy was happy to have a few days off and spent a lot of time talking to her family about the upcoming adoption.

She and Tom also visited Rosemary and Larry to see baby Christian. He was growing so quickly, and Rosemary and Larry were thrilled to be parents. They only had good things to report about being a mom and dad so far. They also assured Tom and Dorothy that the Lutheran agency was very professional, and they had no worries at all that the birth parents might come looking for the baby.

Tom and Dorothy were becoming more anxious as the days continued to roll by, and they hadn't heard a word from anyone at the adoption agency.

Valentine's Day came and went, with Tom bringing Dorothy red roses and taking her out for a lovely dinner at the Hickory House. It was a family-owned steakhouse that had top-of-the-line steaks and fresh seafood. They saw several couples there they knew, and it was a romantic evening.

Soon, March was looming on the calendar, and Dorothy looked at the number 15 on the page. She touched the numbers and thought of her baby Mark. Gone now for two years. They'd go to the cemetery as soon as the ground thawed and plant something special there for him. Her heart missed him every single day. She often wondered what he would be like now. Would his eyes be light or dark? Would he be playing with all kinds of toys? Would he like broccoli? She had so many questions she'd never have the answers to, and it made her sad. But she tried to concentrate on the baby that would come and make their family grow.

Tom, too, was getting more anxious as the weeks passed, wondering when they'd hear about an infant that was to be theirs. Work was going well, and he spent time in the garage tinkering with projects and then getting things ready to clean up the yard and gardens once spring arrived.

The couple talked about the future over nightly meals and on walks through the neighborhood on the weekends if the weather allowed.

March came in like a lion, so they were cooped up in the house for a week or so. The date on the calendar finally reached March 15, and they made their now-annual drive to the cemetery when Tom got home from work that Friday evening. They didn't like to come at other times; it wasn't comforting to see their baby's name on a headstone, surrounded by so many other lost babies and young children.

Tom had brought a hosta plant. It would leaf out and sometimes bloom all season long. Dorothy cleaned off Mark's headstone with a loving hand, talking quietly, telling Mark all that was going on. She certainly spoke to him whenever she felt the urge, but it seemed very appropriate here. Tom joined in, telling his son how much he loved him and was glad he was at peace.

After the hosta was in the ground, Tom watered it, and they packed up the gardening tools. Touching the headstone, Dorothy told her baby he'd always be her first one and she would always love him.

Tom held the door for her as she climbed into the car. With one glance over his shoulder, Tom pulled away from Baby Land, and they made the short drive home.

It was starting to get dark as Tom pulled into the driveway and parked the car. He and Dorothy were quiet, lost in their thoughts about Mark and what might be coming their way sometime soon.

Neither was very hungry, so they just had sandwiches and milk for dinner. The weekend plans were to go see Dorothy's folks for the day tomorrow for an early Easter celebration. It was the only time Dorothy's sisters and their families could all come together.

They were looking forward to seeing everyone, and Dorothy had made a coconut cream pie to take along for the celebration. They'd be back Saturday evening and go to church for Easter service the next morning.

Saturday was sunny and warm, and their drive to Grand Rapids was pleasant. Dorothy glanced at her pie on the floor of the back seat from time to time to be sure it hadn't slid under her seat.

Arriving at her parents' house, she was elated to see both her sisters' cars there and knew everyone would be out on the back screened-in porch.

Tom carried in the pie and set it on the counter with multiple other containers of food. The kitchen smelled wonderful, and they could hear laughter coming from the porch.

Every time Dorothy saw her nieces and nephews, she was always amazed at how much they had grown and changed. Hugs were given all around, and she settled in to hear all their latest stories.

Tom spent time talking to his father-in-law about work and the weather and catching up on sports with his sister-in-law's spouses.

Finally, it was time to eat, and they all gathered in the large dining room off the kitchen. Dorothy's parents had a beautiful mahogany dining room table that had several leaves they'd put in to make room for their large family.

Everyone helped get the food on the table, and Emory said an Easter prayer. Mountains of food were passed around, and plates filled quickly.

The meal passed with stories and laughter and a promise of Easter baskets for the younger kids when they were done eating! Dorothy was happy to help her nieces Shelley and Christy search for their baskets. The other kids had outgrown the Easter tradition and were content to play games out on the porch while the adults chatted in the living room.

Dorothy was glad to spend time with her sisters and families, hoping for the day they'd have a little one to come join in the traditions. The girls found their baskets and spent the rest of the afternoon reveling in chocolate eggs and sharing one or two with their siblings.

Tom and Dorothy said their goodbyes and left for the two-hour drive home around 5:00 p.m. Her mother had packed them several dishes of leftovers to take home. Dorothy was glad she wouldn't have to cook the next day!

Easter Sunday dawned with a pink-stained sky and a light breeze. Lots of families showed up at church, and the service was full of meaning and lessons. Once home, they changed into casual clothes and took a long walk around the neighborhood. Several homes had extra cars in their driveways, with families spending the holiday together.

Tom called his folks in the evening as usual while Dorothy cleaned up the meal of leftovers they'd shared. All was well at the farm; Tom's dad had started planting and was more than halfway done. They asked if Tom and Dorothy had heard about a baby coming, but they didn't have any news to share.

Hanging up, Tom wondered when he would have news to share. He looked at Dorothy and smiled. "I'm sure it won't be much longer, honey." He kissed her forehead and got up, picking up the phone and putting it back on the counter.

They turned in early, tired from a long weekend, ready for another week to start. Dorothy would be on spring break, so she planned to do spring cleaning.

Chapter Forty Two

Tying her brown hair back in a bandanna, Dorothy got to work early Monday morning, deep cleaning the house. She started in the kitchen, going through each cabinet and taking everything out. She wiped down all the shelves and checked the expiration dates on cans.

Cleaning the kitchen took her most of the day, so it was spaghetti for dinner that night. Tom's day was ordinary, he said, so she just told him about cleaning the kitchen over dinner. Tuesday, she moved on to the living room and shoved furniture away from the walls so she could vacuum well.

The week passed like this, and finally, it was Friday. Dorothy was cleaning the bathroom when she heard the phone ring. Walking to the kitchen, she took off long yellow rubber gloves and wondered if it was her mom or one of her sisters calling.

Answering the phone, she heard a voice say, "Dorothy, this is Trudy Belvins. How are you doing?"

Dorothy nearly dropped the phone. Having been over-anticipating this call for so long, she was actually unprepared for when it finally happened!

"Trudy! Hi! I'm fine. I'm fine. Are you calling about a baby? Is there a baby? Oh my gosh, is there a baby?" Dorothy couldn't stop saying it; she was so excited.

Trudy laughed and said, "Almost! There is a baby coming soon! I'm calling to see if you and Tom would be ready for a baby in mid-June, first part of July."

"Oh, Trudy! Really? Of course, *yes*! We are ready right now! It seems like we've been waiting forever. I know we haven't, but it feels like it! Oh, yes, yes!" Dorothy was babbling with excitement, and Trudy laughed again. She had had these reactions many times when she called parents-to-be to tell them a baby was on the way.

"OK, well, I will keep you posted on things. The young lady is due in mid-June and has already signed paperwork to release her baby to Lutheran Social Services for adoption. We feel this child will be a good fit for you based on the information we have from the hospital and the birth parents."

"Oh, Trudy! I'm so excited! I can't wait to tell Tom! Will you call regularly to let us know what's going on?" Dorothy asked breathlessly. She couldn't wait to call Tom with the news. She couldn't wait till he got home at the end of the day.

"Yes, I will call you every couple of weeks to let you know the status of what is going on. How does that sound?" Trudy said, a smile in her voice.

"That's perfect! I'm so excited! I'm going to call Tom and tell him the news!" replied Dorothy.

"OK, that sounds good. An early congratulations to you, Dot!" said Trudy.

"Oh, thank you! Thank you so much!" said Dorothy, grinning ear to ear.

Quickly she hung up and dialed Tom's office. As soon as Tom's secretary put the call through to his office, Dorothy started talking. She rambled on so quickly, Tom had to ask her to repeat herself.

When he finally understood what she was telling him, he, too, was in a state of rambling excitement. It was getting closer for them, and by early summer, they'd be a mom and dad!

Tom and Dorothy decided to call the Steins to ask them about their experience when it was getting close to the time that they picked up their son, and Dorothy called Rosemary after she got off the phone with Tom.

Saturday, they went to see Rosemary, Larry, and Christian to hear about what to expect next. They agreed that the waiting was the hardest part, but the time would end up passing rather quickly.

Rosemary insisted on throwing a baby shower for Dorothy. She would have the bridge club ladies and some of Dorothy's teacher friends, like Mrs. Levy. Dorothy's sisters, mother, and mother-in-law would be invited too.

Dorothy started to get excited about the thought of a baby shower, and Tom agreed that it would be a good thing to do. While the girls talked about the shower, Tom and Larry entertained Christian, rolling a ball across the room to him and playing with blocks.

That evening over dinner, Dorothy said, "This is really happening, Tom! We are going to get a baby soon!"

"It's exciting, I know. I can't wait either, honey."

Chapter Forty Three

The weeks passed, and they were into May. April passed with sunshine and warmer weather than usual. Rosemary sent out invitations for the shower and planned the decorations and food. They'd decided to have it at Tom and Dorothy's house, so all the gifts would be right there for them!

Tom said he'd go spend the day with Larry so Dorothy and all her friends could have their party. Dorothy would have liked him to stay, but she knew he'd feel very out of place in a room full of women.

Rosemary came over early the day of the shower. Larry and Tom decided to take Christian to the zoo so that Rosemary could take care of the shower.

Dorothy helped Rosemary set the table with pink and blue dishes, cups, and napkins. They laughed as they mixed up some punch and set up trays of cookies and tiny sandwiches.

The guests began to arrive in the early afternoon, and Dorothy was so happy to see so many of her friends and coworkers. Both of her sisters and her mother came. Tom's mom was down with the flu, so she wasn't able to come. Dorothy was sorry she would miss it. She did send an afghan that she had knit in a soft shade of green. It was lovely, and Dorothy would send her a thank-you note soon.

Everyone made themselves a plate in the kitchen and went to the screened-in porch to find a spot to sit and eat. Dorothy and Rosemary had set up card tables and chairs so there'd be room for everyone. Rosemary had made a white cake with rich chocolate frosting that said "Welcome Baby" on it in white letters. It tasted so good with the coffee Dorothy had brewed.

Soon it was time for gifts, and everyone oohed over the tiny clothes, books, toys, and practical items as Dorothy unwrapped each one. This time, it was Rosemary's turn to record the gifts as Dorothy opened them. She was so happy for her friend and excited to meet the baby that would come to them soon.

Dorothy's mother and sisters gave them a gift from all of them together. Dorothy took the long white box from her mother, tied with a white satin ribbon.

She untied the ribbon and lifted the lid, parting the light-yellow tissue paper. Inside was a beautiful christening gown! It was all edged with lace and tied with a ribbon. There was a matching bonnet and a long overcoat as well. Tiny white booties with lace and ribbon were under the gown too.

Dorothy lifted the beautiful gown, touching the fabric gently, marveling at the beauty of it. She didn't know if the baby would be a boy or a girl yet, but it didn't matter. Babies were always put in a lace-edged gown like this when they were christened.

Dorothy's mom looked at her youngest daughter and was so happy that it was finally her turn to become a mother. She and her two elder daughters had all pitched in to buy the christening outfit. It had come from an exclusive baby shop in downtown Grand Rapids. Ordinarily, Frances and her daughters wouldn't shop there, as it was an expensive shop, but they had all agreed together that they wanted something perfect for their Dorothy. They all shed a few tears, taking in this moment and the meaning of it for their sister.

Dorothy carefully hung the gown and jacket on the padded silk hanger that came with it and showed it to all the guests. Everyone agreed that it was about the most beautiful gown they'd ever seen.

By the end of the shower, Dorothy had all the things she thought she might ever need for this baby!

As the guests left, there were hugs and kind words of congratulations. Rosemary and Dorothy's mom and sisters stayed to help clean up. Dorothy was so happy, spending time with people she loved so much, she didn't want the afternoon to end.

Tom arrived home just before Dorothy's mom and sisters left. They visited for a bit, and Dorothy showed him the beautiful christening gown. She saw a glint of a tear in Tom's eye that touched her heart.

After everyone had left, Dorothy showed Tom all the gifts they'd received for the baby! He was astonished at all the wonderful things their friends and family had given them. He and Dorothy took their time putting each item away in the nursery, and by then, it was too late to make dinner.

There were still sandwiches and snacks left from the shower, so they nibbled on those and then had some cake for dessert.

Tom told her how he and Larry entertained Christian at the zoo and how much the baby seemed to enjoy the animals.

They called Tom's folks, and his mom seemed to be feeling much better. They thanked her for the lovely blanket she'd made and promised they'd see them soon.

Dorothy was expecting to hear from Trudy this week, and she would be sure to tell her about the baby shower and all the gifts they'd received. They were so ready to get their baby!

All week, Dorothy took a few minutes to write heartfelt thank-you notes to each of the ladies who attended her baby shower. She was glad to have the extra time to do it now instead of after the baby came.

On Friday, Trudy called to say that the birth mother was close to her due date and that she would be calling once a week just to let Tom and Dorothy know what was going on!

Tom and Dorothy couldn't think of anything else and counted the days as they marched by. Memorial Weekend brought a family barbecue at Tom's folks. His sister and her husband came too. Tom's mom had chicken on the grill with peppers from their garden. Tom picked some tomatoes and sliced them too. The sweet corn wasn't ready yet, but it was growing fast. Joan made her rolls, and Dorothy brought homemade peanut butter cookies.

The day was sunny and warm, and they ate on the lawn at the large picnic table that had been there for as long as Tom could remember.

Chapter Forty Four

School let out on June 14, and Dorothy was beside herself with anticipation. Trudy had told her the birth mother was due any day now, and she would call her as soon as she had news.

Tom was anxious, too, busying himself with his gardens and making sure he kept up with lawn mowing. He figured he might be too busy and too tired to stay on top of it once the baby came.

Dorothy spent the following Monday cleaning her classroom at school. She had decided to take the next year off to be a mom, and the school would hold her job for her. She took her time, sorting through her personal items from her desk and cleaning the bookshelves and cabinets that held supplies and odds and ends.

It was bittersweet knowing she was leaving the job she loved for an entire school year, but thinking about being a mom to a brand-new baby overruled the sadness of leaving her students for a year.

Back at the house, she stored her classroom things in the basement closet and labeled each box so she could easily find it next fall.

Every time Dorothy walked by the phone, she stared at it, willing it to ring. It remained silent, so she kept on doing what needed to be done, knowing that the call would come when it would come. Her patience was wearing thin, but Tom kept her on an even keel. He was anxious, too, but he managed to downplay it for Dorothy's sake.

Tuesday passed with them going to dinner at Rosemary and Larry's. Dorothy brought a stuffed lion for baby Christian and watched as he chewed on its ear.

Rosemary assured them that the call would come soon and not to fret. Dorothy and Tom went home that night, more calm than when the evening started.

Wednesday dawned bright and sunny, so Dorothy decided to wash the sheets and hand them on the clothesline to dry. When she brought them in later in the day, they smelled fresh and were warm from the sun.

As she walked by the phone once again, it suddenly rang. Dorothy was so startled, she dropped the clean sheets in a heap on the floor and lunged at the phone.

"Hello?" she nearly yelled.

"Dorothy? It's Trudy. How'd you and Tom like to have a baby girl?" said Trudy excitedly.

Dorothy was so stunned, she couldn't say anything for a moment.

"Dorothy, are you there?" asked Trudy.

"Oh yes! Yes! Yes! We would *love* a baby girl! When was she born? What does she look like? When can we get her? Oh my goodness! I have so many questions!" Dorothy rattled on.

Trudy laughed and waited until Dorothy ran out of questions. "She was just born about an hour ago. She weighs six pounds and has blonde hair and blue eyes. She is healthy, and the nurse at Crittendon says she is beautiful!"

"Oh! I just can't wait! When can we pick her up?" Dorothy asked.

"Well, now it takes just a little bit. We need to make sure she's totally healthy, so she'll be in the hospital for a few days. Then she will be moved to a foster home while all the paperwork and court date are set. So it might be a few weeks yet before you can pick her up," Trudy replied.

Dorothy was silent. Her baby had been born, but she had to wait even longer to get her. She couldn't stop thinking about it being a girl. She was so excited! She hoped Tom would be home soon.

"Well, OK. What do we need to do, Trudy?"

"You can let your family and friends know that the baby has been born whenever you want to and that as soon as a court date is set, you'll be bringing her home. You can also start thinking about names," Trudy said with happiness in her voice.

"Oh yes! We will think of a good name! Tom should be home any minute. Is there anything else you need to let me know?" asked Dorothy, ready for instructions.

"No, that's about it. Just tell who you want to tell, and I'll get moving on the paperwork here. Think of a name, and I'll be calling you next week with details as I get them," said Trudy.

"OK, OK, we will do that. Thank you so, so much, Trudy!" said Dorothy, feeling more excited than ever.

"You're most welcome. Congratulations! It's a girl!" exclaimed Trudy before hanging up the phone.

Hanging up the phone, Dorothy sank into a kitchen chair, still in shock. She tried to imagine this tiny baby with blonde hair and blue eyes. She couldn't wait to tell Tom.

Looking around herself, she saw the sheets she'd dropped on the floor. Picking them up, she shook them out and took them to the bedroom. She quickly made the bed and then went down the hall to the nursery.

She pushed open the door, and a smile broke across her face. A baby girl would be living in this room very soon! Looking up, she sent a prayer to God for thanks and one to Mark, asking for his blessing. She knew he would be happy, though.

Back in the living room, she glanced out the window to see Tom's car pulling into the driveway. She ran out the side door to meet him. He got out of the car and could tell by the smile on his wife's face that she had had news from the adoption agency.

Before Tom could get to the side door, Dorothy threw her arms around him and exclaimed, "It's a girl! It's a girl! Tom, we have a baby girl!"

Tom was thunderstruck and excited beyond words. A baby girl! All their own! He couldn't wait to hear the details as Dorothy took him by the hand into the house. In the kitchen, she relayed all the things Trudy had told her, and Tom took it all in as fast as he could.

"So, blonde hair and blue eyes. I can't wait to see her! We both have dark hair. I wonder if her birth parents were blonde," Tom mused.

"I don't know. We'll have to see what they tell us! Who do you think we should tell? I'm a little nervous to tell a lot of people yet,

Tom. It's still too new. It still hasn't happened! What should we do?" asked Dorothy.

Thinking for a minute, Tom finally said, "I think we tell our families and Father Morgan. Oh, and Dr. Brooks for sure."

"Oh, that's a good idea. Let's wait a few days, though. Let's just have this for us right now," said Dorothy.

Tom nodded in agreement. Then they both went to look in the nursery and imagine how it would be very soon with their baby girl in the crib.

Wanting to celebrate but just keeping it to themselves, they decided to go to the hot dog drive-in! It was called Dog-N-Suds. They had all kinds of hot dogs and burgers and the best root beer in frosted mugs that Dorothy had ever tasted.

Sharing some fries with lots of ketchup, Tom and Dorothy talked about names for their baby. They knew they wanted the middle name to be Joan, after Tom's sister, but couldn't agree on how to spell it! It looked like Joan, but it was actually pronounced Joanne. So they decided to shorten it to Jo.

A first name eluded them for a while. Tom suggested Tonda, which made Dorothy laugh. She thought about Laurel but decided that with the last name Cornell, that was too many *L* sounds.

Dorothy looked over to see a car pull up, and it was her dear friend Pat Norris, along with her son, Danny.

Dorothy looked at Tom. She wanted so much to tell her dear friend about the baby. She'd known Pat and her family forever and just loved them.

Tom nodded, and Dorothy jumped out of the car, rushing over to Pat's.

"Pat! Hi! Hi, Danny! How are you, honey?" said Dorothy. Danny was just three years old. He smiled and waved at Dorothy with recognition.

"Well, hi, Dot! Too hot for you to cook, too? Danny and I came up to get some food to take home to everyone! How are you doing?" Pat asked.

"You're the first one to know! We have a baby coming soon! It's a girl! We just found out she was born this afternoon! We haven't told anyone yet!" called Dorothy.

"Oh, Dottie! Congratulations! I'm so excited for you!" said Pat, climbing out of her car to give her dear friend a close hug. Danny laughed even though he didn't know what he was laughing about.

Tom had gotten out and come over to Pat's car by this time, and she hugged him too. They gave her all the details they had, and she couldn't have been more excited for her friends.

After Pat left and Tom and Dorothy were enjoying vanilla ice cream cones, Dorothy looked at Tom and said, "Patricia. Our daughter's name is Patricia Jo."

Tom looked at his wife. She was right. Pat and Bill Norris had been their friends for many, many years. Pat was always so kind and thoughtful. He agreed that Patricia was a good name, and they would call her Patty Jo for short.

Driving home, they said her name over and over and still liked it the next day. Dorothy went shopping and bought some girl-themed items for the nursery. She also picked up some little pink outfits and sleepers for the baby as well.

Tom told his boss the news and was congratulated and told to take a couple of weeks off when the baby came. Mr. Kline was truly a wonderful boss that Tom knew he could always count on.

Dorothy called her parents and sisters, and Tom called his. Everyone was thrilled with the news and very excited to meet this new baby soon. Tom called Father Morgan, who said he'd love to come along when they went to get the baby, and his wife would come too.

Dorothy called Dr. Brooks, who couldn't have been happier for his patient and her husband. He said he would be happy to recommend a pediatrician, but he'd also like to see the baby. Dorothy agreed and took down the pediatrician's name and number and put it by the phone. There were several things she hadn't thought of, and getting a baby doctor turned out to be one of them.

A few days later, Tom and Dorothy took a walk down to the Norrises' home and knocked on the door. Pat answered and invited them in for lemonade. Her husband, Bill, joined the conversation while their son, Danny, and daughter, Barb, played in the living room.

"Pat, we want you to know we're naming our daughter Patricia after you," said Dorothy, a big smile on her face.

Pat's mouth dropped open, and she didn't know what to say. "Oh, I'm so honored! Oh, that's so wonderful! Thank you so, so much!" Her husband squeezed her shoulder as tears came to Pat's eyes. She leaned over to hug Dorothy, and Tom patted her hand.

"You've always been such a wonderful friend to us, Pat. We just want our baby to have a name that reminds us of someone we care deeply for," said Dorothy with tears in her own eyes.

They visited for a while and said hello to the kids before walking back home. They felt good about their decision on the baby's name and hoped the day they could bring her home would come quickly.

Chapter Forty Five

As the next week unfolded, Tom and Dorothy shared their happy news with their neighboring friends and extended families. They couldn't have been more excited and were counting down the days to taking the trip to Detroit to get their daughter.

A court date was set for July 29 to finalize the adoption. Both Tom and Dorothy were as eager for that day to come as for the day they could pick up their baby.

Father Morgan and his wife were going to ride along to Detroit to pick up Patricia and had cleared their calendar, waiting to hear from Dorothy as to when it would be. They were looking forward to seeing their parishioners become a mother and father, finally, after all they'd been through.

Trudy Belvins called on Monday, July 7, and let Dorothy know that Wednesday was the day they could drive to Lutheran Social Services in Detroit and pick up the baby. Dorothy called Tom immediately at work to tell him the great news. Tom was so excited. He let out a "whoop" that caused his secretary to come dashing into his office. She could immediately tell by the look on his face that he'd gotten the news he'd been waiting for.

Hanging up, Tom asked his secretary to let the team know the good news. He went to see Mr. Kline and told him himself. Mr. Kline insisted that Tom take off Wednesday through Friday and enjoy his new daughter until Monday.

That evening, Tom and Dorothy could talk of nothing else. Dorothy had gone through all the clothes, picking out something to bring Patricia home in. Finally, she decided that instead of a frilly dress, she would dress the baby in a white sleeper with a matching cap, just in case it was breezy. They let their parents know the good news, and everyone planned to come to the house to see the baby and celebrate.

Tom went next door to tell the Wilsons the good news and that the baby would be there on Wednesday afternoon. Mr. Wilson congratulated Tom and then went to talk to his wife. Together, they notified all the surrounding neighbors, and they made a big sign that read, "Welcome to Jefferson Acres, Patricia Jo!" Mrs. Wilson and the other ladies made desserts to bring, deciding the neighborhood would surprise the Cornells when they arrived home with the baby.

As Monday rolled into Tuesday, Dorothy found it increasingly difficult to keep her patience to become a mom. Talking to Tom Tuesday evening during dinner, she found that he was just as anxious to become a dad.

They spent their last evening as just a couple out on the screened-in porch facing the backyard. Fireflies danced through the gardens, and crickets sang their evening songs.

Taking a deep breath, Tom said, "This is it, Dottie. Tomorrow we will become a family of three! I can't believe it. We've been waiting so very long!" He stroked his wife's hand and looked at her, smiling.

"I know! I'm so excited! Won't Patty Jo have fun out here playing when she's old enough? We can get a little pool and maybe a swing set over there!" said Dorothy excitedly, pointing around the yard.

"Oh, how about a sandbox and a little picnic table under the tree!" added Tom, already planning out the changes in his mind.

"It's all just so exciting! What time are we leaving tomorrow? It's two hours to Detroit. Then we have to find the Lutheran Social Services office," stated Dorothy.

"I called Father Morgan and asked them to be here by 10:00 a.m. We will stop and eat lunch on the way down. Then we won't have to stop on the way back. I think we should get the baby home as quickly as possible," said Tom.

"Oh, that's great! I've been so busy planning, I didn't even think about stopping for lunch!" said Dorothy with a laugh.

"Do you think she'll like us, Tom?" asked Dorothy, a worried crease appearing on her forehead.

Tom threw his head back and laughed. "Oh, Dot! You are so funny! Of course, she will like us! We will give her so much love, she won't know anything else!"

Dorothy smiled back at him and thought that he was very wise. They became quiet then, just enjoying the evening, watching as more stars winked at them from the distant sky.

Suddenly, Dorothy found herself thinking about the birth mother of the baby they would be bringing home the next day. Dorothy couldn't imagine being any happier, but how was this young woman feeling? Did she love this baby too? Was she heartbroken? Dorothy herself could not imagine giving a child up for adoption. She thought this birth mother must be brave and quite selfless to give away a part of you, not knowing where your baby would actually be, trusting strangers to love her.

Dorothy felt a lump in her throat as she thought of whoever this young woman was. She would never know her and never be able to thank her for giving her the most precious gift she would ever receive. She wondered about the father of this baby too. Would he remember in all his years to come that somewhere out in the world, a baby he had created was living a life he'd never know about?

Dorothy contemplated these things as the soft breeze ruffled her hair. She was vaguely aware of Tom's fingers brushing her hand, and finally, she looked over at him to see him gazing at her.

"What is it, Dot? What are you thinking about? You're so quiet," he asked softly.

"I was thinking about the birth parents of this baby, Tom. They'll never know that she was given to us. They'll never know how much we love her and haven't even met her yet. I have to say, I can't imagine doing what they are doing, but I could never be more thankful. I don't know how to feel exactly, but my heart feels for them and what they have chosen to do for us."

"That's very kind, honey. I must say, I really haven't thought that much about the birth parents! You've given me things to be thankful for. I have thought about Mark a lot, though. I know he's happy that our nursery is welcoming a baby, and he's always going to be with us a little bit, I think."

Dorothy smiled, thinking of her baby boy. It hurt still and probably always would in some ways, but she knew adopting this baby was the right thing to do.

"Hang on, I'll be right back," said Tom, standing up and walking into the house.

Dorothy leaned back in her chair, gazing up at the night sky. There were more stars than she could ever count. Soon she heard strains of Etta James singing their song.

Tom returned and offered his hand to his wife. "Come on, let's dance once more before diapers, bottles, and sleepless nights become our way of life for a while!" He laughed.

Dorothy smiled up at him and took his hand. As Etta sang, she thought back over the years of her memories of being a couple with Tom. Their journey with Mark and then her painful miscarriage after that. Tomorrow, they would become parents in a different way. She was thrilled and excited, but for now, it was just the two of them, in the moonlight, sharing one last dance as a couple.

Chapter Forty Six

The day broke, sunny and warm. Tom and Dorothy were up early to get ready to head to Detroit. Coffee and English muffins with butter were all they could manage to eat! Father Morgan and his wife arrived promptly at 10:00 a.m., and they eagerly climbed into Tom's car.

On the way to Detroit, they talked about kids, families, and the future. The Morgans had three children of their own and knew the excitement of becoming parents for the first time.

Tom stopped in Northfield, a northern suburb of Detroit. They found a drugstore with a diner inside that looked like a nice mom-and-pop kind of place, and everyone was hungry and could use a stretch by then.

The combination diner and drugstore had everything from prescriptions to gifts and a nice-looking lunch counter with red stools and booths.

The group of four took a booth, and soon, a nice-looking young man with dark hair arrived with menus in hand.

"Hello, folks. Here are some menus for you." As the young man passed out the menus, Dorothy looked at the fountains behind the counter.

"Do you have egg creams here, uh, Curtis?" She spied a name tag on his clean shirt.

"Oh, yes, ma'am! We sure do. They're quite popular. Would you like one?" he replied.

"Yes, I think so! What flavor do you like best? I can never decide!" said Dorothy with a laugh.

"Well, I like the vanilla, but my girlfriend, Judy, prefers the chocolate ones," Curtis's eyes sparkled when he mentioned his girlfriend, Dorothy thought.

"I think I'll have the chocolate! Anyone else?" Dorothy said, looking around the table.

"That sounds great!" said Father Morgan.

Curtis nodded and left them to go make the egg creams while they all decided on what to get for lunch.

Hamburgers all around were decided when Curtis returned with the egg creams. Over lunch, they looked at the map so they would easily be able to find Lutheran Social Services. Tom figured it would just be another half hour away.

When Curtis returned with the bill, Tom asked him if he was familiar with the area they were headed to. Curtis looked at the map and asked where they were headed.

"We're on our way to Lutheran Social Services to pick up our baby! We're adopting a baby girl!" said Dorothy, excitement almost tangible coming from her.

Curtis took a moment and pinched his nose between his eyebrows. Dorothy thought the young man looked upset for a minute and hoped she hadn't said anything wrong.

"Um, let me see. I think if you take this road, it'll get you there a bit quicker," said Curtis, pointing to a spot on the map so Tom could see.

"OK, well, thank you, young man," replied Tom.

They got ready to leave, and Tom left a generous tip for the young man, who'd been so friendly and helpful.

As Dorothy stood up, she looked over at Curtis and said, "Tell your girlfriend that the chocolate egg cream was great! She's a wise young lady!" Her smile lit up her face, and Curtis smiled back. He couldn't help but wonder if the baby girl these people were adopting was Judy and his baby. He swallowed hard and smiled at the woman. She and her husband looked so happy. He hoped his baby daughter would be going to good people like these folks seemed to be.

"I will, ma'am. Uh, congratulations on your baby," he said, waving as the group left the diner.

Back in the car, Tom folded the map, and Father Morgan held it where they could follow the road signs that would take them to Lutheran Social Services.

Soon, they came upon a large two-story building of white concrete with black shutters. There was a short flight of steps leading up to tall double doors. Tom parked, and Dorothy practically ran up steps, unable to wait for the rest of her party.

Once they all were inside the building, a woman walked through a door to the left of the counter. Dorothy assumed this was Trudy Belvins, and that was how the woman introduced herself.

"If you'll give me just a moment, I have someone I'd like you to meet!" said Trudy, smiling from ear to ear.

Tom and Dorothy clung to one another, wildly anticipating the moment they would meet their baby. It seemed like a lifetime, waiting for Trudy to appear. Just then, the office door opened again, and Trudy appeared with a tiny bundle, all of pink! She stepped over to Dorothy's waiting arms and gently gave her the baby.

Dorothy's eyes filled with tears. Tom reached over to stroke the cheek of his daughter. Their hearts were bursting with love! Finally, after such a long time and so much pain and heartbreak, they were finally parents to this beautiful baby girl!

Dorothy was mesmerized by her face. She pushed up the pink cap to see soft curling tendrils of blonde hair. Her first thought was that it would turn dark over time, and she loved that idea since she and Tom both had dark hair.

The baby was asleep, her darker lashes fluttering against full rosy cheeks. Her mouth was a tiny rosebud, pink lips that Dorothy gently kissed.

Tom came around to face Dorothy and took his time looking at this baby, his baby! Then he, too, gave her a little kiss. He smiled up at Dorothy, and they both had happy tears in their eyes.

Father Morgan and his wife stepped up next to them to see the baby and offer congratulations. Trudy stayed by the desk, enjoying the excitement of seeing this new happy family. She filled out some paperwork, giving them a little time to greet their baby and have a few moments before going over everything with them.

Chapter Forty Seven

Trudy stood up, paperwork in hand, and walked over to the new parents.

"If you don't mind, Tom and Dorothy, I just have some papers for you to fill out. Perhaps your pastor or his wife would like to hold the baby for you!"

"Oh yes, of course!" said Dorothy, turning to Father Morgan. He quickly held out his arms and took the pink bundle from Dorothy. His wife cooed and nudged him for a turn to hold her after a few moments.

"OK, as the parents, we just need you to sign and date these forms that state you received the baby and I'll witness it for you and have it notarized. I'll give you a set so you can take them to court with you for the adoption hearing," said Trudy.

"One more thing I think you should know is, the birth mother named this child Shelly. I want you to know that because one day, this child is going to ask you if her birth parents loved her. I can say without a doubt they loved this baby. If they didn't, the mother would not have named her. I just wanted you to know that."

Tom and Dorothy looked at Trudy, and the gravity of what the birth parents went through and their decision to give their baby up coursed through their minds and hearts.

Tom took the papers and looked them over while Dorothy got out her fountain pen. The papers stated the baby's date and time of birth, as well as her vital statistics. The names of the doctor and birth parents had been erased from the forms. They would never know the names of the people who had given them the most precious gift of all.

Tom thought about that for a moment before signing and dating the papers. He sent up a quick prayer of thanks to God above and then handed the papers to Dorothy for her to sign.

Dorothy read the papers carefully and also noticed the names that weren't there. Once again, she thought of the loss these two young people were experiencing and wished them the best in her heart. She was so grateful and thankful to finally become a mother. She would do her very best to care for this little girl as long as she lived. She signed the papers and handed them back to Trudy, who quickly notarized them and gave them copies.

Dorothy took her new daughter back into her arms and thought she'd never want to let go. They all walked out the doors of the building and down the flight of steps into the parking lot. Tom went and got the car while Mrs. Morgan snapped a photo of Dorothy holding the baby. Father Morgan stood by with a big smile, giving thanks for this blessing.

Trudy Belvins shook all their hands and wished them well. She told them what a pleasure it had been to work with them and that she felt confident that this baby was going to have a wonderful life with these new parents.

Tom and Dorothy thanked Trudy for all her help, and then everyone got in the car. Dorothy held her baby close and couldn't take her eyes off her. Tom had the radio playing some quiet music to soothe the baby for the long drive back to Midland.

Father Morgan and his wife shared stories of their children as babies while Tom and Dorothy listened with rapt attention! They were eager to take any advice from other parents since they were new to it!

When there was an hour left to go, the baby woke up and started to fuss! Suddenly Dorothy realized that she hadn't brought a bottle for Patty Jo! She felt terrible! How could she forget something so important!

Tom drove as quickly as he dared to get them the rest of the way home, and as soon as they arrived in the driveway, they spied the huge handmade sign on the garage door that said:

"Welcome to Jefferson Acres, Patricia Jo!"

It looked like half the neighborhood was in the driveway and yard, cheering and clapping! Both Tom and Dorothy had tears in their eyes, seeing how excited their neighbors and friends were for them!

Tom carefully parked the car and helped Dorothy out. By this time, Patty Jo was crying.

"Hi, folks! We can't believe you're all here to welcome us! Thank you so much! We forgot to take a bottle for the baby, so if you'll give us just a few minutes, we'll be right back, and everyone can see her!" Tom spoke loudly and was met with laughter from the gathered friends.

Mrs. Morgan told Dorothy she'd get a bottle warmed while Dorothy changed Patty's diaper. Dorothy was so thankful to have an experienced mom there to help her. Walking into the nursery with her brand-new baby, Dorothy looked around the room and held her baby close. The window was open, and a breeze was making the curtain sway. The room was fresh and cool.

Dorothy whispered to her daughter, "Welcome home, baby. This is your room now. This is your place."

Carefully, she changed the baby's diaper and was just pinning it when Mrs. Morgan arrived with a bottle.

"Here, Dorothy, take the bottle, and I'll find a burp cloth. Everyone's outside, so excited to meet this little one!" said Mrs. Morgan, smiling from ear to ear.

"Oh, thank you so, so much! Let's see if I can do this!" Dorothy took the bottle in one hand while holding Patty in her other arm and headed back outside.

Tom came up beside her and helped her hold the baby and tilted the bottle so she could drink.

The first person Dorothy saw was Pat Norris. She was so excited that the baby's namesake was there first. Pat carefully hugged Dorothy, then Tom, and then looked at the tiny baby, so eagerly eating. "Well now, isn't she precious?" said Pat, a tear in her eye.

Dorothy smiled at her dear friend and thanked her for coming. Pat nodded and said she'd stick around, as others were waiting to see the baby. Many friends and neighbors took a few moments to congratulate the happy couple and look at the baby. When she finished her bottle, Rosemary Stein showed Dorothy how to burp the baby so she would be more comfortable.

Dorothy felt a little awkward but managed to get it done. Then Patty Jo was looking all around, and Dorothy couldn't stop looking at her blue eyes that held shadows of gray.

As the crowd thinned out, Tom and Dorothy stood with Pat and Bill Norris, Rosemary and Larry Stein with Christian, and Marianne and Don May. This group of friends was most dear to Tom and Dorothy, and they couldn't have been more thankful to have them there to meet their baby girl.

"Dorothy, you're going to love this journey!" said Rosemary. "We've had a wonderful time with Christian so far, and we've given some thought about adopting another baby sometime soon. Maybe a girl, like you have!"

"Oh, Rosemary! That would be wonderful! Just think, we'll have kids that can play together!" said Dorothy.

The couples chatted for a while, and Tom took a turn holding his infant daughter. Finally, she looked like she was drifting off to sleep. Everyone took that as their cue to head home and let the new little family be together. Hugs and promises to get together soon and often were spoken as their friends took their leave.

Tom and Dorothy looked at the wonderful sign their neighbors had made. Beulah and Ralph Wilson said they'd be by the next day to see if the Cornells needed anything. Dorothy hugged Beulah and thanked her so much for making the beautiful sign.

Finally, in the house, Tom and Dorothy walked into the nursery for the first time as a family. Dorothy leaned over the crib and gently placed Patty Jo down, careful not to wake her.

They stood there, arms around each other, gazing down at this blessing they had finally received. Tom was thinking of Mark for a little while, thinking that his son would be happy that this baby was going to have his room. The lump in his throat seemed a little smaller, and he let Mark go a little further. He knew his son would always have a special place in his heart, but this child was his daughter, and he was going to do his best to guide her on her way through life.

Dorothy looked around the room again, noting how light and welcoming it was. Fleeting thoughts of Mark crossed her mind. She knew her baby would always be a part of her, but she also knew this tiny girl was meant to be hers.

She thought again of the mother who had given up this child, and her heart filled with love for this woman who would never know the blessing she had given Dorothy and Tom. Silently she thanked the birth mother and father in her mind and gently caressed her baby's cheek. She recalled the words Trudy had spoken—that the baby had been named Shelly. In fact, Dorothy had found a tiny beaded bracelet on the baby's wrist that spelled out SHELLY. She'd slipped it off Patty Jo's wrist and tucked it in her pocket. Someday, her daughter would want this.

Smiling up at Tom, they tiptoed out of the room to go get ready for bed. Offhandedly, she wondered just how much sleep they'd get that night. Just before they went to bed themselves, Tom and Dorothy sat out on the porch once again to talk about their new family.

"This is really something, Dot. I never thought it'd happen for us. I'm so glad it did," said Tom, gazing up at the stars. "Soon our families will come visit, and we'll just be busy all the time. I can't wait!"

Dorothy laughed as she, too, looked up at the infinity of stars in the sky. She thought about family get-togethers, holidays, and birthdays to come. She thought about when her baby would go to school, become a teenager, and grow up! It seemed like it would take a long time, but she had a feeling it'd go fast. Maybe they'd adopt another baby one day, too, like the Steins were planning to do. She was so excited to finally become a real mother!

Her thoughts drifted, and she held hands with Tom. As they enjoyed the warm evening of mid-July, they heard their baby cry.

And so it began!

Thanks and Acknowledgements

First and foremost, I'd like to thank my late parents, Thomas and Dorothy Cornell.

You gave me the very best life you could, and I wish I had appreciated it more when I was younger. You've both been gone for so many years now, yet not a day goes by that I don't miss you both, or mention you in some way.

Your never ending support and love was enough to last a lifetime. I just wish you were still here for my lifetime.

Thank you to Judy Farquharson. I know you are my birth mother, through a lot of research, phone calls, emails, and the website Ancestry.com. I don't know what became of you, or if you are still alive. If you are and these books somehow find you, I thank you for letting me go. I hope that you have had a good life.

Thank you to my birth father. I know that you offered to marry Judy, because the adoption agency told me so. Thank you for your kindness. I hope you've had a good life too.

Thank you to my friends, near and far, who always stand by me and share the laughs and tears!

Thank you and blessings to my publisher, John Paul Owles! I find inspiration in our many conversations with the wide range of topics! You really make me think!

About the Author

Patricia Ploss, originally from Midland, Michigan, makes her home in northwest Indiana with her husband Tony.

Writing has been a passion of hers for many years, but only within the last three, has it become a reality in print.

Patricia and her husband Tony have two grown children. Dawson, 23, lives with them, having survived a car accident that left him with mild brain damage. Her first book, **The Dandelion Picker**, is a memoir based on his story and new reality.

Daughter Rachel, 22, just graduated from IUPII with a Masters in Philanthropy, is newly married to Kyle Hettinger, and resides in Florida.

Patricia spends her time writing, walking, and spending time with her family and pets.

OTHER BOOKS BY PATRICIA PLOSS

Have you ever believed your son was fine? Did you raise him to know right from wrong? Drugs are bad, stealing is not right? Telling the truth is always better than lying? Being a parent is tough! It turns out you can't really make your kids do anything they don't want to do. You try your best and hope they listen, but sometimes they don't.

Emery, a recent widow, finds herself in a love triangle! Mark's feelings evolve from friendship to something more. Bart becomes obsessed with her.

In 1962, seventeen-year-old Judy Bonner finds herself in love with twenty-year-old Curtis Murphy. She learns she is pregnant with his baby! Filled with fear, shame, and secrecy, Judy hides her pregnancy from her family for as long as she can!

Made in the USA
Columbia, SC
15 August 2023